Y0-AGO-819

SECRET LOVERS

"This has been a truly glorious day, Tammi," Ty whispered. "I seem to be having more and more of those . . ." he put one arm around her shoulders, and cupped her face with his other hand, "since you came into my life." The kiss was soft and gentle.

"Oh, Tammi," Ty breathed against her ear, "you mean so much to me." He kissed her again, his lips trailing across her cheek down to the hollow of her throat. "I never thought I'd find you."

Tameka felt herself totally surrender. Why deny it any longer? She was in love with him. And she wanted him as badly as he wanted her.

"Tammi," Ty took her hands, and kissed them, one by one. "You deserve better than a quick, secret rendezvous in the backseat of a car."

They got out of the car, and Ty walked her to the door. He wrapped Tameka up in his arms, his lingering kiss telling her how much he hated to go. They were interrupted by a bright flashing light and the sound of a car whizzing past. "Who is that?" Tameka wondered.

"I think I know," Ty replied. "I recognize the car."

OTHER BOOKS BY RAYNETTA MAÑEES

ALL FOR LOVE was voted a finalist for the Best Contemporary Ethnic Romance of 1996 by the AFFAIRE DE COEUR MAGAZINE annual reader poll. ROMANTIC TIMES MAGAZINE says, "Raynetta Mañees has written a warm, loving romance with the consummate skill of a veteran novelist. Her insight into the hearts of her characters makes *ALL FOR LOVE* a unique reading experience."

WISHING ON A STAR was critically acclaimed even before it's official release. ROMANTIC TIMES MAGAZINE calls *WISHING ON A STAR* "a delightful romance that explores the selflessness of true love, and the wealth of compassion in the soul." RENDEZVOUS MAGAZINE called the book, "fast-paced ... enlightening ...", and concluded, "I couldn't put it down!"

FOLLOW YOUR HEART is Ms. Mañees' third novel. Her fourth, as yet untitled, is scheduled for a June, 1999 release.

FOLLOW YOUR HEART

Raynetta Mañees

Raynetta Mañees

9/1/99

To Lela
God Bless!

P

Pinnacle Books
Kensington Publishing Corp.

http://www.arabesquebooks.com

PINNACLE BOOKS are published by

Kensington Publishing Corp.
850 Third Avenue
New York, NY 10022

Copyright © 1998 by Raynetta Mañees

All rights reserved. No part of this book may be reproduced in any form or by any means without the prior written consent of the Publisher, excepting brief quotes used in reviews.

If you purchased this book without a cover you should be aware that this book is stolen property. It was reported as "unsold and destroyed" to the Publisher and neither the Author nor the Publisher has received any payment for this "stripped book."

Pinnacle, the P logo and Arabesque, the Arabesque logo are Reg. U.S. Pat. & TM Off.

First Printing: September, 1998
10 9 8 7 6 5 4 3 2 1

Printed in the United States of America

DEDICATION

This book is dedicated with love and gratitude to my mother, Lebertis Knight Mañees Wright, my first—and best—Bible teacher.

Love and kisses to my fella. He knows why.

Chapter 1

"Danny! Danny, would you come over here, please?"

Danny took his sweet time swaggering across the studio to where Meeko sat trembling with anger. "Yeah?"

"What is *this*?"

"What does it look like, baby?" he replied with a smug grin. "It's your score."

Meeko looked him up and down. "We've been through this, Danny," she told him through clenched teeth. "I'm not recording this nasty trash, and that's final."

Danny leaned against the wall, and crossed his arms, "Looks like you *are*, sugar. If you'll trouble to check the musician's scores, their music is the same."

Meeko glared at him a long moment. She opened her mouth to speak, but stopped. Instead, she hopped down from her stool and took off her headphones, carefully hanging them across the suspended microphone in front of her.

Danny suddenly straightened. "What do you think you're doing?"

"What does it look like I'm doing?" Meeko flung his words back at him. "I'm leaving."

Danny's eyes narrowed, but before he could speak, Squeak Simon, the musical director, approached them. "What's up, ya'll?" He turned to Meeko, "Is there a problem with the music, honey?"

"No, man," Danny quickly put in. "Meeko's just . . ."

"Yes, Squeak," Meeko answered as though Danny hadn't spoken. "There's a big problem with the music. Namely—it's not the music it's supposed to be."

Squeak was sincerely puzzled. "I don't understand. Danny and I discussed it in detail when he gave me your list, and . . ."

"Then Danny's memory is getting as slippery as his mind," Meeko shot a frosty glance in Danny's direction. "Because I most distinctly told him there was no way I would ever record this song."

"Now, wait a minute, Meeko . . ."

"No, you wait a minute, Danny. If you think . . ."

Their rising voices caught the attention of the musicians and technicians milling around the studio. The crew grew silent, tuning in to the brewing storm in their midst.

"Look, Squeak," Danny said, glancing about him, "why don't you all take five while my protegée and I sort this out?".

"Protegée, my foot! Who the . . ."

"Come on, *Tameka.*" Danny took her arm, and hustled her into the small office adjoining the studio. When Squeak followed in confusion, Danny slammed the door in his face. Danny turned on Meeko, his face hard and menacing. "Now just what was that little scene supposed to prove?"

"It proved what I've been telling you since Day One. I'm selective about what I will do—and what I *won't* do. Singing that song is in the 'won't do' category. I've managed to do pretty well so far without lowering myself to that kind of . . ."

"*You've* managed? Don't let that little gold statue go to

your head, girlfriend. I'm the manager here, not you. Where do you think you'd be today without me? Just poor—and I do mean poor—little unheard of Tameka Morgan, from Hole-in-the-Wall, Georgia, singing your heart out in some second-rate supper club, like where I found you."

Meeko paused a moment to compose herself. "Look, Danny, you've done a lot for my career. I don't deny that. Although I've had to fight every step of the way to keep you from going too far, and in more ways than one, but you know where I stand. There's no way I'd ever do a song like that, and you know it. Why do you keep trying to push me—trick me—into doing things you know I don't go for?"

"Why?" Danny repeated to the empty room at large, his arms flung wide. "The woman asks me 'why!' " He spun Meeko around to face the mirror behind the desk. "There! Take a good look, sweetheart! That's why!"

Meeko blinked back at her image in the mirror. At her sculpted face with its enormous black eyes fringed with thick black lashes. She pursed her lips in exasperation, and in spite of her ire, her trademark dimples materialized. The black satin of her chin-length mushroom cut hair gleamed even under the muted lights of the room, and the baggy T-shirt and jeans could not hide the slender shapeliness of her figure.

Meeko was honest with herself, and knew she was a beautiful woman, just as she knew she had a beautiful voice. And she was thankful. But she saw no reason to get conceited or stuck-up about either. After all, she had not been the creator of either.

"I've told you a million times, girl," Danny was rattling on. "Sure, you've made a terrific start, but you could be ten times the star if you'd just use a little of what Mother Nature so generously gave you." Danny put his hands on Meeko's shoulders, his voice suddenly dropping to a whisper. "And the best place to start practicing your new image . . ." His hands slipped to her breasts, "Is right here, right now—with me."

Meeko spun quickly, slapping his hands away. "And I've told *you* a million times. That's not going to happen. Now or ever! I'm sick of your come-ons. Don't ever try to put a hand on me again, unless you want to draw back a nub!"

Meeko strode to the door. "If I'm going to make it, I'm going to make it on my voice, my talent. Not by slithering around on stage half-naked, singing filth that would make a streetwalker blush!"

Danny shook his head. "You can take the girl out of the country, but you can't take the country out of the girl. You've been in L.A. three years now, honey. Haven't you learned anything?"

"Uh-huh. A lot. One of the things I've learned is making it in this business doesn't mean a thing if you can't look yourself in the mirror because of *how* you made it."

"Meeko, Meeko, how many times do we have to have this argument? It's time to put your preacher's daughter hang-ups aside, little girl."

"That's deacon's daughter. And I'm a small woman, but I'm not a little girl. And I'm also not about to 'shake what my mama gave me,' as you've so delicately put it. I'm going to do what my father taught me."

"Well, look," Danny gave her a cocky smirk, "today it's moot, anyway. You've already got a studio full of very highly paid people waiting on the other side of this door for you to come out there and do what pays the bills. Don't you realize how much it costs just to set up a session like this? I don't think the suits at the record label will be very happy if you leave them holding the bag—and the bill."

Meeko put her hand on the doorknob. "Well, explaining it to them is what I have you for, now isn't it?"

Danny looked suddenly worried. "Now wait a minute. You can't be serious about this. You can't just . . ."

"Oh, no?" Meeko stared him down. "Watch me!"

"Come back here! Meeko, you . . ."

But she had already opened the door, and resolutely reentered the studio, heading for the exit.

"Meeko, where are you going?" Squeak managed to get in as she swept past him. The musicians and studio techs were watching in silent, wide-eyed amazement. Danny pushed Squeak aside as he rushed after Meeko, catching up with her just as she reached the exit door. He roughly grabbed her arm, spinning her around to face him.

"Now, look here, girl. This ain't your Sunday school Easter pageant. This is the big time. You can't have a hissy fit and flounce out of here. You've got a contract."

Meeko snatched back her arm. "That's right. I do. One that gives me artistic control over my music. Me. Not you. So when you think you can set up a session to record music I've approved, you know where to reach me."

"You!" Danny exploded. "Just who the hell do you think you are? I created you, Miss Meeko Moore! And don't you ever forget it!"

Meeko stood her ground and looked him dead in the eye. "I haven't heard your voice on any of my recordings." She moved in closer, not in the least intimidated by his towering over her petite 5'3" frame. "You created Meeko Moore. But it's Tameka Morgan's voice on that CD. And I was Tameka Morgan long before you came along. Tameka Morgan is walking out this door. Unfortunately for you, she's taking your Meeko Moore with her!"

Danny's face darkened as he reached for her again, "You little . . . I'll show you who . . ."

Meeko shrank back, but before Danny could touch her, Squeak grabbed him in a bear hug from behind, pinning Danny's arms against his sides.

"Look, I don't know what the hell is going on here, but you're not talking to Meeko like that! Not if I have any say about it! And you're damn sure not going to shove her around!"

"Let go of me! Mind your own business, music man. This don't concern you. This is between Meeko and me!"

Danny struggled, but his slight build was no match for Squeak's muscular arms. And several of the other men stood ready to lend Squeak a hand.

"You better go now, Meeko," Squeak told her. "Don't worry about him." Squeak tightened his grip on Danny, it seemed to Meeko a little harder than was required. "He's not going to stop you. And he better not mess with you after you leave, either, if he knows what's good for him!"

Danny suddenly stopped struggling. "Okay, okay! I lost it a minute. But I'm all right now. So would you be good enough to take your big, ugly hands off me, man?"

Squeak hesitantly released him, but didn't step away, ready to renew his restraint, if need be.

Meeko knew that was wise. Danny was a master manipulator. A true chameleon, he would change his expression, his actions, or his standards in a flash, if he thought it to his advantage.

"Look, honey," Danny purred now, in his slickest conciliatory manner. "We need to sit down and discuss this calmly. Why don't you and I go down to the cafeteria . . ." he fastidiously took Meeko's elbow, "and talk this over like two rational adults?"

"Uh-uh." Meeko removed his hand with finger and thumb as though it were slime. "That's impossible. One of us doesn't meet the criteria."

Danny's face hardened again, but he glanced over at Squeak, who was still at his elbow, and paused a moment before saying, "Then let's just record the song as scheduled, love, okay? I know you'll feel differently once it's on tape. And if you don't like it then . . ."

"Then you'd find a way to get it released, anyhow, wouldn't you?" Meeko interrupted. Danny started to sputter as she picked up her jacket. "It won't work, Danny. I know your tricks too well. No. I'm outta here." She again headed for the exit. "You give me a call when *my* music is ready to record."

Danny made a move toward her, but thought better of

it when Squeak made a move toward *him*. Danny stayed where he was, but called, "Meeko, you better get back here . . . if you want to stay in this business!"

"I don't respond well to threats, Danny," Meeko threw over her shoulder, still heading for the door.

Danny lost all his fabricated cool. "Then respond to this, you self-righteous, country wench! I've got other clients. Who have you got? I made you . . . and I can break you!"

As she drove away, Danny's last words rang in Tameka's ears all the way home. She knew he was capable—from both a business and moral standpoint—of doing just that.

The press called Meeko Moore an overnight success story. That wasn't the case. Tameka had been in L.A. for a year trying to break into the music industry before Danny found her. She knew his first attraction had as much to do with her looks as her voice. As she later found out, that was hardly the first time Danny had tried to lure a girl to his bed with promises of stardom. He was usually more successful at it, too. But by the time Danny learned Tameka was no pushover in the bedroom department, he'd taken the time to really listen to her.

Scuzzy as he was, Danny was no fool, and no novice to the inner workings of the recording world. He knew he had a rare talent in Tameka—one that could make him a lot of money. So he did an about-face, turning all business, and skillfully maneuvered Tameka into a representation contract with him as her manager.

After renaming her, Danny quickly landed Tameka a recording contract. The first single from her CD "Meeko Moore, Myself" had made the Top 10. And the second single, "Follow Your Heart," had gone platinum. It was the song that, to Tameka's immense surprise, had won her a Grammy award for the "New Artist of the Year."

There was a time when Tameka would have viewed winning a Grammy as assuring her future as a vocalist. She knew better now. In this business you were only as good as your last hit. The Grammy record books had many a one-hit wonder. Tameka didn't want to become one. And just when she needed him the most, Tameka's deteriorating relationship with Danny had finally hit bottom.

Over the two years he had been her manager, Danny's true nature had slowly resurfaced. Their battles over her image and her struggle to fend off his increasing advances intensified. She was grateful to Danny for opening the door, giving her a start. But Tameka wasn't naive enough to believe he'd done it out of the kindness of his heart. He had no heart—or kindness, either. Danny received a very lucrative ten percent of everything she earned. Tameka didn't resent that, but she did resent him acting like he owned her. And she more than resented his continuing attempts to be compensated in ways other than monetarily.

I've got to get out of here, Tameka told herself. *I need time to think things through, to regroup.* She turned on the radio. Stephanie Mills was in the middle of "Home," one of Tameka's favorite songs. *You're right, Stephanie. That's where I need to be right now. And that's where I'm going.*

"Tammi! I don't believe you're here!" Mama threw her arms around Tameka right there on the front porch. "Why didn't you tell me you were coming? I could have met you at the airport. Oh, honey! Let me look at you!" Mama stood back to appraise Tameka. "Child, what you been eating out there in California? You're thin as a lame excuse."

"Oh, Mama," Tameka laughed. "You say that every time you see me. I'm only a size seven, but I'm very healthy, I'll have you know, Mrs. Morgan."

"Huh . . . size seven," Mama spurned that idea. "Seven is a shoe size, girl—not a dress size."

Tameka laughed again as they went into the house, from years of habit heading straight for the kitchen. "Tammi, why didn't you tell me you were coming?" Mama repeated once they had both taken a seat. She peered at Tameka closely. "That skinny man pestering you again?"

Tameka had to smile in spite of herself. "That skinny man" had been Mama's handle for Danny since the first time she met him. Mama's seasoned instincts proved more on target than Tameka's. Mama had distrusted Danny on sight.

"Is he ever *not* pestering me?" Tameka tried to make light of the situation.

But this was Mama. No use trying to fool her. "Honey, you're a big star now. You don't need to put up with his foolishness. After all, he works for you. Why don't you just fire him and get another manager?"

Tameka stood and went to the window, looking out at the back yard where she'd played throughout her childhood, the warm June sun having brought the flowers into full bloom. "I've sure thought about it, Mama. But it's not that simple. Low down as he is, Danny's got a lot of clout in the industry. And if I let him go, he's vindictive enough to use every trick in the book to throw a monkey wrench in my career."

She turned, facing Mama. "One hit album doesn't make a 'big star'. I'm at a real turning point right now. And if I don't handle it right, I could easily become a has-been before I even get to really be an 'is.' "

Tameka's face suddenly brightened, "But let's not talk about that now. I'm home. And I haven't seen my mama in four months. And . . . that's not peach cobbler I smell, is it?"

"Lord have mercy!" Mama ran to the oven. "It was almost burnt peach cobbler! I forgot all about it!" She gingerly removed a dish.

"Umm-Umm," Tameka sighed as she sniffed the tangy air, "my mama is still the best cook in town!" Tameka looked at Mama with mild reproach. "Is this for one of your catering jobs, Mama? You know you don't have to do that anymore."

"Honey, I've kept my business going because I want to, not because I have to. I love it. And, girl, I'm only fifty-two. I'm too young to retire."

"I know Mama, but . . ."

"Dear, I know my highly successful and overly generous daughter would gladly support me, but I don't want to be supported, nor do I want to leave my home and move to L.A. I've lived here all my life, and I don't want to leave my home nor my friends. Anyway, the first time the ground shook, I'd be on the first flight out! But this isn't for a catering job. The church is having a bake sale to raise money for the Young People's choir."

"New choir robes?" Tameka asked, deeply inhaling the steaming delight.

"No. They've been invited to the Gospelfest in Atlanta this year." Mama removed a second cobbler from the oven. "We're raising money for their trip."

A far away look came into Mama's eyes. "I remember when you used to sing with that choir, honey. I only wish your daddy was here to see you now. He'd be so proud of you." Tameka's eyes followed Mama's gaze as she turned to look into the living room. Tameka's Grammy sat in proud display on the mantle, right between her high school graduation picture, and a picture of Mama and Daddy at their wedding.

Tameka wrapped her arms around Mama from behind, and buried her face in Mama's hair. "He is here, Mama," she whispered. "And he always will be."

Mama turned, and hugged Tameka in return. "You're right, baby." She smiled as she gazed deeply into Tameka's eyes. "I see him every time I look at you . . . Well," Mama continued briskly, "I've got to get this cobbler down to the church. Deacon Bradfield was going to come by for it, but he just called to say his car wouldn't start. You want to come with me?"

"No, Mama. I'm so happy to be home that I think I'll just sit out on the porch for a while until you get back."

Mama frowned, "Here I haven't seen my only baby in months, and I go rushing out almost the moment you get here. I'll call Sister Rakestraw. Maybe she could come by on her way down, and . . ."

"Mama, I'll be fine. You'll only be gone an hour or so. That'll give me a chance to unpack and . . ." Tameka eyed the remaining cobbler, "get reacquainted with my mama's cooking."

Mama laughed, "That sounds more like my Tammi!" Tameka carefully wrapped the still piping hot cobbler while Mama went upstairs for her purse.

"You're sure you'll be all right, honey?" Mama asked as Tameka walked her to the door.

Tameka laughed. "Mama, please! I was born in this house, remember? Where could I be more 'all right' than here? Don't worry about me," she added as Mama stepped out onto the porch. "But don't be too disappointed if there's none of that other cobbler left when you get back!"

Tameka stood in the door watching as Mama got into her car, waving as she pulled away. *Well, better get unpacked.* Tameka started for her bags, but her eye fell on her old piano. She went to it, rubbing her hand lovingly over its carefully polished cherrywood finish. Her father had gotten it for her eighth birthday. Tameka remembered how he had thrown back his head and laughed at her speechless delight when she came down the stairs that morning and there it sat, sporting a huge red bow.

Without consciously meaning to, Tameka pulled out the bench and sat down, flipping the cover to expose the keys, now mellowed to more ivory than white. She ran a quick arpeggio, relishing the still resonant sound. Her fingers

moved almost independent of thought as she began the
introduction that was so familiar, and began to sing:

> "Why should I feel discouraged?
> Why should the shadows fall? . . ."

"His Eye Is On the Sparrow"; it had been her father's
favorite song. She sat here in this room singing it for him
more times than memory could count. He would always
sit in his chair, next to the piano, his eyes closed as he
nodded in time to the music. And he would stay that way
until she finished, only then opening his eyes to gaze on
her with such love and pride she felt her heart would burst.

Tameka closed her own eyes as she sang, and it felt as
though her father was still there next to her. As though
he was telling her through the words of the song he loved,
"Don't worry, baby girl. Everything's going to be all right."

Tameka finished the song, her heart lighter than it had
been in months. She was still deep in memory, when her
meditation was broken by the sound of vigorous applause.

She whirled to see a towering silhouette outlined by the
screen door. Startled, she stood so quickly the piano bench
toppled, hitting the floor with a bang.

"I'm sorry," came a deep, husky voice. "I didn't mean
to frighten you."

"How . . . how long have you been there?" Tameka
stammered, a hand to her throat.

"Quite a while, I'm afraid. Eavesdropping is not usually
my thing, but how many chances does a man get to enjoy
a Meeko Moore concert?"

Tameka laughed in spite of her trepidation. "I'm not
Meeko Moore in my mama's living room," she said, going
to the door. "Here I'm just plain Tameka Morgan, proud
survivor of Sister Richardson's piano class."

He laughed, and stepped back slightly, out of the
shadow, as she approached the door. The sun fell warmly
on his chiseled features, making his deep mahogany skin

seem to glow. His chocolate brown eyes sparkled as he smiled down at Tameka. "From where I stand . . ." his teeth were dazzling white as he smiled, "there ain't *nothing* plain about Tameka Morgan."

Tameka peered up. He seemed like a giant. *But then, you're so close to the floor, almost* everybody *looks like a giant to you,* she told herself ruefully. He could have only been about six feet tall, but it wasn't his height that brought thoughts of a colossus to mind. It was his bearing. He had a presence, an air of substance, that had nothing to do with his physical stature. *Although there's certainly nothing wrong with the physique, either,* Tameka's thoughts tumbled on, noting the muscular chest and arms that strained his crisp white shirt.

Tameka suddenly realized he was still staring at her, waiting for her to respond. "Uh . . . I'm afraid you have the advantage," she finally said. "You know who I am, but I don't know who you are."

"Well, that's not surprising." His grin expanded, "I haven't won many Grammys lately." His gentle laugh had the reverberance of distant thunder. "I'm Tyler Barnett, from the church. I came by for Sister Morgan's cobbler, for the bake sale. I went by to help Deacon Bradfield with his car, and he told me he was supposed to pick it up."

"She already left to take it down herself."

"Oh. Sorry I missed her." He stopped smiling, his gaze intense. "But I'm sure not sorry I came by."

Tameka felt herself flushing under the open admiration in his scrutiny. She couldn't think of anything to say. She couldn't say what she was thinking: *Neither am I.*

"Well," he added after a long pause, "guess I'd better be heading on down there myself, if I want to get a piece of that cobbler before it's gone. It was great to meet you. I play your CD so much it's a wonder it hasn't worn out." He reluctantly turned to go. "Hope to see you again soon."

Tameka found her voice just as Tyler started down the

stairs. "Uh . . . Would you like a hot piece?" *Ouch! Rotten phasing, girlfriend!* she silently rebuked herself.

Tyler turned slowly. "Excuse me?" he asked, lifting one eyebrow.

"The cobbler," Tameka hurriedly explained. "You can get a piece *of cobbler* here . . . with me . . . I mean, Mama made an extra one. I was just about to have some." She lamely finished, "Won't you join me?"

They stood staring awkwardly at each other a moment, both a little embarrassed by their mutual awareness of Tameka's unfortunate double entendre. Then the silliness of the situation struck them, and they simultaneously burst out laughing.

"Well," Tameka shrugged, "I'm a singer, not an orator."

"Darn good thing, too," Tyler teased, coming back up the stairs. "But if the invitation's still open, I'd love to have a piece . . ." a devilish grin crossed his handsome face, "of cobbler."

Tameka laughed again as Tyler followed her into the kitchen. "Your mother talks about you all the time," he said. "I'm surprised she didn't mention that you were coming."

"She didn't know." Tameka motioned him to a seat at the table as she got two plates out of the cupboard. "I just decided to come this morning. I went out to the airport, and just got on the first flight headed this way."

"Just like that? No special reason?"

"No. I just missed Mama. I . . . I hadn't seen her in a while," Tameka evaded. Tyler looked at her perceptively as she cut the cobbler, but didn't comment. Tameka felt as though he knew she wasn't leveling with him. *That's silly*, she chided herself. *How could he know?*

"Milk or coffee?" Tameka asked, changing the subject.

"Milk, please. Buttermilk, if you have it."

"Buttermilk? With peach cobbler? Not!" Tameka pronounced with a shudder, opening the refrigerator.

"To each his own, Miss Moore . . . I mean, Morgan."

"That's Tameka," she said, pouring the milk. "Although around here, everybody calls me Tammi."

"Middle name wouldn't be Faye, would it?" Tyler put in, that roguish grin again adorning his face.

"No!" Tameka laughed as she set their plates and glasses on the table, and took a seat. "I'm afraid we don't have any buttermilk, Mr. Barnett. Just the sweet stuff."

He gazed deeply into Tameka's eyes. "Well, the 'sweet stuff' is just fine with me," he said deliberately.

Against her best efforts, Tameka found herself blushing again. She was intensely aware of his nearness, of his muted, subtle cologne.

"Anyway, it's Ty," he was continuing. "And as to the 'Mr.,' it's actually . . ."

"Why, Reverend Barnett! What a surprise! I saw your car outside." Intent on each other, neither Ty nor Tameka had heard Mama entering the front door.

Ty stood. "Came by for the cobbler, Sister Morgan. Deacon Bradfield told me he was supposed to pick it up. Sorry I didn't get here in time to save you a trip." He smiled down at Tameka. "But my trip certainly wasn't wasted."

Tameka looked up at Ty in confusion, "*Reverend?*"

"That's right, honey. Remember I wrote you Pastor Hawkins had a new assistant pastor? This is him, Reverend Tyler Barnett." Mama peered at them closely. "Didn't you two even introduce yourselves to each other?"

"Your daughter needs no introduction. I'm a big fan. I would have recognized her anywhere." He smiled at Tameka again, "Even though TV and the pictures I've seen don't do the real thing justice."

Tameka didn't say anything, too flabbergasted by Mama's revelation to speak.

"I see," Mama commented, checking out the situation. "Well, I've got to prepare the lesson for my Sunday school class tomorrow. You two go ahead and finish your dessert."

She gave Tameka a knowing glance as she headed for the stairs.

"Mama, since time immemorial you've been organizing your Sunday school lesson on Wednesday nights, right after prayer meeting. Isn't it already prepared?" Tameka put in, giving Mama a knowing glance of her own.

"Well, then, I'll go over it, dear," Mama shot back in her sweetest voice. "See you at church tomorrow, reverend," she added before going upstairs.

Ty reclaimed his seat. He and Tameka were silent for a moment. Then Tameka abruptly asked, "Why didn't you tell me you were a minister?"

"Well, I did say I was from the church. And, anyway, I was about to tell you when your mother beat me to the punch."

"You could have told me out on the porch," Tameka insisted.

"Yes, I could have," Ty admitted. "But sometimes people start acting funny when they find out I'm a minister. And just then I didn't want you to think of me as a man of God . . ." He leaned forward, his gaze one of candid fascination, "But, rather, as just a man."

Tameka blushed, and looked down at her hands, clasped in her lap. When she didn't reply, Ty looked embarrassed. "I'm sorry. I'm usually not so presumptuous. It's just that . . ."

Tameka looked up at him, "Not all presumptions are bad." She smiled, the dimples out in force. "Especially when they're mutual," she finished shyly.

Ty's face broke out in a heartbreakingly winsome smile. "Really?"

"Yes, really . . ." Tameka gave him a playful glance, "Reverend."

Ty laughed as he stood. "I'd better be heading on down to the church. Walk me out?"

Tameka had been too startled by Ty's sudden appearance to notice his car earlier. She didn't know cars, but she didn't need to know cars to know this one was a treasure. "Wow! What's this?"

"A 1957 Buick Roadmaster." He stood back from the car proudly. "Ain't she a beauty?"

"She" indeed was. Its classic lines gave it a solidness and substance even most modern luxury cars could not match. It was two-tone pink and black, its diamond finish twinkling in the afternoon sun.

"It's fantastic! How long have you had it? Where did you buy it?"

"I've had it about seven years now. And I didn't exactly buy it. I sorta made it."

"Made it?"

Ty chuckled. "In a manner of speaking. I found it in a junkyard when I was in college. It was in great shape, considering. So I started rebuilding it. Took me three years to get it road worthy." He ran his hand lovingly over the gleaming hood. "There's very little original stuff on the inside. In some cases I even had to fabricate a part. But she looks great, and runs like a champ." He looked uncertainly at Tameka. "Maybe you'd like to take a spin one day?"

Tameka smiled, "I'd love to."

"Great! Well, better be on my way." He got behind the wheel. "See you at church tomorrow?"

"Yes. I'll be there."

"Okay ..." Ty's eyes lingered on Tameka's. "It was really wonderful meeting you."

"Same here." Her eyes twinkled in return. "And I'll make sure we have buttermilk next time."

Ty laughed. "I'll hold you to it! See you tomorrow."

Tameka remained there at the gate, waving as he pulled away. And she stayed there, deep in reflection, long after Ty's car had disappeared down the road.

Chapter 2

"Hurry up, honey, or we'll miss devotion!"

Tameka came flying down the stairs. "I'm ready, Mama. Will you zip my dress?" She turned her back to Mama, while peering into the mirror over the piano to apply her lipstick.

"Oh, Tammi, don't you look pretty! When did you get this dress?"

"I've had it a while, but I've never worn it before. In L.A. I'm usually dressed in one extreme or the other—super casual or evening wear. Not much call for a Sunday-go-to-meeting dress."

"Just 'cause you're away from home don't mean you can't go to church somewhere else, child," Mama gently chided.

"I know Mama, and I've tried. I went to a couple of churches in L.A., but none of them felt right. And since the album, once somebody recognizes me I can't even enjoy the service without being stared at. Once a girl leaned over and asked me for an autograph during communion!"

Tameka turned to face Mama, "How do I look? Are you

sure this dress is all right?'' Tameka twisted her torso, squinting down the back of the dress. "I should never have put this thing on. It's too short! I knew I should have kept on the green one! It'll only take me a second to change." She headed for the stairs. "Be back down in a minute!"

"Oh, no, you don't, young lady!" Mama took her arm. "What's the matter with you? That dress looks wonderful! And if it was too short, believe me, your mama would be the first to tell you."

Mama looked into the mirror herself to secure her flower-laden hat with a huge hat pin. Giving a satisfied nod, she put her handbag over her arm, and started for the door. "You're going to church, girl, not the prom. What's gotten into you this morning? You've already changed twice."

Mama stopped suddenly, "Your preoccupation with your appearance wouldn't have anything to do with Reverend Barnett's visit yesterday, would it?"

"Oh, Mama." Tameka proceeded her onto the porch. "I just met him. And anyway, Ty's our pastor, well—assistant pastor, which is practically the same thing."

"So it's Ty already, huh?" While Tameka locked the door, Mama went to the shiny green Cadillac Tameka had given her the year before.

"Well . . . uh . . . yeah. That's what he told me to call him." Tameka got in the passenger seat. "What's wrong with that? I mean," she continued delicately, "we're both about the same age and . . . and why stand on ceremony?"

"Why, indeed." Mama smiled, backing out of the driveway.

"I like uh . . . Reverend Barnett. He's very . . . nice. But there's nothing more to it than that. My goodness, just because he's an attractive, single man . . ." Tameka stopped short. "He is single, isn't he?"

Mama chuckled. "Now, honey, do you think I'd let a married man grin in my daughter's face in my own kitchen? Of course he's single. I was wondering how long it would take you to get around to asking me that. And he is very attractive, isn't he?"

Despite herself, Tameka blushed. "Now, Mama, don't start." She paused before asking, "Hasn't some woman at the church staked a claim on him by now?"

"No, although many have tried. But Reverend Ty's very circumspect in his fellowship with the younger female congregation. As well he might be. Some of the elders are leery enough as it is about having a single minister, especially such a young one. But he's been above reproach. Although Odetta Slayton's girl is trying her best to give everyone the impression she's got the inside track."

"Dee-Dee Slayton? I thought she was engaged to some big shot attorney from Atlanta."

" 'Was' is right. Something went amiss there. She's back home with her mother."

Tameka looked out the side window. "And Ty's interested in her?" she whispered.

"I said she's interested in him. But from all I've seen, I don't think it's reciprocated. I haven't seen the good reverend show particular interest in any young lady . . ." she glanced meaningfully at Tameka, "until now."

Tameka made no reply as they pulled into the church parking lot. The "I'm home" feeling hit her all over again as she looked at the graceful, old-fashioned structure. She had been baptized here. Memories flooded in of all the choir rehearsals and church socials she'd attended here. Her parents had been married in this church. *And Daddy's funeral was here, too,* she mused, suddenly melancholy.

"Thinking about Daddy?" Mama asked softly, reading Tameka's thoughts.

"Yes, Mama. I don't think I could ever come here without thinking about him. So much of his life was centered around this church."

Mama reached over to pat her hand. "Yes it was, honey. For a time after your Daddy died, I thought I was going to have to join another church, that this place held too many memories for me to ever be comfortable here again. But instead, coming here helps me remember all the good your father did, and I feel better, stronger. Maybe it will be that way for you, too."

Devotion had indeed started. They entered, and took a pew near the middle of the sanctuary. Tameka found herself getting lost in the familiar ritual, to the point where she almost didn't mind the small stir rippling through the church at their arrival.

She and Mama had purposefully decided to attend the early service. Preferring to sleep in on Sunday morning, most parishioners attended the 11:00 service, rather than this one at 8:00. After the service Mama would stay for her 9:45 Sunday school class, catching a ride home with a fellow teacher later. That would leave Tameka free to take the car, missing the larger crowd at the later service.

Mama couldn't understand why Tameka wanted to do it this way. "Don't you want to see all your old friends?" she'd asked Tameka in bafflement.

"Yes, Mama, of course. But not all at the same time," Tameka had only partially explained.

How could she explain to Mama the isolation she felt when people she'd known all her life, people she grew up with, treated her like an . . . an outsider. Like she was somehow different than the person they had known for so many years. Some assumed she had gotten stuck-up. Some treated her like visiting royalty. Not all, thank God. But too many treated her like Meeko Moore, a dazzling stranger in a strange land. Like someone they didn't know, rather than as Tameka, Deacon Morgan's girl.

But Percy Stallworth, the church organist, wasn't in that group. He beamed across the assembly, straight at Tameka. She grinned back. Percy had accompanied her more times than she could remember. At his urging she had finally decided to make the move to L.A., to try her luck in the recording industry.

Percy threw a musical flourish into his accompaniment

of the devotional hymn. Tameka almost laughed out loud. He'd incorporated the intro to her single "Follow Your Heart" so smoothly no one caught it but Tameka. She grinned, and wagged a reproving finger at him.

But as Tameka looked around the church, she realized her evasion strategy hadn't worked. The church was as packed for this early service as it normally was for the later one. "Mama, when did so many people start coming to early service?" Tameka whispered. "There's hardly an empty seat."

"Oh, it's been that way recently," Mama whispered back with a cryptic smile.

Tameka saw movement out of the corner of her eye. She turned, and there sat Eddie Mae, her best childhood friend. Eddie Mae was trying her best to look indignant, no doubt because she hadn't been told Tameka was coming home. But the welcome in Eddie Mae's gaze belied that pretense. Tameka smiled, and Eddie Mae gave her a what-am-I-gonna-do-with-you head shake in reply.

Devotion over, the deacons took their seats. The organ began the pulpit processional. The door from the pastor's study opened, and the ministers exited, starting up the steps to the platform. Tameka's heart began to race. Pastor Hawkins was there, but in a brown suit, not his pastoral robes, which he always wore when he preached. Instead, the man in a flowing black garment was Ty.

"Mama, is T . . . Reverend Barnett preaching this morning?"

"Yes, honey. He's been giving the early sermon for a couple of months now."

"Well, you could have told me," Tameka chided.

Mama just smiled, "Yes, I could have. But I didn't. Now, hush!"

Tameka tried her best not to stare at Ty, but against her will, her eyes returned to him again and again. The masterful strength emanating from him was even more pronounced now. The black robe seemed to accentuate this, as though he was born to wear it.

Her eyes were inexorably drawn to Ty yet again, and she realized with a shock he was returning her gaze.

It's just your imagination, girl. Where else could he look but out into the congregation? He's not looking at you. But then his almost imperceptible nod and discreet smile made it evident he was.

Tameka smiled and nodded in return, then quickly looked away, right into the eyes of Dee-Dee Slayton. Tameka smiled warmly at Dee-Dee. She was surprised by the frosty nod Dee-Dee telegraphed her in return.

Now, what's gotten into her? Tameka wondered. *True, we haven't seen each other since high school, but . . .* Then she remembered what Mama said about Dee-Dee having a thing for Ty. *Surely she couldn't think, just because he smiled at me . . .*

But apparently Dee-Dee did think just that . . . or something equally disagreeable, from the dry expression she continued to exhibit.

" . . . and, praise be to God, she's with us this morning!" snapped Tameka's attention back to the pulpit. Pastor Hawkins was at the lectern, beaming down directly at her.

"I baptized that child. I married her parents," he was continuing. "And the Lord has blessed me to see the day she returns to this church as a Grammy winner! Of course," the pastor maintained with an airy wave of his hand, "I knew it was coming. I knew it the day her daddy stood her on a chair to sing 'Jesus Loves Me' when she was three years old!"

That brought a surge of laughter from the congregation, along with several "Amens" and "Hallelujahs."

"And proud as I am of Sister Morgan's professional triumph, I'm even prouder of her personal victory. In today's recording environment, especially rap music, where so many have disgraced themselves and dishonored their people, she has always presented herself with respect, dignity, and pride. There's not a one of her recordings I wouldn't want my grandchildren to hear."

There was a tremendous ovation from the congregation. Many were on their feet. Tameka's eyes brimmed with tears. Mama put one arm around Tameka's shoulders to hug her, her own eyes misting as well.

"I wouldn't dream of imposing on a visiting celebrity, but girl, you're no visitor here. You're family. And you've owed me a favor ever since you spit up on my best shirt the first time your parents brought you to church!"

The congregation again burst out in laughter. Pastor Hawkins had to wait for it to subside before asking, "Would you favor us with a song?"

Tameka was surprised, but then realized she shouldn't have been. She'd been a regular fixture in the choir here since she was a child. Much as she'd planned to maintain a low profile, there was no way she could refuse. And she didn't want to refuse.

Tameka rose from her seat. Ty's eyes never left her as she mounted the few steps to the choir loft, the admiration on his face unmistakable.

Tameka had grown up with most of the choir, and most of them were clapping and waving, calling greetings. But even there, Tameka noticed a few tight jaws, and eyes that did not smile, even though the lips beneath them did.

Percy rose from the organ bench to embrace Tameka, "Lord have mercy, honey! This is just like old times. What do you want to sing?"

"Oh, Percy!" Tameka hugged him in return. "It's so great to see you! Gosh, I don't know. I didn't come prepared to sing."

"Well, I don't know why not," Percy grinned as he reclaimed his seat. "You didn't think the Hawk would let you out of here without a song, did you? And you don't need to 'prepare to sing.' The Lord took care of that the day you were born. Why don't you sing 'Peace! Be Still?' That was always one of your favorites. The choir still does it.

We'll back you up." Before Tameka could answer, Percy's talented fingers began to whip out the familiar refrain.

Tameka hadn't sung the song in years, but nothing could erase the words from her memory—or her heart. She turned to the mike, looking down on the sea of parishioners. During the brief intro, she spotted the occasional taciturn face, but most were upturned up in eager anticipation.

"Master, the tempest is raging . . ."

The suddenness of the situation, and the occasional disapproving stare made Tameka's first few notes tentative. But then she threw her head back, closed her eyes, and let the music take over.

"The billows are tossing high . . ."

The voice *Rolling Stone* magazine called "one of the most beautiful sounds ever recorded" came forth, true and strong. When she sang, Tameka was in a world unto herself. The music seemed to encompass her, to engulf her, until they became one. Time receded, and she was no longer the 23-year-old, nationally known singing sensation. She was 11-year-old Tameka again, singing this song for the first time with the junior choir.

"And then I heard the Lord say . . ." Tameka spoke the words as she flourished her hand outward in invitation to the choir. They stepped right in with the chorus: "The winds and the waves shall obey my will . . ." Tameka began to sway in time to the music, the choir behind her moving in sync.

"Sing your song, girl!" and "Praise the Lord!" rang out from all about the room. Sister Rakestraw started to shout. A member of the nurse's guild came rushing forward to remove Sister Rakestraw's glasses and ventilate her with a cardboard fan on a stick, courtesy of Rushton's Funeral Home.

As the song ended, the cries of exaltation did not. The church had been ignited. Percy began to play the song again, softly this time, as the hosannas continued. Many were now on their feet, waving hands, handkerchiefs, and fans.

Tameka didn't realize she was crying until a tear rolled into the corner of her mouth. She gave the assembly a shaky smile as she maneuvered the now blurry steps, and returned to her seat. Mama's hand was trembling as she reached over to take Tameka's. "Thank you, Lord Jesus," Mama whispered, tightly squeezing the hand she was holding. "Thank you for my child."

Ty rose, and slowly approached the altar. He stood there, nodding his head, silently acknowledging the Spirit that permeated the building. As the tumult began to subside, Percy brought the music to a close with a long, lingering chord. Ty's eyes swept the audience, seeming to single out each person in his piercing examination. "Praise the Lord!"

"Praise the Lord!" the congregation echoed.

"No, I don't think you heard me," Ty asserted. "I said 'Praise the Lord!' "

"Praise the Lord!" the assembly repeated, even louder.

"You said that mighty feeble. Are you not glad you woke up this morning? A lot of folks didn't. Are you not glad you had a bed to sleep in last night? A lot of folks didn't. Are you not glad you had a good breakfast this morning? A lot of folks went hungry. Whatever the troubles in your life, the Lord allowed you to walk into this building on your own two feet. A lot of folks would give anything just to have two feet. And all these folks would make a loud, joyful noise unto the Lord if only they could be here. Now . . . what I said was . . . Praise the Lord!"

"Praise the Lord!" The strength of the response made the old walls seem to tremble.

"Amen! A joyful noise unto the Lord. And I want to thank our sister for sharing the gift the Lord has given her with us this morning." Ty looked down at Tameka. But it was somehow different this time. This time he wasn't the

guy who liked buttermilk and rebuilding classic cars. This
time his thoughts were on things eternal.

"And how are you sharing your gift?" Ty challenged the
group at large. "If your answer is 'What gift?,' we need to
talk. Maybe you can't sing, but you can teach a Sunday
school class. Maybe you can't teach, but you can lead the
devotional prayer. In His bountiful goodness, the Lord has
given us all a talent, a gift, to be used to help our brethren
. . . and to His glory."

Tameka understood now why the church was so packed.
As Ty progressed into his sermon, it was like being born
along with the unstoppable tide of the ocean. The congregation was alternately lifted high on the wave of a resounding phrase, only in the next moment to be soothed by
serene reassurance. Ty's voice was a clarion, calling them
all to bear witness to the wonder of God's love, and their
place in His eternal plan.

For that span of time, Tameka's thoughts were not of
the man, but of the messenger, whose business it was to
comfort the despairing, to rededicate the disheartened; to
rekindle the flame that daily living strove to make dim.
This time Sister Rakestraw wasn't the only one who shouted
out to the Lord in praise and supplication. The church
echoed with the cries of those moved outside of themselves.
Moved to open themselves to the wisdom and inspiration
being offered to them.

The sounds of thanksgiving continued even as Ty concluded his sermon. Percy and the choir began "You Have
A Talent—Use It for the Lord". Ty stepped from behind
the pulpit, arms spread wide, the full sleeves of the black
robe fluttering, looking like the wings of an enormous
black eagle. He "opened the doors of the church" for
membership to any seeking a church home.

A young couple with a babe in arms shyly came forward.
Ty came down from the pulpit, and warmly greeted them
both to the church's chorus of Amens, before the deacon

board led them into the pastor's study to talk with them privately.

During the following song from the choir, while the offering plates were passed, Tameka watched Ty in wonderment. He wiped his brow with a white handkerchief as he casually leaned forward, smiling and nodding at whatever Pastor Hawkins was whispering in his ear. Ty seemed totally oblivious to the fact that he had electrified the room just a few moments before.

Benediction quickly followed, and Tameka soon found herself and Mama surrounded by people who wanted to welcome Tameka home.

Sister Rakestraw was the first, "Oh, baby, you come here!" She grabbed Tameka in a bear hug, almost smothering her with the stole made up of a string of minks biting their own tails that she always wore on Sundays, winter and summer, rain or shine.

"I remember when you were in my Sunday school class! And look at you now!" The good sister pulled a hanky from her generous bosom, dabbing a sudden tear from her eye. "The Lord bless you, darlin'! And you keep on singin'."

Eddie Mae was next, "Okay, girl . . . They don't have phones in California now, or what? Why didn't you tell me you were coming?" she demanded, trying to look ticked off. But the twinkle in her eyes gave her away.

"Stop fussing, and give me a hug," Tameka laughed as they embraced. "Eddie, you look fabulous! Looks like teaching agrees with you."

"Yep. I've been promoted from kindergarten to fourth grade," Eddie Mae said with a grin. "But really, girl, I love it. I love it so much I even teach Sunday school, as well."

"You, the terror of the junior choir, a Sunday school teacher? Will miracles never cease! Who would have ever thought . . ."

"Well, well, well. Welcome back, Miss Morgan . . . or is it Miss Moore now?" a sardonic voice interjected before

Eddie Mae could answer. Dee-Dee Slayton stood at Tameka's elbow, a smirk on her face in place of a smile.

"It's neither. I'm Tammi, like I've always been," Tameka ignored her snide tone. "How are you, Dee-Dee?"

"I guess my complacent little life can't compare to the . . . uh, pandemonium you must have in yours, but I'm happy with it. By the way, I go by Deirdre now. After all, we're not children anymore, now are we?"

"Depends on how you look at it," Eddie Mae put in, rolling her eyes in Deirdre's direction.

Deirdre frowned, but before she could comment further a number of other church members closed in. Even surrounded by well wishers, Tameka noticed a number of others standing off to the side watching, their lips pursed.

When one young man asked for an autograph Tameka said, "I'd be happy to . . . but not here in the sanctuary. Let's wait until we're outside, okay?"

"Okay," he responded, clearly not comprehending why.

"Good morning, Margaret," a deep, honeyed bass voice said from nearby. "Tameka, good to see you home, girl." It was Jesse James, the town sheriff. Uncle Jesse had been one of her father's closest friends. Needless to say, the poor man had taken a good deal of ribbing about his name all his life. That he had turned out to be a cop made the joke that much richer. His laid-back, unassuming demeanor might have made the uninitiated doubt his qualifications as a lawman. But Tameka, who had seen him in action during some of the town's few criminal emergencies, knew better.

Tameka stood on her toes, and kissed his cheek. "It's good to be home, Uncle Jesse." Jesse had never married, and since he had no children of his own, had always been a special patron to Tameka, especially since her father's death, five years before.

"Jesse, if you're not on duty, why don't you come over for dinner this evening, so we can celebrate Tammi's homecoming?" Mama said warmly.

"You know I never miss an opportunity for your cooking, Margaret. I'll be there," he promised, with a smile.

Tameka felt Ty's presence before she turned to see him standing there. "Good morning, Sister Morgan . . . and Sister Morgan," Ty nodded to Mama, with a smile.

"Good morning, Reverend," Mama smiled in return.

"Good morning, Reverend Barnett," Tameka said, her voice somewhat husky as her throat felt suddenly constricted. She bashfully shook Ty's offered hand. "Your sermon was magnificent."

"Thank you. Your song was magnificent, also."

Ty had taken off his robe, and was now in a dark blue suit. Tameka found herself wondering how his tailor had managed to mold the jacket to fit those massive shoulders. Ty was quickly surrounded by others congratulating him on the sermon.

Tameka and Mama gradually made their way to the exit, and out in the church parking lot, Tameka made good her promise, signing autographs for all who wanted one. As she finished the last one, Mama said, "I'd better get back inside, baby. It's almost time for my class."

"All right, Mama." Tameka kissed her cheek. "Are you sure you have a ride home?"

"What's this about somebody needing a ride?" Ty had come up behind them.

"Tameka's taking the car home while I stay to teach my class," Mama told him. "But I'll be fine, Reverend. I know several people who'll be heading out my way."

"I've got a better idea. I'm leaving now, too. Why don't I escort Sister Morgan, junior, home . . ." he looked at Tameka with a smile, "and then Sister Morgan senior can keep the car."

"You're not staying for the second service?" Mama asked.

"Not today. I'm speaking this afternoon over at Glouchester Memorial. I've got to get on the highway now to make it in time."

"That's very thoughtful of you, Reverend. Isn't it, dear?" Mama said pointedly Tameka's way.

"Yes ... Yes, it is," Tameka found her voice. "Well, if you're sure it's not out of your way ..."

"I'm very sure it's not out of my way," Ty smiled down at her.

"See you at home, honey," Mama pronounced. "Have a safe drive, Reverend, and thank you." Mama turned and headed back into the church.

"Shall we?" Ty delicately took Tameka's elbow to guide her toward the Roadmaster. Several parishioners were watching as he held open the passenger door, and helped her inside.

Neither of them spoke for several moments before Ty finally said, "I'm glad for this chance to talk to you alone. There's something I'd like to ask of you."

Tameka was surprised. "Yes, Reverend?" Her voice came out in little more than a whisper.

Ty turned to her with a quick smile. "I think we can go back to Ty and Tammi now ... don't you?"

Tameka felt ill at ease. "Yes ... I guess so ... but it just seems strange now that I've heard you ..."

"Tameka, I'm surprised at you," Ty chided. "I would have thought you of all people would have no problem separating the person from what he does for a living."

Tameka was somewhat piqued by this mild rebuke. "What you do is more than just 'a living,' Ty, and you know it."

"Yes, it is," Ty turned suddenly serious. "A whole lot more. But isn't your singing more than just 'a living' to you?"

Tameka had never really looked at it that way before. "Yes," she reflectively admitted, "I guess it is."

"I saw the way some of the folks related to you. Like you were somehow different, somehow set apart. I would imagine it happens to you all the time."

"It does," Tameka again admitted.

"Happens to me, too." He sent Tameka a sharp stare. "Don't you believe in God?"

Tameka was again vexed. "Of course I believe in God! How could you even ask me that?"

Ty smiled, "Just wanted to get it on the record. I do, too. And since *you* do, why does it trouble you that my chosen profession is preaching His Word?"

Tameka looked out the side window. "It . . . it *doesn't* bother me."

"Oh, come on, now. You should have seen your face when your mother called me reverend yesterday. I hope you're not one of those people who think ministers go home and stand propped up in a corner in their suit and tie all week, waiting for Sunday to roll around again."

Despite her discomfort, Tameka had to laugh. "Oh, Ty, please!"

He joined her laughter. "I'm glad you're not, because I don't think Grammy winners walk around with their noses stuck up in the air, waiting for someone to come peel them a grape, either."

By then they'd reached Tameka's house. Ty pulled the Roadmaster into the driveway, and turned to Tameka with a gentle smile, "So let's just go back to being the two people who enjoyed each other's company over peach cobbler yesterday." He offered his hand as his eyes searched hers. "Deal?"

Tameka felt a quiver run down her spine as they shook. "Deal."

Their hands remained joined for a long moment as they looked into each other's eyes, both aware of the understanding that had just developed between them.

"So . . . is that what you wanted to talk to me about?" Tameka finally asked.

"No." Tameka could feel Ty changing gears. "I wanted to talk to you about the Young People's choir."

"The Young People's choir? What about it?"

"Well, you know the fundraiser yesterday was for them—

to help send them to Atlanta for the Gospelfest next month?''

"Yes. Mama told me. And I'd be glad to contribute . . .''

"Good. That's what I'd like for you to do. Make a contri-bution—but not in money.''

Tameka was confused. "Well, in what, then?''

"Your time. Do you know Clarise Swanson?''

"Yes, of course. I've known Clarise since we were little girls. Why?''

"She's been directing the Young People's choir for the past couple of years. But she's pregnant, and things aren't going smoothly.''

"Oh, no. I hope she and the baby are all right.''

"The doctor has her stabilized now, but she's going to have to take it very easy for the next few months.'' He looked at Tameka purposefully. "She won't be able to work with the choir.''

Tameka was puzzled for a moment, then grasped his intention. "And you want me to . . .''

"To take her place. I don't know how long you're plan-ning on being home this trip, but if you could meet with them even a couple of times, it would mean a lot. Percy would be there to help you.''

Well, why not? Tameka thought. *I'm in no hurry to get back to L.A. just now. And I think I really could be of some help to those kids. It's time I did more to give back than just send money. And . . . who am I fooling . . . I'd enjoy it.*

Ty watched Tameka anxiously as these thoughts ran through her mind. Finally she smiled at him and said, "I'd love to do it. When do I start?''

"Really? You mean it?'' Ty looked at her with delight.

"Yes,'' Tameka laughed at his elation. "I'm looking for-ward to it.''

"You know, I probably shouldn't swell up that monster ego of yours any more than it already is,'' Ty teased, "but I think you're pretty terrific—for a singer.''

"Thanks, Rev,'' Tameka grinned back as she reached

for the door handle. "You're not bad yourself—for a minister."

"Uh, Tammi," Ty touched her arm lightly. "I was wondering . . . that is, I thought maybe . . ." Tameka was astounded to hear the confident, articulate Ty fumbling for words.

What on earth is he trying to say? "Yes, Ty?"

"Well, this thing over in Glouchester is no big deal, just a church supper after the service. But it's such a beautiful day for a drive . . . and I would certainly welcome the company . . . and if you don't already have plans for the afternoon, I thought maybe you'd . . ."

Tameka's heart melted as he continued to stammer over the invitation. "I'd love to go with you, Ty."

His eyes lit up. "You would?"

"Yes, but . . ."

His eyes dimmed. "But . . . what?"

"Well, Ty, you know how idle talk travels. Word will probably get back before we do. I . . . I don't know if my going with you would be such a good idea for a man of your . . . your status."

Ty grinned. "My status? What status is that? Being single? I should think that's the best status for a man who's just asked a pretty woman for a date."

"Ty, you know what I mean. Some people assume with me being a recording artist and living in L.A., I'm into all seven of the deadly sins—and have probably invented an eighth."

"Well . . . are you?" Ty asked with a twinkle in his eye.

Tameka laughed. "Only four or five, tops," she teased back. She stopped laughing, "But, Ty . . ."

"Tammi, my grandma used to always say, 'Honey, they talked about Jesus. What makes you think people ain't gonna talk about you?' There are only two consciences I answer to. One is my own. I think you know Whose the other one is." He took Tammi's hand. "And I'm fairly certain both would be very pleased to have you go to church with me this afternoon," he whispered.

Tameka looked deeply into his eyes for a long beat before saying, "It'll just take me a moment to go in and write Mama a note."

Chapter 3

"So have you ever met Babyface?" Reggie asked eagerly.

"Yes, Kenny and I worked together on some of the cuts from my CD, but . . ."

"Man, who cares about Babyface?" Marc told Reggie. "What about Brandy? Now that's who I'd like to get to know . . . real good!" Marc turned to Tameka, "Do you know her?"

"Yes, but . . ."

"Oh, Miss Moore, I can't believe you're really here in our church, at our rehearsal!" Opal gushed.

"Well, it's my church, too, Opal," Tameka said with a grin.

Not to be deferred, Opal timidly touched the sleeve of Tameka's silk blouse. "Did you get this on Rodeo Drive?" Only she pronounced it "*Ro-de-o*".

"Don't be pulling on her clothes, girl! What's the matter with you?" Calvin glared at Opal, and turned to Tameka. The shining glaze across Calvin's eyes was one Tameka had seen very often of late. "Miss Moore . . . we . . . ah, I mean . . .'' Calvin didn't seem to know just what he meant as he continued to stare at Tameka, stammering.

"Uh-uh! Thought you were gonna rock her world, my brother.'' Marc gave Calvin a playful shove. "Looks like you better get those 'rocks' outta your mouth before you start trying to rap to Miss Moore!''

Calvin flushed and whirled to shove Marc back—hard. "You shut up or I'm gonna put a rock in your mouth—one with five fingers on it!''

"Step up off me, man! Just because you got a love jones ain't no reason to be getting bad with me! You better . . .''

Tameka had gone over to the piano, and banged down heavily on the keys with both hands. The loud discordant blare stopped the teens cold.

"Excuse me . . .'' Tameka announced, her cool gaze encompassing them all, "but have you all forgotten where you are?''

The teens all looked shamefaced—especially Calvin—and quietly took their seats once again.

"That's more like it. Now, let's establish a few ground rules. First, I'm Miss Morgan, not Miss Moore. Moore is my stage name. I'm not on stage here. Second, we're here to advance your singing, not mine. Understood?''

Thirty-seven heads nodded in silent unison.

"Third,'' Tameka continued, this time with a smile, "I'm tickled to death to be here, and I'm going to try my best to help you win that trophy . . . if you'll let me.'' Tameka put her hands on her hips, dimples twinkling. "So . . . you down for that, or what?''

The choir breathed a joint sigh of relief, realizing Tameka wasn't really ticked over their preliminary foolishness.

"Yes, ma'am!''

"You know it!''

"Well, alllll-righty, then,'' Tameka pronounced in her best Jim Carrey imitation as she sat down at the piano. "Brother Stallworth will be here shortly. Why don't we do some warm-up exercises in the meantime. I want to see what you can do.''

Tameka started them off on a series of scales. She was impressed with the power and richness of their young voices. *If they sound this good just warming up, we really do have a shot at that trophy,* she thought with satisfaction, not consciously realizing she'd made a transition from "they" to "we" in how she viewed the choir.

By the time Percy arrived Tameka had pinpointed a few problem areas that would need individual attention. The sopranos were wonderful; Latrisse could even hit high E over the staff. But too many of them had what Tameka called "the soprano syndrome"—singing through their noses. Being a soprano herself, she knew exactly how to deal with it.

The boys presented a more diplomatic problem. They were too loud. They drowned the girls out. She'd somehow have to find a way to tone them down without losing the fullness and vibrancy of their sound.

But, all things considered, Tameka felt really encouraged by rehearsal's end. She had a good group here. With hard work, and with God's help, she hoped to mold them into a great group.

"What do you think, Tammi?" Percy asked as the choir members where milling around, preparing to leave. "You think we've got a shot?"

"For a trophy? More than a shot. These kids are good. Clarise has done a wonderful job with them. But, Percy, why didn't the church just ask you to take over the choir when she became ill?"

"No way I could do it. I'm already playing accompaniment for all six of the church's choirs, as well as playing for all the services. I knew I couldn't do justice trying to direct this one as well, especially with them preparing for a special performance." Percy grinned, "So I think Reverend Ty had a dynamite idea in thinking of you as the replacement. But then . . . I guess Rev T has been thinking about you a good deal lately."

Tameka scrutinized Percy, "And what's that supposed to mean?"

Percy laughed. "Now, come on, Tammi. You know good and well the whole church knows about him taking you to Glouchester Memorial Sunday. Some of the good sisters over there were on the phone as soon as they got home. Did you expect them not to notice a handsome, young, single minister? Especially one as together as Ty. He's considered a prime catch around these parts."

"He'd be considered a prime catch anywhere," Tameka said spontaneously, before she could check her tongue.

Percy gave her a knowing grin, "So you *have* noticed. And you're not exactly low profile yourself."

"Be that as it may, I don't see any reason for folks to go gossiping . . ."

Percy grinned even wider, "Since when did folks need a reason to gossip? And where is the reverend this evening? I'd have thought he'd be here to wish you well on your inaugural stint with the choir."

Tammi had been wondering the same thing. Ty had called Monday evening to tell her about the Thursday rehearsal, and they had chatted about a little of everything: his love of classic cars, her recording career (although she didn't tell him about her difficulties with Danny). Ty seemed reluctant to hang up when she had finally brought the call to a close. He hadn't *said* he'd be here for the rehearsal, but Tammi had assumed he would be. She could have used his moral support and . . . *And who do you think you're fooling, girl,* a voice said from within. *You just plain want to see him again.*

"Percy, why should Reverend Barnett come to a choir rehearsal?" Tammi said aloud, and got his "yeah, right" look of skepticism in return. "I'm sure he's got a hundred other things to do," she hurried on, "and . . ."

"Miss Morgan?" Calvin's tenuous murmur interrupted them.

"Yes, Calvin?" The boy looked like he was about to cry. "What's the matter? Is something wrong?" Tameka asked in concern.

"No . . . yes . . . I mean . . ." Calvin looked down at the floor. "I . . . I'm sorry about that cra . . . stuff Reggie was talking. I mean, I would never say anything disrespectful like that about you, Miss Morgan." He looked up suddenly, the unbridled devotion on his face unmistakable.

Uh-oh, Tameka recognized with déjà vu. She remembered her own childhood crushes, and how serious they had been to her. She couldn't hurt this boy's feelings.

"I know you wouldn't, Calvin," she responded softly. "See you Saturday, okay?"

Calvin suddenly brightened, "Okay, Miss Morgan!" He turned and started to run out, then remembered where he was, and stopped. He looked back with an enamored grin so shyly wistful Tameka's heart ached for him. "Bye."

Percy peered at Tameka, "Uh-oh. Crush Central, dead ahead."

"Yeah, I know," Tameka sighed, gathering up her things.

"Well, just because a man is only sixteen doesn't mean he can't recognize quality when he sees it."

"Percy, cut it out," Tameka said with a worried laugh, giving Percy's arm a swat as they walked to the back of the sanctuary. "It also doesn't mean he can't hurt or be humiliated either. I'm going to have to be very careful with that situation."

"You can handle it, Tammi. And you can handle the choir, too. You were great with them this evening."

"Thanks . . . Postscript," Tameka grinned, harkening back to her old nickname for Percy, which came from him marking *P.S.* in big red letters on all his music.

"Ouch! Thought you'd forgotten about that," he grinned back.

"Not a chance."

By then they'd reached the front lobby, where several of the teens were still hanging around, waiting for rides, or just goofing off. "Need a ride home, Tammi? I didn't see your mom's car in the parking lot."

"She had some shopping to do after she dropped me off. No, thanks, Percy. It's such a lovely evening, I think I'll just walk home."

"You sure?" He looked down at her feet. "Think those Gucci loafers can deal with a mile and a half hike?"

"Gucci, my foot," Tameka laughed. "I got these out of Penny's catalog. And, yes, I'll be fine. It won't be dark for at least another hour, and I need the exercise. I don't have my trainer here to keep me on the straight and narrow. I've been enjoying Mama's cooking a little bit too much the last few days."

The outer door opened, and in charged Thelma Fuller, balancing a bawling baby on one hip. "Reggie!" she hollered at her oldest, who was standing with his back to the door, whispering something in Opal's ear. "Boy, didn't I tell you to wait for me outside after rehearsal? I've been sitting in the parking lot ten minutes!"

"Yeah, man, better get a move on. Yo' mama's here," Calvin taunted, obviously relishing the opportunity to do a little teasing of his own.

"Off my case, man," Reggie murmured under his breath, with a mortified glance at Opal.

"You better get your narrow hips on out to the car. We'll be late picking your father up from work! How many times have I told you . . ." Thelma's tirade stopped suddenly when she looked up to see Tameka standing with Percy. "Tammi! Uh . . . What are *you* doing here?" Thelma self-consciously brushed at her disheveled hair while hiking the baby up higher on her hip.

"Well, hello, Thelma. Long time no see," Tameka pointedly responded, puzzled and somewhat piqued by Thelma's greeting.

"Oh . . . sorry," Thelma said quickly, switching the still crying baby to the other hip. "These kids are about to drive me crazy! I heard you were in town, but I'm surprised to see you here on a Thursday night."

"Since Clarise is out sick, Tammi's going to help with the choir while she's here," Percy informed her.

"She is?" Thelma's incredulity was plainly not based in delight.

"Anything wrong with that?" Percy challenged.

"No . . . no, of course not," Thelma stammered, giving Tameka a dubious eye. "It's just that I'd have thought she'd be too busy to bother with us with all her . . ."

"Thought you were in a big hurry, Mama," Reggie sullenly piped up.

"Don't smart-talk me, boy!" She thrust the baby into his arms. "Here! Take your sister on out to the car. And don't you dare turn on that radio!"

Tameka remembered when she was a small girl, how she had looked up to Thelma, who was about ten years older. Thelma was one of the prettiest teenagers at the church at that time. Thelma prided herself on also being one of the sharpest dressed. The rumpled and harried woman before Tameka now barely resembled the breezy teenager she remembered.

Not that any of that was important to Tameka. Thelma's appearance was her own business. And Tameka had long since learned to appraise people for what was on the inside, not the outside. But Thelma evidently felt the competitive leaning Tameka had begun to experience frequently of late from other women, as though they felt uncomfortable around her.

"It's really, uh . . . nice of you to volunteer, Tammi, but maybe you should have cleared this with one of the church officers before . . ."

"Reverend Barnett asked me to step in with the choir, Thelma," Tameka quietly informed her.

Thelma seemed to find this piece of information extremely interesting. "Oh, he did?"

"Yes, I did," a resonant voice came from behind them as Ty entered from the church office. He was casually dressed in high-top sneakers, jeans, and a sweatshirt with the sleeves ripped short. Tameka couldn't help but notice the rippling biceps in his powerful upper arms. Despite herself, Tameka felt her breath quicken. Then it all but stopped as he gazed down at her with one of his heartwarming smiles.

"And I think we're extremely blessed Sister Morgan was willing to help out." Ty continued. He turned a steady gaze on Thelma, "Don't you?"

"Why, yes . . . yes, of course, Reverend Barnett. I just thought . . ."

"Yes?" Ty came back smoothly. "You thought . . . what?"

"Mama!" Reggie burst back in the outer door. "Kayla just spit up all over the front seat!" he informed his mother—with obvious disgust.

"I've . . . I've got to be going." Thelma said hastily. She left quickly, hustling Reggie out the door ahead of her.

Ty turned back to Tameka. "I planned to get here earlier, to wish you well. I help coach the basketball team at the high school on Thursday nights, and the game went into overtime. I didn't even get a chance to change. But how did rehearsal go?"

"Great, Rev.," Percy answered for Tameka. "I think we've got a winner here."

"We sure have," Ty said earnestly, his eyes never leaving Tameka.

"Uh . . . I meant the choir, Rev. T," Percy remarked with a meaningful grin.

Ty didn't seem to hear him. "Were you as pleased with the rehearsal, Tammi?" he asked softly.

"Yes, Ty. These kids are marvelous. Working with them is going to be a joy."

"Great! I'm so glad you feel that way." He moved a little

closer. "Now that we've found you, we sure wouldn't want to lose you."

Percy cleared his throat, "Ahem . . . well, guess I'll be on my way."

Ty seemed to come back to the situation at hand. He looked at his watch, "Guess it is getting late." He looked back to Tameka. "Just give me a minute to put some things up in the office and I'll see you home."

"Okay, Ty," Tameka said softly. "I'll wait for you outside," she called as he re-entered the office.

"Thought you were walking home, girlfriend," Percy quipped.

"Well, I . . . I was," Tameka stammered, "but . . ." *But what?* she quizzed herself. *I was planning to walk home. I wasn't waiting around, hoping Ty would show up . . . or was I?*

"Yes?" Percy prompted.

"Oh, Percy," Tameka laughed self-consciously. "Stop instigating and start ambulating!" She aided him in that effort by walking him out the front door, and down the few steps at the front of the church.

It was a beautiful evening. A warm breeze was blowing softly, carrying the scent of the roses planted all about the entryway. The song of crickets added to the quiet serenity of the twilight.

"See you Saturday," Percy called, heading around to the parking lot, at the side of the church. He couldn't resist adding, "Don't do anything I wouldn't do!" with a roguish look in his eyes.

"That gives me a lot of room to maneuver!" Tameka called back. Percy's laughter trailed off, along with his footsteps.

Tameka noticed headlights approaching. It was a squad car. The car pulled to the curb and stopped. "Tammi! What are you doing out here all by yourself?"

"Hi, Uncle Jesse," Tameka greeted him, walking up to the open car window. "Choir rehearsal just ended."

"So that's what's going on. I was cruising by on patrol, and I saw all the activity over here, and thought I'd better check it out. But why was there a rehearsal on a Thursday night?"

"It's for the Young People's choir. Since they're preparing for the Gospelfest, they're going to be rehearsing twice a week now, on Thursdays and Saturdays."

"Oh, I see. But if it's the Young People's choir, what are you doing here?"

"Well, I am still relatively young, Uncle Jesse," Tameka teased.

Jesse chuckled softly, "Don't get sassy with me, girl. You know what I mean. The Young People's choir is for kids thirteen to seventeen. Young you may be. A teenager you are not. Hey, are you going to sing a solo for the Gospelfest? That would be fantastic!"

"No, Uncle Jesse." Tameka drew herself up to her full height—what little there was of it. "You're looking at the new directress of the Third Avenue Church Young People's choir," she giggled. "Well, temporary directress, anyway."

"That's wonderful, honey! How did this happen?"

"Since Clarise Swanson won't be able to work with them for a while, I'm going to help out. The concert's only a little over two weeks away. I can stay at least that long. Reverend . . . Reverend Barnett asked me about it Sunday."

"Oh, Reverend Barnett did, huh?" Jesse asked, seeming to pick up on something.

"Yes, he did. What's wrong with that?" Tameka asked, a little bit too energetically.

Jesse grinned, "Not a dang thing, honey." He paused, "Uh, is your mother at home now? I mean, I stopped by earlier, and she wasn't there."

"No, she went shopping. Why?"

"Oh, I was just wondering." He seemed a tad self-conscious. "I didn't want anything special. I was on patrol, and just thought I'd stop by to see how you two were doing," he rambled on.

Oh, us two, huh? Tameka thought, picking up on a little something of her own.

"So is that why you're standing here? Is she coming by to pick you up?"

"Ah . . . no," Tameka replied, looking down at the sidewalk.

"Do you need a ride home? Jump in, I can run you by."

"Ah, I've got a ride, Uncle Jesse." *Why do I feel so secretive about it?* Tameka wondered. *It's no big deal.* "Tyler Barnett already offered me a ride home," she finally admitted.

"Oh, I see," Jesse replied, as if he really did see. He smiled. "Okay, darlin'. Catch you later then. Tell your mother I said hello." He gave her a jaunty wave as he drove away.

Tameka slowly strolled back from the curb. Sitting down on the steps, she drew up her knees, and wrapped her arms around them. Ty should be out soon.

I'm trembling, she realized with wonder. She hadn't felt this way in a long, long time. She was suddenly reminded of sitting in her parents' living room, waiting for her high school sweetheart to pick her up for the senior prom. But then she had been just a girl. Now she was a woman, and the feelings coursing through her were much more intense, much more complex.

She suddenly felt frightened. *This shouldn't be happening. I can't have these sort of feelings about Ty. He's my pastor for goodness' sake! This just isn't right.* But it felt right. It felt very right.

" . . . and she has the audacity to pretend she's interested in the choir . . . when all she's really interested in is him!" a strident voice burst in on Tameka's meditation. The voice was a ways off, but still audible in the hush of the evening. It was Thelma, still in the parking lot around the bend.

"Oh, Thelma, I wouldn't say that," another voice demurred. "And I think it's wonderful she's directing the choir. After all, to have a big star like her . . ."

"Exactly," a third voice volunteered. " 'A big star like

her.' My son has pictures of her all over his bedroom! I think it's disgraceful for a blues singer to be leading one of our choirs—especially the children's choir! God knows what she's putting in those kid's heads."

"Oh, I don't think . . ." Tameka's supporter began.

"Well, she sure seems to have put some ideas in Tyler Barnett's head," Thelma cut her off. "And I don't think they have much to do with her musical talents, either! You should have seen the silly grin on his face when he was talking to her!"

"Mama!" Reggie called urgently. "Kayla did it again!"

"Well, you know how to wipe, don't you?" Thelma snapped back. "Look," she continued to her companions, "I gotta be going. My old man's gonna pitch one about me being late picking him up. And speaking of husbands, quiet as it's kept, I'd advise you ladies to keep a sharp eye on your husbands while Miss Thang is in town. You know how foolish men can get over women like her!"

Thelma's parting shot silenced the other women. Even Tameka's defender had no rebuttal with the contemplation of her man straying from the fold occupying her thoughts. Their hurried good-byes were followed by the sound of their cars pulling out of the parking lot.

Tameka looked up at the late evening sky, the pink glow of the sunset clouds shimmering through the tears that suddenly filled her eyes.

"Ready to go, Tammi?" Ty's voice from behind startled her.

Tameka quickly drew a hand across her face, hoping to wipe the tears away before he saw them. "Y . . . yes, Ty. I'm ready." In spite of her best efforts, her voice wavered.

Descending the stairs, Ty looked down in concern, "Tammi? You all right?"

"Of course," she fibbed. Tameka forced a smile. "Why wouldn't I be?"

"That's what I'm trying to find out." Ty sat down next to her on the step. He reached over and with his thumb softly wiped away a bit of moisture from Tameka's cheek. "You missed one," he said quietly. "You were so up just a moment ago. What on earth could have happened so quickly to bring you down?"

"I . . . I don't know what you're talking about." Tameka started to rise. "We'd better get going. I . . ."

Ty took her hand, and gently pulled her back down to the step. "You're not very good at fibbing, Tammi." He smiled tenderly, "Probably due to lack of practice. Come on; come clean. Listening to troubles is one of the things I do best. After all, I am your assistant pastor."

"Yes . . . Yes, you are," Tameka replied hesitantly, looking down to their hands, still clasped. "And that's one of the things that troubles me most," she finished in a muted tone.

Ty's grip on her fingers tightened slightly. "But I thought we had that all sorted out. When we talked Sunday you said . . ."

"Your being a minister isn't a problem for me, Ty. It's just the opposite. I'm anxious that your . . . your friendship with me not provoke . . . problems for you . . . being a minister."

Ty was sincerely puzzled. "What brought all this on? Tammi, what are you talking about? I know my conduct is under more vigorous scrutiny than most other guys, and I accept that. But what does that have to do with you?"

"Your conduct includes your choice of the people you . . . you associate with, does it not?" Tameka asked, looking away from him.

"Yes, of course," Ty replied, still mystified. "But what . . ." A light suddenly dawned in his eyes. "Okay . . . what tacky gossip found its way to you?" he probed.

Tameka looked up at Ty. The concern and indignation in his eyes on her behalf was unmistakable. Embarrassed as she was, Tameka could keep the truth from him no longer. "I overheard Thelma and some of the other mothers talking in the parking lot," she admitted. She gave him a synopsis of the conversation.

For a moment Ty just sat staring out into the dusk, but the muscle working in his jaw gave away the turmoil within. Finally, he turned to Tameka, and said quietly, "Well, is any of it true?"

Tameka's shock cleanly banished her melancholy. "What? What do you mean, 'Is any of it true?' Of course it's not true!" Tameka leaped up from the step. "I'm not interested in Thelma Fuller's husband, or anybody else's husband, for that matter! And I decided to work with those children because I wanted to, because I want to help them, and for no other reason!" Tameka put her hands on her hips, her neck snapping. "Don't flatter yourself, friend. I didn't do it because of you. And I thought you understood that, Tyler Barnett!"

Ty rose slowly, and stood looking down at Tameka with a wily gleam in his eyes. "I do understand that," he chuckled. "I just had to find a way to remind you of that . . . Tameka Morgan."

Tameka's wrath flooded away as quickly as it had come, only to be replaced by even more embarrassment than before. "Ty . . . I'm . . . I'm sorry . . . I should have known . . . I didn't mean . . ."

"Yes, you should have known better than to think I'd believe that trash. And yes, I know you didn't mean to bite my head off . . ." he rolled his head around, "but you nonetheless did. Man! You may be little, but you sure pack a wallop! Is my neck still attached?"

Tameka couldn't help but laugh at his tomfoolery. "Oh, Ty, stop it! I said I was sorry!"

"So you did. Well, it was worth a tongue-lashing to put those dimples back in your cheeks." He stopped smiling and touched her cheek lightly. "Dimples become them much more than tears," he added in a whisper.

Tameka sensed him almost unperceptively moving closer, leaning down to her. And although she wanted him to, at the last moment she quickly turned away. "Ty, you're right—we haven't done anything wrong. But sometimes a lot of harm can come from people's perception of right and wrong, whether it's true or not. You're doing such important work here. You're held in such high regard. I wouldn't want to be the cause of . . ."

Ty moved directly in front of Tameka, and put both hands on her shoulders. "Tammi, that a woman with your talent and beauty, not to mention fame, should be so sweet and unpretentious is nothing short of a miracle. But then . . ." his hands left her shoulders and gently cupped her face. "I'm in the miracle business," he whispered as he leaned down once again, "so I'm somewhat predisposed to acknowledge one when it comes my way."

Ty's kiss was sweet, tender, as his soft, full lips pressed down on hers. The kiss was discreetly brief, yet even in that fleeting moment, Tameka could sense the power and passion that lay just below the surface. She felt light-headed, and was unaware that she was standing on her toes, in her need to be even closer to him.

His eyes searched hers as he reluctantly pulled away. Tameka felt herself getting lost in his eyes. A long moment passed with the only sound being the crickets' serenade as they stood facing each other. Ty suddenly gave Tameka a sheepish grin. "You know, when I offered to see you home I completely forgot. My car's at home. I walked to the gym for the exercise . . ." the chagrin deepened, "then I ran over here, hoping to get here before you left. I guess I'll have to impose on you for a ride."

Tameka smiled back. "I don't have a car here either. Mama dropped me off, and I was just going to walk home . . ." now it was Tameka's turn to look sheepish, ". . . for the exercise."

A beat passed before they both laughed, realizing how much they'd both been anticipating seeing the other. Then Ty smiled tenderly as he held out his hand. "Well, in that

case, Sister Morgan . . . it would be my very great honor
to walk you home."

Tameka shyly reached out, and took his hand. As they
strolled slowly down the tree-lined street under the newly
unveiled moon, neither noticed the car in the very back
of the parking lot.

But its occupant noticed them.

Chapter 4

"Honey, why aren't you going in? You've been swimming like a fish since you were a baby. Don't you feel well?"

"Yes, Mama. I feel fine." Tameka drew the belt of her beach robe tighter about her waist. "It's a little chilly. I think I'll wait until later, see if it warms up."

"Chilly? Warms up? Girl, it's got to be more than eighty degrees. And what 'later?' " Mama held her wrist out of the shade of their umbrella to better see her watch. "It's almost six o'clock now. It'll be time to head home shortly."

Tameka didn't want to tell Mama what was really bothering her—but knew she had to. She knew Mama didn't buy her weak excuses for a second, but would not try to force the issue. Mama had always been heedful of Tameka's personal space, even from Tameka's childhood. It just was one of the many endearing—and wise—facets of the Mama that Tameka loved.

But this was different. Mama was bound to hear—or overhear—the gossip sooner or later. And Tameka had much rather Mama hear it from her. "Well, Mama," she began slowly, "I really don't feel comfortable in this swim-suit. Maybe it's a little too revealing, and . . ."

Mama looked at her in wonder, " 'Too revealing?' Baby, as far as swimsuits go, that one's about as modest as they come." Mama grinned, the dimples she had conferred on Tameka in mischievous mode. "Unless you could dig up one of those monstrosities with bloomers they used to wear in silent movies."

"Mama!"

Mama laughed along with Tameka at first, but then looked her in the eye. "Tammi . . . you're not upset about the talk going 'round about you and Reverend Ty, are you?" she asked point-blank.

"Talk? What talk, Mama?" Tameka replied, not returning Mama's gaze.

"Honey, please," came Mama's amused although slightly exasperated retort.

"My goodness, just because we went to the movies the other night . . ."

"Why are you two good sisters just sitting here? Let's go over and get some of those bones!" Eddie Mae burst upon them, unceremoniously plopping herself down on the beach blanket next to Tameka.

"Eddie Mae," Mama smoothly said, brushing off her legs and the hem of her flowered sundress, "if I had wanted sand in my ice tea, I would have put it there myself, dear."

"Oh. Sorry, Miz Morgan. But why aren't you two over at the food tent? You're missing out on some mighty good eating."

"Not to mention some mighty good swimming," Mama added, looking pointedly at Tameka.

"Girl," Eddie Mae turned keen eye on Tameka, "you're not still hung up over those harpies wagging their tongues, are you? I told you forget that mess," she tossed her hand in dismissal.

"Speaking of wagging tongues," Tameka crossed her arms, and gave Eddie Mae a little scrutiny of her own, "yours wouldn't be the one that told Mama about all this, would it?"

Eddie Mae looked scandalized, as Mama clucked over them both. "I didn't need Eddie Mae to fill me in, Tammi. You forget I was born and raised in this town. There's not much that goes on that I don't know about." The dimples appeared again. "And even if I hadn't clued in on my own, a couple of ladies saw it as their Christian duty to call and tell me."

"I should have known," Tameka said with an I've-been-here-before sigh.

"I told her not to pay those jealous heifers no mind, Miz Morgan."

"I knew you'd stand by Tammi, honey," Mama smiled warmly at Eddie Mae, who was almost like a second daughter to her. "That was good advice."

"Although not very grammatically worded, Ms. English Teacher," Tameka threw in Eddie Mae's direction. "Just what are you teaching those kids in your class, anyway?"

"Solid standard English," Eddie Mae airily replied, biting into an apple. "But what's wrong with a little ebonics between friends?"

"And it was good advice," Mama repeated, getting back to matters at hand. "Honey, most of the people here in town are proud of you, and wish you well. But they'll always be those who can say the words 'thou shalt not covet' on Sunday, but not live by them the rest of the week." She looked closely at Tameka. "What does Tyler say about all this?"

"The same as the two of you—'just ignore it.' "

"Then why won't you just go enjoy the picnic? And what on earth does all this have to do with why you won't go swimming?"

"Oh, I can answer that," Eddie Mae piped up. "Tammi almost caused a riot when she came out of the changing room. Bert Thomas 'bout had a heart attack, and told his boys, "Man! She's built like a brick s . . .""

"That's enough, Eddie Mae," Mama said firmly, holding up one hand. "I get the picture."

"Oops! Sorry, Miz Morgan." She turned to Tameka, "Sister-girl, you couldn't help but draw attention!" Eddie Mae looked down wistfully at her less than effervescent bosom, "Sure wish I had some of what you're trying so hard to cover up! And there's nothing wrong with your swimsuit, either." Eddie Mae rolled her eyes. "It's a lot more discreet than that getup Dee-Dee is almost wearing! She looks like a hundred pounds of potatoes in a fifty-pound sack!"

"Eddie Mae McElroy!" Mama struggled to keep a straight face, but Tameka just burst out laughing as she hugged her friend.

"Much as I hate to break up this lovely display of sisterly devotion . . ." Ty's voice came from behind them, "if one of you ladies don't take these plates quick, your barbecue will have sand-flavored sauce!" They turned to see Ty struggling to juggle three food-laden paper plates.

Tameka hopped up to take two of them from him, and hand them to Mama and Eddie Mae. "Ty, what . . ."

"Well, I had to make sure you didn't miss out on the best barbecue I've ever made."

"That was really sweet of you, Ty, but you didn't have to."

"And please . . ." Ty turned around quickly, revealing two cans of Pepsi stuffed in the back pockets of his baggy Bermuda shorts. "Take these things out! Besides sending a bigger chill down my spine than *Anaconda*, if they drag my pants down any farther, I'll wind up in jail!"

Tameka took the cans as Eddie Mae started laughing. "The striptease preacher! I love it!"

Tameka sat back down, trying her best not to laugh at Eddie Mae's irreverence, and Ty's swift one-handed hoist of his pants.

"And now . . ." Having gotten the rapidly slipping britches under control, Ty pulled a number of napkins from the front pocket of his shorts, and handed Tameka's plate to her with a flourish. "Madam's dinner is served!" To which all three women burst out in laughter and applause.

"May I join you?" Ty asked with a twinkle in his eye.

"Most certainly, Reverend." Mama answered, wiping a tear from the corner of her eye. "I don't think I've ever been served in such an uh . . . interesting manner."

"My pleasure," Ty replied, sitting down on the blanket next to Tameka. "What a glorious day! Having the picnic at the beach was a terrific idea. Never let it be said Third Avenue Church doesn't throw one mean church picnic!"

"Aren't you eating, Ty?" Tameka asked, sampling some of the truly wonderful barbecue.

"Already did—while I was 'cuing. I sampled so much of this and that I was full by the time I finished."

"So you're the one we have to thank for these marvelous bones?" A voice asked.

Jesse James was in uniform, but he had a plate of ribs in hand. "I'm on duty today, but that's one of the privileges of being the boss . . ." He settled down on the blanket, where Mama had scooted over to make room, and grinned at her. "I can take a rib break whenever I like!"

Mama laughed, "Jesse, be careful. You're getting sand all over your uniform."

"It's worth it for a meal like this," he smiled again, "And company like this." He looked at Ty, "Rev., I take my hat off to you. You can not only preach up a storm, but you can burn at the grill. These are the best ribs I've had since I was young and good-looking!"

"I haven't started mine yet, but if smell is any prediction, I heartily agree," yet another voice put in.

Eddie Mae looked up at Percy, "About time you showed up," she said as he sat down next to next to her, gingerly transferring his own overflowing plate from one hand to the other.

"Yes, Percy. I had wondered why you weren't here," Tameka added.

"Oh, I guess I forgot to tell you, Tammi. About six months ago I started hosting a weekly religious music show on AM WXAL. Since I can't do it live on Sunday mornings, when it airs, I tape it the day before."

"Why did it take so long today?" Eddie Mae asked. "You're usually finished long before now."

"I had to go by home to change, honey. I couldn't go to the station dressed like this . . ." he gestured to his tank top and cut-off jeans. "Now could I?"

"Let's hope not," Eddie Mae winked at him. "One look at those sexy legs would have driven the station secretaries wild!"

The group chatted on while they ate. As they were finishing, Ty asked, "Tammi, don't you swim? I haven't seen you in the water once today."

"She got her Red Cross card in elementary school," Eddie Mae volunteered, savoring the last of a particularly tasty bone. "Took most of the rest of us until junior high."

"Well, what are we waiting for?" Ty stood. "After slaving over a hot grill all day, I'd love to get in a dip before we head back." He extended his hand to Tameka. "Care to join me?"

Tameka hesitated only a moment. Then she smiled and took Ty's hand as he helped her up.

"Aren't you folks coming?" Ty asked the others.

"No, I don't swim, Reverend," Mama told him.

"Wish I could, but I've got to get back on patrol," Jesse said.

"I'm too full to swim," Eddie Mae said, stretching out on the blanket. "You guys go ahead, with my blessings."

"Well, I'll go with you all," Percy said, starting to rise.

But Eddie Mae grabbed his arm, "Percy, I think I'd like some more ribs." She stared at him meaningfully. "Would you mind getting some for me?"

"But I thought you said you were . . . Oh, okay," he

amended, finally catching Eddie Mae's drift. "Sure, I'd be glad to."

Ty had his swim trunks on under the baggy shorts. Tameka felt herself flushing as he discreetly peeled them off, revealing his muscular thighs and slim hips. Which wasn't helped any by Eddie Mae giving Tameka a wink and big okay sign with thumb and forefinger while Ty's back was turned.

"Well?" Ty said as Tameka continued to hesitate.

Tameka gingerly removed her robe, and leaned over to lay it on the blanket near Ty's shorts. Although he tried his best to hide it, she couldn't help but notice how Ty's eyes widened as she straightened and reached up to secure her hair into a ponytail.

Although she was used to being on stage, and accepted as part of the territory all the positive and negative regard by strangers that it entailed, Tameka hated being ogled by men. But this was different. Ty's stare was not like the lustful, tawdry glances so many men had thrown her way. Ty's gaze, while admiring and appreciative, was also respectful, almost reverent. Tameka didn't feel self-conscious and wary as she usually did when some men—men like Bert Thomas—stared at her. Instead she felt prized, cherished. She smiled, and took the hand Ty had silently offered.

"Have a good time, you two," Mama called softly after them. But Tameka barely heard her. As they strolled along, she was only aware of Ty's nearness, and the brilliant loveliness of the day, which seemed to echo the glow that was building inside her.

They just walked along the beach, hand in hand for several minutes without speaking, before Tameka softly said, "Penny for your thoughts."

Ty looked down at her with a slightly embarrassed smile, "Sure you want to know?" he whispered.

She looked up into his warm brown eyes and suddenly knew nothing this man ever did or said—or thought—

would ever hurt her. "Yes. Yes, I'm sure," Tameka whispered in reply.

Ty stopped, and turned to face Tameka. "I was just thinking this is one of the most beautiful days I've ever seen." His fingers tightened on hers, "And that I'm blessed to experience it with the most beautiful woman I've ever seen by my side."

From another man this might have seemed corny, contrived, a practiced make-out line used many times over. But as Tameka continued to gaze up into Ty's eyes, his simple sincerity was unmistakable.

"Thank you, Ty," Tameka said, just as sincerely. "That's the sweetest compliment I've ever received."

Their contemplation of each other was broken by a wildly colored beach ball tumbling along to bump up against Ty's leg, followed by a rowdy bunch of children, who were chasing it.

"Hey, Rev. T!" one of the boys called. "Over here!"

Ty laughed, and bent to pick up the ball. He tossed it high in the air, and caught it with a masterful kick as it came down, sending it careening off over the kids' heads.

"Hey, all right!" the boy said with admiration. "You oughta be in the NFL!" He took off with the other children, in hot pursuit of the ball once again.

"You're quite the sportsman, Ty," Tameka matched the child's admiration. "You coach basketball, and you kicked that thing like a pro punter."

"Well, I *was* a punter—in college."

"Really? Where was that?"

"In Chicago. That's where I'm from. I lost both my parents in a car accident ten years ago. But I have an older sister and younger brother. They're both still there."

"I'm sorry about your folks, Ty."

"I miss them." He looked over the water. "I guess I'll always miss them . . . Anyway," he returned to the present, "I thought about a career in sports. If not pro sports, then as a phys-ed teacher . . ." His gaze grew reflective. "But then I became more concerned about the care and feeding of souls than of bodies."

He turned back to Tameka, "But speaking of bodies, I did pick up enough along the way to know it's not wise to go swimming right after a meal. I don't think you should go in just now, Tammi."

Tameka gave him an impish grin, "Then why did you ask me to go swimming?" she posed, already knowing the answer.

Ty laughed, unabashed at being caught. "Okay, you got me. But I had to think of some way to get you off to myself."

"And now that you've accomplished that, sir," Tameka diffidently replied, only partially joking, "what do you plan on doing with me?"

It was Ty's turn to grin. "Come along, my dear . . ." he took Tameka's hand again, and again started along the beach. "I'm sure we'll think of something."

By this point they were drawing closer to where the bulk of the picnickers had gathered, and Tameka began to feel uncomfortable. "Ty . . ." she began, and he could feel the hand he was holding tense, "I don't know if it's such a good idea for us to walk around . . . holding hands like this. It's just going to add fuel to the fire." She began to draw her hand from his. "I mean, there's enough talk already, and . . ."

"Talk? What kind of talk?" Ty asked, keeping a firm grip on her hand. When Tameka didn't answer, he continued, "Oh, you mean the talk about me being sweet on you? Why should I mind that . . ." he questioned softly, stopping to put his other hand under her chin, so that she looking up directly into his eyes, "since it's true?" he finished softly.

"So here you are, Ty," broke the mood and the moment. Dee-Dee Slayton was standing a few feet behind them, her hands on her not inconsiderable hips. Tameka saw what Eddie Mae was talking about. A string bikini was not the most prudent choice for a church picnic. Especially one about two sizes too small. *God help us if one of those straps snaps,* Tameka thought. That took her back to a recent concert, when her bass player suddenly popped a string with a loud *twaaang.* In spite of herself, Tameka couldn't suppress a giggle.

"What are you laughing at?" Dee-Dee challenged, seeming to know, and also seeming to regret her choice of attire as Ty unsmilingly checked her out with what was clearly not the reaction she'd hoped for. Before Tameka could reply, Pastor Hawkins came trotting over to join them.

"Where have you been, Number One?" The pastor puffed as he hurried down the beach. Tameka barely stifled another laugh at the sight of the usually conservatively dressed pastor in beachcombers, with a riotously colored Hawaiian shirt covering his ample girth.

"Just enjoying the beautiful scenery, pastor," Ty smiled, looking down at Tameka.

"Ahem ..." the pastor gave them a smile, "I see." He removed his straw hat, and mopped his almost completely bald pate with a large kerchief. "A lot of the folks are getting ready to head home, and it's time for closing prayer. But, seeing as how you're already otherwise ... er, occupied ..." the pastor grinned benevolently on the two of them, "I'll just lead it myself."

"No, pastor, I'll be glad to lead the closing prayer," Ty told him. "Sister Morgan and I will be right along." He looked down at Tameka, "Won't we, Tameka?"

"Yes ... Yes, of course," Tameka replied, not certain that it was wise for her to accompany Ty, but seeing no tactful way out.

"Good." The pastor turned to Dee-Dee, "Come along then, Sister Slayton." The pastor took Dee-Dee's elbow. "Although that unfortunate headache of yours didn't allow you to help with the cooking, I'm happy it didn't affect your appetite. And I know now that you're feeling better you'll want to help with the cleanup." He looked at Dee-

Dee with one eyebrow raised. "Maybe you'd like to get your robe first. I'll help you fetch it."

Dee-Dee had no choice but to trail along with the pastor, casting one last baleful look in Ty and Tameka's direction as they went.

Ty started to chuckle. Tameka gave him a sidelong glance. "To quote our recently departed companion 'What are you laughing at?' "

Ty shook his head in admiration, "The Hawk. That sixth sense of his always knows how to get gracefully out of a ticklish situation."

"Dee-Dee? I have to admit, she certainly hasn't been very friendly since I've been home this trip." Tameka looked pointedly at Ty. "Is that because of you?"

Ty was uncomfortable, seeming both embarrassed and annoyed. "Probably. At least partially. Ever since I got here eight months ago she seems to have assumed that I . . . that she and I . . ." The usually articulate Ty was at loss to explain this particular situation. "Well, that . . ."

"You mean she's got a thing for you," Tameka supplied.

Ty's smooth chestnut complexion flushed with a deep crimson blush. "Well, yeah. I guess so. I don't know why. I . . . I've never done anything to give her the impression that I . . . I mean . . ." Ty stammered on. "I don't understand it," he finally finished.

"Well, I do." Tameka impulsively replied, surprised to find a curious emotion—was it jealousy?—causing her to speak so candidly. Her voice softened as she turned to look across the water. "I mean . . . it . . . it isn't very difficult to understand why any woman could find herself attracted to you, Ty," she whispered.

"Oh, really?" His face broke out in a delicate smile, as he gazed deeply into Tameka's eyes. "Any woman?"

His eyes held her defenseless, unable to look away, and unable to camouflage the feelings that were welling within her. "Yes, Ty," she replied, her voice, although a mere whisper, steady and definite. "Any woman."

The smile left Ty's face as he came a step closer, and took both Tameka's hands in his. His eyes seemed to blaze, the warmth of their radiance flowing over her, causing the warmth of the sun on her back to pale in comparison. "Now that's the sweetest compliment I've ever received." He squeezed her hands gently, "Because you're not just any woman, Tameka Morgan." He moved even closer. "You're a special woman. A singular woman." He raised one of her hands to his lips, his eyes continuing to consume hers. "A once-in-a-lifetime woman," he murmured so mutedly she barely heard him. But she didn't need to hear him—his eyes said it all.

Spontaneously, the hand Ty had kissed lifted to touch his cheek, the smoldering heat of his skin warming her palm, "Ty . . ."

"Honey, that's too much for you to carry," came Mama's voice from nearby.

"No, it's okay, I can handle it."

Tameka and Ty turned to see Mama, Eddie Mae, and Percy approaching, with Calvin struggling along beside, carrying Mama's picnic basket and cooler, and the beach umbrella thrown over one shoulder.

Ty laughed. "Hey, hold on, my man! Looks like you're a little overloaded here." Ty stepped toward the foursome, reaching for the umbrella. "Let me give you a hand."

"No, I said I'm okay!" Calvin insisted, pulling back from Ty, clutching the umbrella possessively.

"Calvin insisted on helping us get the things to the car," Mama told Ty with a straight face, but with laughing eyes.

"Yeah. And Mr. Macho insists on carrying almost everything himself," Percy added, looking more than a little amused himself.

Eddie Mae handed Ty his shirt and shorts, "Your raiment, Reverend Barnett."

Calvin unceremoniously dropped the items he was carrying, and pulled a bundle from beneath his arm. "And here's your robe, Miss Morgan," he said, handing it to Tameka, eyes sparkling.

"Why . . . uh, thank you, Calvin," Tameka told him, not quite knowing what to make of the situation. She and Ty slipped into their outer garments.

Still stubbornly refusing Ty's offers of assistance, Calvin shouldered his burdens once again as they made their way to the tent where most of the church group was convening.

Seeing Ty enter, Pastor Hawkins held up both hands, "May I have your attention?" The hubbub of talk and laughter gradually subsided. "This has truly been a wonderful day of food, fun, and fellowship. Not being much of a swimmer myself, I would never have thought of holding the church picnic at the beach. But then, my number one assistant . . ." he gestured to Ty, "has had any number of righteous ideas since God sent him to join us . . . and he 'cues some mean ribs as well! Let's give Reverend Barnett a big hand!"

The applause was sprinkled with a hearty number of cheers and "Amens!" Ty gave the group an jaunty salute in response.

"And now, Number One, if you would close us out with a prayer . . ."

Ty joined the pastor at the front of the tent. "Let us pray . . . Heavenly Father, we thank Thee for Thy bountiful goodness, for the blessing of this beautiful day by the sea. And as we leave, let us keep in our hearts the message and spirit of He who walked the waters, and caused the waves to obey. Amen."

"Amen," quietly echoed the assembled parishioners. Tameka felt her eyes mist, touched by the succinct eloquence and simple majesty of Ty's prayer.

Tameka's meditation was broken by a sharp jab from Eddie Mae's elbow. With a start, Tameka realized everybody was looking at her.

" . . . uh, Sister Morgan?" From the mischievous glint

in Ty's eyes, Tameka discerned it wasn't the first time he had called her name.

"Oh . . . I'm sorry, T . . . er, Reverend Barnett, what did you say?"

Ty chuckled. "I said 'Would you lead us in a hymn as we shake hands and go our separate ways?' "

She pondered a second what to sing, then began, "Blest be the tie that binds . . ." Instead of joining her in the song, the assembled group just stood, listening, some swaying, some nodding their heads to the simple song they knew so well. Tameka saw some put their arms around a spouse or a friend, or take a child's hand.

At the second verse, Ty stepped to where Tameka stood, and joined in with a surprisingly rich baritone, taking her hand, and reaching for Eddie Mae's hand as well. The circle continued to grow as each person took up the refrain, and his neighbor's hand. Tameka's eyes weren't the only moist ones by the song's end.

"Amen!" Pastor Hawkins intoned, again pulling his kerchief to dab quickly at his eyes this time. "Drive safely on the way home! And get a good night's sleep so I can see you in church bright and early tomorrow morning!"

A titter of laughter greeted this none-too-subtle reminder. The crowd began to drift off in small groups.

"Pastor Hawkins hasn't changed a bit since I was a little girl," Tameka began, turning to Ty. "Even back then he always . . . Ty?" Ty was staring at her as though transfixed.

He hastily drew a hand across his own eyes. "Your voice is truly a gift from God," he murmured hoarsely. Then he gave her a gentle smile, "And the rest of you is, too." His voice was barely a whisper.

"Rev. T!" Reggie came rushing up, "We need your car keys so we can load up Maybeline!"

"Okay, brother-man, here, catch!" Ty reached in a pants' pocket, and pulled out a bunch of keys, tossing them to Reggie. "And don't turn on that radio!" he called to Reggie's rapidly retreating back. Ty turned to Tameka,

"The last time I gave him my keys he ran the battery down playing WYAL!"

"Uh . . . Maybeline?" Tameka queried.

Ty grinned, "Sure. That car was built in Chuck Berry's hey-day. Don't you think it only fitting she be named after one of his songs?"

He took Tameka's hand, heading for the changing rooms. "I brought a carload of your choir members with me, since a lot of them didn't have a way to get to the picnic. But there's no way I'm driving that bunch of Bebe's kids wannabes back without some moral support. You're coming with me. Let's go tell your mom, and I'll load up the hellions while you change."

Before she knew it, Tameka found herself ensconced in Maybeline's front passenger seat with Ty. But they were hardly alone. Calvin had perched in the front seat between them, and Reggie, Opal, Marc, and Latrisse were piled in the back. The trunk was so loaded with barbecue and beach equipment that it gave a loud *THUMP* every time they went over a bump. Although that could barely be heard over the teens' overlapping questions about Hollywood. Added to that was the jazz station Latrisse insisted they listen to when Ty gave them a firm no on the local rap station, and a lively argument among Reggie, Marc, and Ty as to who was better—the 49ers or the Broncos.

Tameka couldn't remember when she had enjoyed herself more.

They dropped the teens—along with their respective beach paraphernalia—off one by one. Calvin insisted on being last. "Good-bye, Miss Morgan," he meekly told Tameka after she had slid from the car to let him out, while Ty went to the trunk to get Calvin's things.

"Good-bye, Calvin. Did you have a good time at the picnic?"

"Yes, ma'am," Calvin replied with a solemn and pensive face.

"You sure don't look like it, son," Ty remarked, handing Calvin his stuff. "Is something wrong?"

"No," Calvin replied shortly, looking at the ground. He looked up at Tameka, "See you tomorrow at church?" he said wistfully. Their choir was singing that Sunday.

Tameka playfully punched his shoulder, "The Lord willin', and the creek don't rise," she quipped.

That got a small smile from the boy, who reluctantly turned for his front porch. "Okay . . . well . . . bye."

"Good night. Sleep tight. Don't let the bedbugs bite." Tameka called after him. Calvin gave her a shaky grin.

"Good night, Calvin," Ty called. Calvin didn't reply. The boy turned to glance worriedly back at the two of them just before entering his front door.

Tameka gazed after him just as worriedly as Ty held the door for her, and she slid back into the car.

Neither said anything for a while as they drove along. Then Ty suddenly said, "I've been wondering what was bothering Calvin. Now I know." He turned to look earnestly at Tameka, "Do you?"

"Yes. Yes, I do," Tameka told him.

A beat passed before Ty said, "The poor kid. Puppy love can hurt just as much as the real thing. I remember. I had a massive crush on my tenth grade math teacher." Ty chuckled softly. "I never missed a class. That was the only *A* in math I ever got."

When Tameka didn't reply he said, "Don't worry about it, honey. He'll be all right. Well . . ." Ty reached over to squeeze Tameka's hand, "at least little man has great taste in women."

Tameka squeezed Ty's hand in return just as they turned into her mother's driveway. "Why is Mama sitting out on the porch? No, that couldn't be her. She was going by my Aunt Shirley's before she came home. And that's not Mama's car in the driveway, anyway." Tameka peered closely at the shadowy figure slowly rocking on the front porch. "Who is that?"

Ty pulled Maybeline up to the rear bumper of the shiny late model car ahead of them. "Do you recognize the car?" Tameka asked.

"No, I've never seen it before. Hey, it's a rental. See the sticker on the bumper?" Ty said, pointing to the Hertz emblem.

Tameka hopped out of the car as soon as Ty brought it to a stop, calling, "Hello? Who's there? Can I help you?" as she approached the front steps.

"Almost certainly, my runaway songbird," came the reply in a voice Tameka knew only too well.

Tameka stopped cold. "Danny! Danny, what are you doing here?"

Danny stood, and slowly stepped out of the shadow to the railing. He leaned against one of the corner posts, and crossed his arms. "I might well ask the same, sweetheart, seeing as how you've got an album to record that's about two weeks off schedule."

"How . . . how did you know where I was?"

"Did you think I wouldn't find out where you had gone?" Danny smirked. "I've got friends in high places—friends like airline executives, no pun intended. And anyway . . ." he curled the fingers of one hand to look down at his manicured nails, "it wasn't hard to figure out that my plantation girl would come running home to Mama."

Ty had gotten out of the car, and had quietly taken in this initial exchange. The plantation barb clearly didn't sit well with him. "Do you know this . . . person, Tameka?" Ty put in, giving Danny a hard scrutiny.

"Yes, Ty," Tameka told him. She crooked her head in Danny's direction. "This is my manager, Danny Dorsey."

Danny coolly appraised Ty. "And who might you be, cowboy?"

Ty unflinchingly returned Danny's stare, "I *might* be anybody, but I *am* Tyler Barnett. Reverend Tyler Barnett, to be exact."

"Reverend?" Danny seemed to find this amusing. He

checked Ty out from head to toe, taking in the now wrinkled shirt and shorts Ty was still wearing. "Don't they pay you boys enough these days to afford a suit and tie?"

Ty bristled, and seemed to swell in size. Trying desperately to defuse the situation, Tameka hastily asked, "What do you want, Danny?"

"What do I want? What do you think I want?" Danny shot back, coming to the top of the steps. "I want you. I've come to take you back to L.A. with me. This foolishness has gone on long enough. It's time to come back from Oz, Dorothy, and get back to taking care of business."

Tameka crossed her arms, "And what if Dorothy doesn't feel like coming back—Toto?"

Danny darkened, and menacingly came down a step, "You better watch yourself, little girl. This dog's bite is worse than his bark."

Ty quickly stepped forward, in front of Tameka, "Then I suggest you take your bark and your bite, and wag your tail right on out of here."

"Step aside, preacher-man," Danny almost growled at Ty. "This is a private business transaction between me and my client." He came slowly down the last of the stairs. "So why don't you get lost, and go find somebody to pray over?"

Ty moved a step closer, looking Danny dead in the eye, "You're the one who's going to need prayer if you don't get on your way with a quickness."

Danny looked at Ty, seeming to finally realize—a tad too late—that he'd underestimated both Ty's gumption, and his size. Danny's ever-present self-preservation mode kicked into gear. "Now, look here, my man," he began in his best just-between-us-guys tone. "There's no need for unpleasantness here. After all, I am her manager, and I only want what's best for her career. I only want to *talk* to Meeko."

"The lady's name is Tameka, and I don't think she wants to talk to you." Ty turned to Tameka, "Or do you?"

"That depends," Tameka replied. She turned a piercing stare on Danny, "Have you corrected the music rundown for the recording session?"

"Well . . . no, honey. Look, we've already signed a royalty contract for the music. If you don't record it, we'll have to pay off the songwriters with a big one-time fee. That's just a waste of money, don't you see?"

"Yes," Tameka came back, "I do see. It would be a waste of money—your money. Neither the recording company nor I would be liable for the songwriters' compensation since I didn't approve the music." When Danny's eyes narrowed, Tameka knew she had hit on the real reason he was so adamant she record the song.

"But you should have thought about that, Danny, before you signed a contract without my approval." Tameka went on. "Which, may I remind you, my contract with you calls for."

"But, Meeko, that's my job, to advise you on . . ."

"Yes. To advise me. But you can't make decisions *for* me. You're my manager, Danny, not my daddy. The sooner you realize that the better."

Danny's appeasing act was rapidly coming apart at the seams. "Looks like you need a daddy, or somebody, to knock some sense into that hard-ass head of yours. You know what they say, 'a hard head makes for a soft behind.' "

He'd gone too far then. "I had a Daddy," Tameka snapped, "and he was a far better man than you'll ever come close to being! I told you I wasn't coming back to the studio until *my* music was ready. I meant it then, and I mean it now. Good-bye, Danny." Tameka turned her back to him. "You can get off my Mama's 'plantation' now."

"But, Meeko . . ."

"That's it, buddy. You heard her." Ty had visibly glowered at Danny's "hard-ass" comment, and was now all too ready to give him a hand moving along. "Let's get packing." Ty advised, taking another step toward Danny.

Danny backed away, and speedily got into his car. But he wasn't going without a parting shot. He didn't want to tussle with Ty physically, but was damned if he'd leave without landing one more verbal blow. "All right, I'm going! But you're going to have to come my way sooner or later, Meeko—someday when choirboy here doesn't have your back!" Danny gunned the engine, racing around the circular drive.

"Say, ain't it a little late for house calls, Your Holiness? Or were you planning on showing her your religious etchings?" Ty stiffened as though slapped. "You might as well," Danny screamed over the roar of the engine. "Everybody in Hollywood has had some of that—including me. Why should you be the odd man out?" His lunatic laugher rang down the street as he ran over the curb, and was gone.

Ty raced for his car. "Ty! Ty, where are you going?" Tameka called as she ran after him.

"After that son of a . . ."

"Ty, don't!" Tameka grasped his arm. "He's not worth it!"

Ty seemed to come to himself, but his eyes still flashed fire as he looked down at Tameka. "I'll suffer no man to talk that way about you, Tameka."

"You don't believe him, do you?" Tameka came back, still gripping his arm.

Ty stood panting for a beat, and then his eyes softened. "No. No, of course I don't believe it, Tammi."

"Then, just let it go," she whispered. Tameka released the breath she had been holding when Ty slowly released the car door handle.

Tameka sank down to the step, so angry, confused, and ashamed she was trembling. "Ty, I'm so sorry. I had no idea he would be here. I'm so embarrassed."

Ty sat down next to her. "That's why you came home so unexpectedly, isn't it?"

"Yes."

"Tell me about it, honey. I'm not sure I understand what this is all about. And maybe it would help for you to talk it out." Ty gave Tameka a gentle smile. "Confession is good for the soul, so they tell me."

Ty's steadying presence had calmed Tameka already. "Sure you want to hear it? It's a long story."

He leaned back, both elbows on the step above him. "I don't have anywhere to be until eight o'clock tomorrow morning."

Ty listened silently as Tameka outlined the situation, nodding occasionally as if to urge her on. Somewhere during her story Tameka had leaned over, her head on Ty's shoulder. And somehow his arm had found its way around her waist.

"I don't know what to do, Ty," Tameka finally concluded. "Danny has helped my career tremendously up to this point. And he would fight me like the very devil if I tried to break our contract. What's the answer?"

"I think you already know the answer, Tameka," Ty asserted.

"I do?"

"Yes. It's in the title of one of your songs." Ty looked deeply into Tameka's eyes. "You have to follow your heart, Tammi. That's all. Just follow your heart." His other arm encircled her. "And when you do . . ." his face was mere inches from hers. "I'll be right there beside you."

His kiss was warm, sheltering, engulfing. Tameka felt all the tension of the past half hour drain away as Ty's arms tightened around her. She could smell the adventures of the day upon him: a hint of hickory smoke, the crisp freshness of the sea. And underneath it all was the faint male muskiness of the day's exertions. The combination of it all caused her to literally melt into his arms. She gasped involuntarily at the sensation of her breasts crushing against his chest. Her nipples were swollen, and her excitement was only heightened by knowing Ty could feel them harden.

The trouble with Danny, her concerns about her career, everything, faded away as they sat there on the step, lost in each other, with only the moon and stars as witnesses.

Or so they thought.

Chapter 5

"Hey, Rev. T, how about letting me drive part of the way, man?" said Reggie, hanging over the front seat. Reggie neglected no opportunity to exercise the rights conferred on him by his new learner's permit.

"Don't make me forget I'm a man of the cloth, my brother." Ty coolly threw over his shoulder, not even favoring Reggie with a glance. "Or you might find yourself walking to Atlanta."

Tameka stifled a laugh as a duly chastened Reggie settled back to his seat behind them. They were carrying eleven passengers in all, three teens each on the three bench seats behind them, Tameka and Ty in the front seats. Percy was following them in the second church van. Five cars followed Percy, carrying the remaining choir members, the choir's instruments, and several chaperoning parents.

"Okay, y'all," Tameka turned sideways, planting her feet in the aisle between the two front bucket seats. "Let's go over 'Goin' Up Yonder' one last time."

A groan rose from the rear of the van. "Miss Morgan,"

Marc moaned, "I think if I sing that song one more time I will go up yonder."

"We'll have no blasphemy in this van, young man," Ty told him with mock forbidding.

"Yeah, man. Miss Morgan's right," Calvin volunteered. "You need all the practice you can get. You're the one who keeps dragging the whole section flat, anyway."

"Who died and made you Luther Vandross?" Marc retorted.

"All right, now look, guys," Tameka put in. "We're too cramped in this van to start getting on each others' nerves."

"He got on my last nerve before we left the church," Marc informed Tameka. "What's been wrong with you lately, anyway, blood?" Marc questioned Calvin. "You've been tense as a hog going to breakfast at Bob Evans."

All the other teens burst out laughing, but Calvin didn't appreciate Marc's sense of humor. "You shut up, man! Shut up and mind your own damn business!"

"Calvin. That's enough," Ty said quietly.

Calvin glared sullenly at Ty's back, then glanced sheepishly at Tameka. "I'm sorry, Miss Morgan."

"That's all right, Calvin. Okay, group, we'll be there in about twenty minutes. Time to loosen up those voices. It's either 'Goin' Up Yonder' or vocal exercises. Your choice."

A group lament arose this time. The teens thought the vocal exercises Tameka had insisted they do before and between every rehearsal were "a drag." But even the most rebellious of them had to admit—the exercises had improved their sound.

Tameka had also taught the sopranos to sing from their diaphragms, instead of their chests, so that the tinny nasal quality disappeared from even the highest notes of their register.

Tameka also restructured their performance grouping. Instead of standing grouped by voice; sopranos with sopranos, and so on, she had arranged them strictly by height. Tameka had the males and females all intermingled, so that each small section had one person from each voice, soprano, alto, tenor, and bass.

The choir had found this last move very difficult to handle at first. "How am I supported to hold my part when there are no other tenors around, and I'm surrounded by females?" Reggie had peevishly asked.

"You're supposed to know your part, Reggie," Tameka had told him. "Know it so well that you can hold it on your own, no matter what anybody around you is singing." Which was true enough, and tremendously helped the precision of the vocals, since there could be no faking, none of the uncertainty of leaning on one's neighbor on any sections of music not quite mastered.

But that wasn't the main reason Tameka changed their groupings. Now they had no choice but to listen to one another—really listen to one another. The quality of their blend improved dramatically, and the boys no longer over-powered the girls. They now truly sounded like a choir was supposed to sound. Like the root meaning of the word *chorus*: "in simultaneous utterance," or more simply, "as one voice."

Tameka hummed the introduction to the song, and they were off. *They sound fabulous, even if I do say so myself,* Tameka thought with satisfaction.

Ty was singing along as well. He'd attended so many rehearsals he knew the songs as well as the choir. Tameka watched him as he drove along, singing his heart out, never fathoming how much he meant in the lives of these children. For some of them he was the closest male role model they had, and between his basketball coaching, and ferrying kids back and forth for church functions, many of them saw Ty more often than they saw their own fathers.

He just has no idea how important he is to them, Tameka reflected, watching Ty's finely formed profile. And the thought followed closely on its heels, *or how important he is to me.*

Before Tameka knew it they were on Peachtree Avenue,

and then they were approaching the convention center where the Gospelfest was to be held. The closer they got, the heavier the traffic became, until they were barely crawling along.

"Man!" Ty exclaimed. "I expected this thing to be well attended, but I didn't expect anything like this! It's still almost two hours before the program's scheduled to start. Who would have thought so many people would be here so early?"

Fortunately, they had passes for the special nearby parking provided for participants. Ty lead their little caravan into the lot after showing the attendant his pass. The lot was already filling up with an assortment of buses, vans, and cars bringing choirs from all around.

"Okay, we're here!" Ty called out as soon as he had brought the van to a stop. "Now, everybody stay together, and let's all pitch in to get the robes and instruments inside."

A short while later they were heading for the stage door, Tameka and Ty in the lead, Percy and Eddie Mae bringing up the rear. Ty stopped so suddenly that Calvin, who was walking right behind him, almost ran into his back.

"What's the matter, Rev. T?" Percy cried out above the bustle surrounding them.

Ty didn't speak for a moment, then turned to Tameka. "I think I know why so many people are out today." He silently pointed to the side of the building they were approaching.

A large banner flapped in the wind: "*GOSPELFEST '98 FEATURING GEORGIA'S OWN MEEKO MOORE.*"

Tameka was thunderstruck. "Who told them . . . How did . . . What's going on here?" she stammered. "I'm not here to perform. This is the choir's day, not mine. Who told them I would be on the program?"

"Don't look at me," Percy said quickly. "All the stuff I sent in just said 'Third Avenue Church Young People's Choir, Percy Stallworth, accompanist.' "

"A lot of people at home know you're directing the choir, Tammi." Ty reasoned. "There's any number of ways word could have gotten out you'd be here today."

"I know, Ty," Tameka replied with dismay. "But I'm not the headliner here. Those poor kids. They've worked so hard. So have all the choirs here. Who am I to breeze in and steal their thunder?"

"There's only One who can produce thunder, Tameka." Ty said softly.

"Yes, I know, Ty. That's not what I meant. I meant . . ."

"I know what you meant, Tammi. You planned to stay in the background." Ty looked up at the banner. "But that's evidently not how it's destined to be." He looked down on Tameka with a smile. "Honey, you're about the least vain-glorious person I've ever known. But I just wanted to remind you there's only one Star here. Anyone who thinks your name being spotlighted is taking something away from them clearly doesn't understand that. So why worry what they think?"

Tameka gratefully touched Ty's arm. He always knew what to say to put things in perspective.

They marched on toward the stage door, and were greeted by a cadre of reporters and cameramen. Seeing Tameka, they surged forward en masse.

"Miss Moore, when were you signed to perform for the Gospelfest? Do you know why you're not listed on the program?"

"Look this way, Meeko! Smile!" A photo flash went off in their faces.

"There are rumors that you're boycotting your record label. Any truth to them?"

Ty and the rest of their group were looking at the reporters in amazement. Some of the teens were being jostled by reporters trying to get close enough to stick a microphone in Tameka's face.

"No, I'm not performing this evening," Tameka told the reporters as she continued on toward the entrance. "I have no idea why my name is on the banners. Please let us by.''

Some security personnel saw the crush in the parking lot, and blessedly came over to run interference for Tameka and her party, helping them get past the throng, which now included several autograph seekers. With the guards, joined by Ty and Percy, holding back the growing crowd, they were able to make it into the building.

"Man! That was intense!" Reggie exclaimed as they were being shown to the huge room where the competing choirs were assembling.

"I'm sorry. I didn't know that was going to happen," Tameka said, checking through the children. "Do we have everybody? Are you all okay?''

"Yeah, we're all here," Marc told her. "That was all right!" he went on. He looked at Tameka. "Do you think they're going to be out there when we leave?" he asked eagerly, as though he was looking forward to the possibility.

"Not if I can help it," Tameka grimly replied. "All right, let's stay together now!"

There were no reporters in the corridor they were traveling. But word had spread that Tameka was there, and groups of people stopped cold to stare at them as they passed or to point and whisper, "It's her!" Their progress was further impeded by the occasional fan who came up to say hello, or ask for an autograph. Tameka was cordial to those who greeted her, but politely—though firmly— declined to give autographs.

They found their way to the large ready room that was to serve as a sort of dressing room for the choirs in the competition. As soon as they entered the room, a buxom woman in a flowered dress came sailing over to meet them. "Miss Moore! We're so very glad you're here!" she cried, pumping Tameka's hand up and down as though it were a well handle. "Having a star of your celebrity perform for us is such an honor! And I . . .''

"Excuse me," Ty smoothly interrupted, offering his

hand. "I'm Tyler Barnett, the assistant pastor of Third Avenue Church of Halcyon. And you are . . ."

The buxom lady stopped abruptly, and put her hand to her throat as she stared at Ty, apparently thinking Third Avenue Church was fortunate indeed.

"Oh, please excuse me, Reverend Barnett! Where are my manners? I'm M. Lee Pinkett, from Greater Grace in Augusta. I'm the organizer of the Gospelfest," she went on proudly, "and I'm serving tonight as stage manager for the concert."

"I'm so happy to meet you, Sister Pinkett. It's an honor for our choir to have been invited. But we've had a long drive. I think the choir would like a chance to relax and refresh themselves a bit before they prepare to go onstage. I wonder if you could show us to our uh, quarters."

Tameka had spied a couple of tables, a long coatrack, and several chairs over on the far side of the room, with a sign reading "Third Avenue Church Young People's Choir" taped to the wall. Ty had to have seen it, too. But his strategy worked. It got Mrs. Pinkett off the subject of Tameka, and on to the business at hand.

"Oh, yes, of course! The poor little dears!" She reached out—or rather up—since he was as tall as she, to pat Reggie on the head. "They must be exhausted after your long drive. This way, please." She started off toward their area. Fortunately, she turned her head just in time to miss Reggie crossing his eyes, and following her with an almost perfect imitation of her somewhat knock-kneed walk.

"Hush!" Tameka admonished the other teens, as they started to sniggle at Reggie's tomfoolery, although she could barely manage to keep a straight face herself. "Thanks, Rev.," she leaned over to whisper to Ty.

Ty winked. "You're welcome . . . Meeko."

The next hour was a flurry of organization as each choir was instructed in where and how to enter, and given a brief few moments onstage to familiarize themselves with the layout before the doors were opened to the public.

When their turn came, Tameka was finishing her final arrangement of the choir when Mrs. Pinkett returned with a tall, distinguished looking older gentleman in tow.

"Miss Moore, I'd like you to meet Carlton Johnston, our Master of Ceremonies this evening."

"A very great pleasure to meet you, Sister Moore." Although his wooly shock of hair was entirely white, a youthful twinkle remained in his eyes.

"The pleasure is mine," Tameka replied enthusiastically. "The Johnston Cavaliers are one of the greatest gospel groups in history. I've admired you all my life."

"Thank you, my dear." Johnston shook his head, "But I'm afraid the Cavaliers are now a was, not an is. Everybody's gone Home now, 'cept me. And I've been retired probably longer than you've been alive. But I'm surprised—and touched—that you've heard of us. We were long before your time."

"Your music is timeless, Mr. Johnston."

"I think yours is, too." The sparkle in his eye brightened as he leaned forward. "All you've got to do is wait until you're an old fossil like me so they can make it official."

Tameka introduced Johnston to the group. "It's a pleasure to meet you, young man," Johnston said, shaking Ty's hand. "I know Reverend Hawkins well. He's not with you tonight?"

"No, sir. He's preaching a revival in Detroit this week."

"That's too bad. It would have been wonderful to see him again after all these years." He turned to Tameka, "What are you performing for us this evening? I don't know what the problem is, but you're not listed in the program for some reason."

"I'm not singing tonight, Mr. Johnston."

"You're not? I don't understand."

Before Tameka could respond, Mrs. Pinkett burst in. "Not singing? What do you mean?" She seemed almost frantic.

"Oh, boy—here it comes," Percy murmured under this breath.

"Why not?" Mrs. Pinkett insisted. "Has anybody here done anything to offend you? Because I can assure you, if they have . . ."

"No, that's not it at all, Mrs. Pinkett. It's just that I'm not here as Meeko Moore tonight. I'm sorry if anyone told you differently. Third Avenue is my home church, and I've been filling in lately as director for the choir."

"But still, you can favor us with at least one selection, can't you?"

"I'm afraid you don't understand. I . . ."

"But I told the entire organizing committee you'd be here!" Mrs. Pinkett wailed. "As soon as Deirdre Slayton called me, I put the word out you were coming! It's even on the banners outside!"

"You know Deirdre Slayton?" Ty inquired sharply.

"Yes . . . yes, of course. She was engaged to my nephew at one time. She told me how eager Miss Moore was to be a part of the concert, and even with such short notice we've done our best to . . ."

Carlton Johnston was more perceptive than Mrs. Pinkett. He realized there was more going on there than star temperamentality. He took Mrs. Pinkett's elbow, "Come on, Mary Lee. You've got several other choirs to get situated. Let's let Reverend Barnett and his group finish their setup."

"But Carlton . . ."

"See you later on in the evening," he told them, leading the still protesting Mrs. Pinkett away.

Tameka gave him a small smile of gratitude as they left.

"Why aren't you going to sing, Miss Morgan?" Calvin was at her side.

"Well, Calvin, I just don't think if would be . . . fitting."

"Why not?" Calvin was obviously sincerely puzzled.

"Yes, why not, Miss Morgan?" Opal put forth. "It would

be great! We could even back you up. Singing backup for Meeko Moore! Wow!'' she breathed reverently.

"Yeah! . . . You know it! . . . Come on, Miss Morgan, go for it! . . .'' the other teens urged, gathering around Tameka."

Tameka was moved by their loyalty and support. "Look, guys, I appreciate your encouragement, but . . .''

"Look, y'all," Percy helpfully interrupted, "we've got to get off stage and let the next group have their prep time. Let's go catch a quick bite while we still have time."

Percy lead the teens offstage, but Calvin lingered a moment. "We really want you to sing, Miss Morgan. Really."

Tameka felt her eyes sting as she looked into the fresh honesty of his gaze. "I . . . I'll think about it, Calvin," she murmured. Calvin took off after the group, giving Tameka a sad little smile as he went.

Ty was standing at the piano, plunking out a little one-fingered tune. Tameka waited for him to speak, but he seemed totally absorbed in the keyboard.

"Well?" Tameka finally asked.

Ty stopped and looked up. "Well? Well what?"

Tameka sighed in frustration. "Well, don't you have anything to say about all this?"

He gave her his mischievous smile. "Nope." He went back to harassing the piano.

In spite of herself, Tameka was a little miffed at his indifferent pose. "If I wouldn't be disturbing you, Reverend Barnett, surely you have an opinion."

"Yes, I do," Ty responded without looking up.

Tameka went over and sat on the piano bench. "Look, Ty, all kidding aside, I could really use a little advice right about now."

Ty stopped once again, looking intently down at Tameka. "I have an opinion, Tameka. Are you sure you want to hear it?"

"Y . . . yes. Yes, Ty, I'm sure," Tameka answered, but

was not certain that she really was. Ty was wearing his "no nonsense" look.

"Okay." He sat down on the piano bench next to her, fixing her with his gaze. "Just remember that you asked me to give it."

Ty paused a moment staring down at his hands, clasped between his knees. When he suddenly looked up, right at her, the intensity of his gaze gave Tameka a little start.

"I understand where you're coming from, Tammi," Ty began. "You know this means a lot to the kids, and you don't want to diminish their accomplishments by throwing them into your shadow, right?"

"Right, Ty, and . . . and . . ."

"And you also don't want to give the impression you're show-boating. 'Local girl makes good,' and all that."

"What a way to put it!" Tameka laughed, then grew serious. "But, yes, I guess that's pretty much it."

"Both those positions have a lot of validity. But I don't think you're looking at the whole picture . . . or at your real reasons."

"The whole picture? And what 'real' reasons. What do you mean?"

"Tammi, God gave you a talent, a gift. You don't own it. You're just the custodian of it. The Bible says 'To everything there is a season.' Yes, there's a time to stand quietly in the background. There are times when that has its place. But there are also times to stand up and be heard. Times to share what the Lord has given you. To proudly exhibit your talents as your offering—not to others, but to Him."

"So you're saying you think I should perform tonight?"

Ty's eyes were so passionate they were glowing. "No. No, you should not perform. That's definite. But that's not to say you shouldn't *sing*. But only you can make that decision."

Tameka's head began to throb. "Huh? I don't follow you. What are you saying?"

Ty gently took both of Tameka's hands. "I'm saying,

honey, that when you perform, you do that for other people. But when you sing, you do that only for yourself—and the Lord."

Tameka sat silently for a long moment, absorbing the principle—and the wisdom—of his words.

"And, anyway, Tameka," Ty softly interrupted her meditation, "are you sure it's the choir you're concerned about?"

Tameka stiffened, and looked away. "What do you mean?" She tried to pull her hands away, but Ty held on tight.

"Tammi, those kids know you. They love you. And they know you're not some egotistical attention seeker. If you didn't already know that, they've just told you so. You know everybody here for the concert would love to hear you sing. That's what all this excitement is about. And you love to sing. Your singing is as much a part of you as breathing. So whose opinion *are* you worried about?"

Tameka still refused to look Ty in the eye. "I'm sure you have a theory on that, as well," she rigidly replied.

"Since you ask, yes, I do." Ty stopped. When he didn't continue, Tameka looked at him, wondering why he was so hesitant to go on. But he wasn't hesitant. He was just waiting to get her full attention.

Ty's probing eyes were so enthralling she couldn't look away. "Tammi, isn't this all about the gossips back home? Aren't you worried about what they might think? About what they might say?"

Tameka was this time successful in pulling her hands from Ty's grasp. "No! Of course not! I couldn't care less about what they have to say about it. How could you even think that?"

"Because I know what a hard time some people have given you these past few weeks. And I know how hurt you're been to be treated that way by some people you've known all your life. And I also know you've tried your best to keep a—what have you called it?—low profile."

Ty leaned closer, "But, baby, there's only just so far you should go to try to keep peace with other people, especially when they're wrong." He gave her a little smile. "Ever heard the phrase, 'bending over backwards?' " Tameka gave him a distracted little nod. "Well," Ty went on, "That's a good way to *break* your back—if you go too far."

Tameka didn't reply. She just sat staring down at her hands.

A guy came up to the front of the stage. "Excuse me, folks . . . oh, it's you, Miss Moore! Excuse me, Miss Moore, sir, but it's time to open the doors for the audience."

"Okay," Ty told him, as he and Tameka stood.

As the guy headed for the back of the auditorium, Ty put both his hands on Tameka's shoulders. "I'm no Danny, Tammi. I'm not trying to tell you what to do. I just want to be sure you're making your decision with your eyes, and your heart, open. Remember what I told you that night?" Tameka nodded once again. "Then that's the only real advice I have for you. As long as you do that, you'll be fine. And whatever you decide . . . I'm behind you."

By the time they found their way back to the ready room, the choir was finishing the snacks Percy had taken them to get, and starting to put on their robes. The girls were nervously combing their hair and applying lipstick. Tammi got her own robe down from the rack, and put it on. She stared at herself in the mirror a long time before opening her purse for her comb.

Percy came up to her. "What's it gonna be, Tammi? Are you singing? 'Cause if you are, I need to know what you're singing."

"Does it look like I'm singing tonight? Have I rehearsed anything to sing?" Tameka snapped at him. "Percy, you of all people know I haven't."

"Okay! Mercy! I just asked," Percy shot back. "Anyway, I've told you my opinion about your need to 'prepare to sing.' "

"I know, Percy, I know," Tameka said contritely. "This

whole situation caught me so unaware it's got me on edge. But that's no reason for me to take it out on you." She put her arm around his shoulders. "I'm sorry."

"No apology needed, girl." He gave her a peck on the cheek. "I just hope you know what you're doing."

Tameka sighed. "So do I, Postscript. So do I."

She turned, and saw Ty sitting just behind them. He didn't speak, but his expression spoke for him.

Irrationally, Tameka found herself angry at Ty, as though the whole debacle was his fault. She breezed past him without a word, rounding the choir up for warm-up vocals. She tried to ignore him, to act as though his words were forgotten. But she couldn't. They weren't.

Before she knew it, the choir was being motioned forward. They were next. Occupied though she was with herding the children to the wings, and shushing them while they waited for the choir on stage to finish, her whirling thoughts continued. A few of the chaperoning moms hovered about, tucking in this collar, or brushing back that stray hair.

Carlton Johnston was standing near Tameka. He seemed about to speak when Ty suddenly grasped Johnston's elbow, and pulled him aside, whispering something in his ear.

What is Ty saying to him? Tameka wondered, her groundless anger mounting. *Probably telling him to introduce me, to force me into singing! After he told me he'd respect my decision, whatever it was!* The anger was replaced by a kind of lonely melancholy. Her disillusionment was crushing. *Well, what did you think he was, anyway,* she scolded herself, *some sort of superman?* And then another voice from deeper inside piped up to say, *Yes, I guess you did.*

The sound of spirited applause broke into her revery. The choir on stage had finished, and was filing off via the wings on the other side of the stage. Carlton Johnston rushed past Tameka as he went on stage and up to the mike.

"Amen! Amen! Wonderful! That was the Inspirational choir from Prince of Peace Church, who came all the way from Laurel, Mississippi, to be with us today." Johnston told the audience. "Let's give them another hand!" The audience enthusiastically responded.

"And now, we're going to hear from the younger generation. The media would have you believe all our children are out sinning and killing and selling drugs. One of the best rebuttals to that fabrication is waiting in the wings to sing for you. Ladies and gentlemen, accompanied by Percy Stallworth, and directed by Tameka Morgan, I give you the Young People's Choir from Third Avenue Church of Halcyon, Georgia!"

Tameka was thunderstruck. *How did he know my real name?* she thought. And Johnston had introduced them exactly as he had the other choirs, with no special emphasis on just who their director was. *But how* . . .

Tameka pivoted to see Ty at her elbow, giving her a fragile smile. "Break a leg, Sister Morgan," he whispered.

Tameka's heart melted as she realized what Ty had done, and at the same time she flushed with shame that she had ever doubted him.

"Tammi, come on," Percy prompted, tugging at the sleeve of Tameka's robe. "Surely you don't have stage fright! Let's go, we're on!"

Tameka rushed to join Percy and the choir as they filed on stage, only pausing a second to turn and silently mouth the words *thank you*. She was rewarded by Ty's most dazzling smile.

The teens formed flawlessly into the semicircle Tameka had devised for them. As she stood facing them, she could hear the murmur of the audience behind her grow louder as word was passed that the Meeko Moore they'd been anticipating was no other than the woman who had been so modestly introduced.

But the undertone faded away as Tameka focused on the choir. She could see how nervous they were from their fidgeting stances and trembling hands. She gave them a confident smile, dimples flashing, as she clasped her hands in front of her in a prize-fighter victory shake only they could see. The smiles she received in return told her they were ready.

Tameka nodded to her right at Percy, who started the introduction for their first song, "Steal Away." Tameka loved the old hymns, and wanted to be sure this younger generation was exposed to them, as well as the wonderful music of the Winans, Kirk Franklin, and other contemporary gospel artists.

Tameka felt near tears at the simple beauty of the choir's presentation of the lovely old refrain. Their harmony was perfection, with each part sustaining the other in flawless balance. From behind her Tameka could hear some of the audience joining in, a sure sign that they too were touched by the vibrant young voices' rendition of this song that had been sung by their grandparents and their grandparents' grandparents.

At the song's end the ovation was tremendous, with "Amens" and "Hallelujahs" liberally augmenting the vigorous applause. Tameka turned to face the audience, and at her discreet hand signal she and the choir bowed in union.

Tameka then turned to the choir again as Calvin went to the drums that were set up near Percy's piano, and tambourines were passed among the choir. Opal shyly stepped forward to the single microphone to Tameka's left. Tameka gave her a concealed thumbs up, and lifted both hands. At Tameka's downbeat, Percy and Calvin started in on the lively intro to "Goin' Up Yonder." Opal took a deep breath—from her diaphragm, as Tameka had taught her, and launched into her solo.

As the dynamic clarity of Opal's bountiful alto rang out across the room, the audience's cries of appreciation joined in. As Opal came to the end of the first verse, Tameka gave the signal to the right, and the entire choir began to sway. They added the tambourines to the chorus, and those without tambourines started to clap in time to the music. Calvin was almost tearing the skins off the drums with his manic tattoo. Tameka would not have been surprised to see smoke rising from the keyboard as Percy hunched his shoulders, and gave himself over to the music.

They ended the song with Opal's improvising over the choir's final run, to which Calvin stood to give the cymbals a resounding crash. Percy's fingers were a blur as he ran the closing arpeggio from top to bottom of the keyboard.

The audience leapt up as one body, their shouts and applause making the building seem to quake. Tameka turned once again to face them, her arms held out wide. As she and the choir took another bow the acclamation increased in volume. Tameka gestured to Opal, Calvin, and Percy, who each took an individual bow.

Then suddenly Ty appeared on stage, handing Tameka a huge bouquet of red roses. The choir began to whistle and cheer as Tameka took a bow of her own, with Ty, who had disappeared back into the wings, adding his own applause to the cheers. Then Tameka led them in one final group bow before they exited the stage.

Back in the ready room, the parents present enthusiastically hugged their children as the teens ran around like young lunatics, pumped up by their performance. Tameka stood by and watched them proudly.

Seats had been reserved at the front of the auditorium for each of the choirs use after their performances. After giving them a short while to settle down, the adults herded the group together, and with them unobtrusively slipped into their seats. Ty had made sure he was seated next to Tameka, and in the dark of the room, quietly took her hand.

During the applause for another choir, Tameka leaned over to whisper, "You got the roses, didn't you?"

Ty was scandalized, "Me? Gracious no. They're from the choir."

"But you gave them the idea." This was a statement, not a question.

Ty just smiled.

The balance of the concert was truly marvelous. Tameka was impressed with the variety and talent of the groups on hand. Tameka wasn't so sure now that they would win a trophy, but that didn't matter to her. She hoped it didn't matter to the choir, either. They had come and had given their very best. Tameka hoped the kids would be happy and content with that, even if they went home empty-handed.

The final choir finished. Carlton Johnston took the stage once again. The concert's organizing committee was introduced, along with the judges, as the first, second, and third place trophies were placed on a table near the front of the stage.

"This has been truly a blessed evening. I know I'll leave here tonight with my heart uplifted," Johnston said. The audience emphatically agreed.

"And now, on to the awards. I'm only sorry we don't have an award for every group represented here tonight. They each deserve one." The audience again signaled their approval.

"The third place award goes to . . ." Mary Lee Pinkett handed Johnston an envelope, "The Inspirational Choir, Prince of Peace church, Laurel, Mississippi!"

A roar arose from the section of the auditorium where the choir was seated as its director ran onstage to gratefully accept their trophy.

And the second place award goes to . . ." Tameka squeezed Ty's hand tightly. "The Men's Chorus, St. Matthews Temple, Atlanta!"

As the excited choir director ran onstage, Ty smiled over at Tameka, "Two down, but one left to go!" She smiled wanly back, the butterflies in her stomach worse than those on the night she won her Grammy.

"And our first place choir . . ." Johnston tore open the

envelope, his face breaking out in a huge grin, "The Third Avenue Church Young People's Choir of . . ." The pandemonium of the group all around Tameka drowned out the rest. The teens were jumping up and down, hugging one another and their parents. Ty grabbed Tameka in a bear hug that lifted her feet from the floor. "Well, Madame Directress," Percy told Tameka with a peck on the cheek, "go get our award!"

The audience was on its feet as Tameka ran to the stage, so thrilled she almost tripped over her choir robe. Johnston was beaming as he handed Tameka the trophy, and she hugged the precious statuette to her bosom. The room grew quiet as she went to the mike.

"We'd like to thank the committee who invited us here, and the judges who voted for us," Tameka breathlessly began. "We'd like to also thank all of you . . ." she gestured to the audience, "for your kind reception." The audience roared once again. "But I, personally, give thanks to the Lord, for giving me one of the most joyous experiences of my life, in the privilege of working with this wonderful group of talented young people."

The audience's applause turned into a clamor as the chant clearly arose from Tameka's choir, "Tam-e-ka! Tam-e-ka!" They were quickly joined by the rest of the crowd, chiming in with "Mee-ko! Mee-ko!" They wouldn't let her leave the stage. The din grew ever louder as claps and stomps were added to the tribute.

Tameka's heart was full to bursting as she looked about her. She looked down and her eyes met Ty's. He was standing with the group, not chanting with the rest, but just clapping quietly, his eyes shining with pride. And then Tameka understood. She understood that their request was not prompted by some misguided starstruck adulation. It was based in their sincere respect for her talents, and the manner in which she had resolved to present them—and herself.

Tameka bowed her head, and stood motionless. The

room grew gradually silent. She lifted her head, and held out her arms, as the exquisite sound poured from her slender throat:

> "Our Father, which art in heaven,
> Hallowed be Thy name . . ."

The golden beauty of Tameka's voice needed no accompaniment. The auditorium, which had been so uproarious only moments before, grew hushed and still.

Chapter 6

"Alone at last," Ty chuckled.

Tameka looked into the back of the van, where the teens were all sound asleep, leaning one against the other. "Yes, I guess so. Even Reggie finally gave in." She glanced over to where that worthy gentleman sat, propped against a side window, with their trophy securely tucked under one arm.

"You need to get a few winks yourself, lady. You've had a busy day."

"And leave you up all alone at the wheel? I think not. Your day has been as long as anyone else's—probably longer. Nope. I'm going to stay awake to keep an eye on you."

"I should let you drive." He smiled at Tameka. "Then instead of watching the road, I could watch you."

They drove on in silence for a long while.

"Ty?"

"Uh-huh?"

"I'm sorry."

"Sorry for what, honey?"

"Sorry for getting angry at you this afternoon. You were

only telling me the truth. I got angry because I didn't want to hear the truth." She bowed her head, "Although I needed to hear it. I think in reality I was angry at myself, not you.

"And when you were talking to Carlton Johnston, I momentarily lost faith in you. I should have known better. I'm sorry. And thank you for caring enough to tell me what I needed to hear, not what I wanted to hear."

Ty looked out at dark road ahead for a moment. "Caring about you comes easy, Tammi." He paused again. "In fact," he whispered softly, "I'm finding it's impossible not to."

Tameka didn't reply. The conversation had suddenly taken a turn she wasn't prepared for.

"Tammi . . . you don't have to say anything." Ty went on in the face of Tameka's silence. "I know how improbable this whole thing is. Tonight, for the first time, I really got a glimpse of what your life must be like. You're so for real and down-to-earth, it's easy to forget you're a celebrity. A woman who is known to millions and sought after by fans all over the country couldn't . . ."

"Ty," Tameka softly interrupted, "I think we already had this conversation."

"We did? When?"

"The day after I met you, when you brought me home from church." A smile crept into her voice. "We talked then about what we both did for 'a living', remember?"

"Yes, I remember. But that was different. Then I liked you, I was attracted to you, but I didn't know I'd come to feel . . . to feel . . ."

"Yes?" Tameka wasn't aware that she was holding her breath.

"Tammi, I know I haven't got any right to hope. A woman like you . . . There are men all over the country who'd give anything to be with you. Men with far more to offer than I."

Tameka's heart spoke for her before she could stop it.

"Ty, a man couldn't possibly have more to offer a woman than you. A man who's strong enough to be gentle. A man who respects himself, and has dedicated his life to helping make the world a better place. A man who uses both his head and his heart." Tameka touched his cheek. "That's a pretty unique combination."

Ty took her hand, and gently brought it to his lips. "You mean this country preacher might actually have a chance?" he whispered.

Tameka smiled tenderly, "A pretty good one, I'd say." Tameka paused this time. "But, Ty," she finally went on, "I'm really starting to get concerned about all the gossip. You were right. That was one of the reasons I had decided not to sing today. Some people seem determined to distort everything we do, trying to turn it into something cheap, something ugly.

"Ty, you know how . . . how puritanical people can get in what they expect of clergymen. Just like some folks assume I've turned into some kind of 'fly girl' since I've become a recording artist. You have a talent, too, Ty. And more importantly, you have a mission. I don't want to impede that mission."

Ty was silent, and Tameka knew he was mulling over her words in his usual perceptive way. "Tammi," he said at last, "I have to admit there's a lot of truth to what you say."

Tameka's heart began to sink. She braced herself for the "Maybe it's best we don't see each other anymore."

"I do have a mission," Ty went on. He took Tameka's hand, "Tammi, I'm a man of God, but I'm also just a man." He squeezed her hand tighter, "And you're the most exceptional woman I've ever known. And I want you to stay in my life. I need you in my life." He paused, biting his lip. "Tammi, I . . ."

A lethargic yawn came from the back of the van. "Oooh! My back is killing me! Are we home yet?"

"Not yet, Latrisse," Ty informed her, quickly reorienting himself. "We should be there in about half an hour."

Hearing their voices, Reggie woke up, too. "Huh? What did you say? What's going on?" he asked, sleepily rubbing his eyes.

"Nothing, Reggie. Go back to sleep, honey." Tameka said.

"Reggie, let me hold the trophy for a while, okay?" Latrisse requested.

Reggie cackled wickedly as his eyes rolled in a suggestive leer, "What'll you give me for it?"

"How about a pop upside your head?" came Latrisse's reply.

That dampened Reggie's romantic ardor. "Well, if you're gonna be that way about it—here."

"Ouch!"

In the transfer the trophy had fallen—squarely on Marc's stocking feet. That ended all chance of Tameka and Ty continuing their private conversation. It woke everybody up. Having had a chance to get their second wind, the group was livelier than ever, and began rehashing the day's events.

"Hey, Rev. T," Reggie called out, "now that we're in the big-time, you can have us on your TV show. 'The Reginald Fuller Singers,'—has a nice ring to it, doesn't it?"

His fellow choir members didn't think so. They started pelting Reggie with shoes, socks, and balled up paper bags from McDonald's.

"What TV show, Ty?" Tameka asked.

"One of the local cable stations is trying to get Reverend Barnett to host a weekly show," Opal volunteered.

"That's not for sure yet, Opal. We're still working out the details. And I'd have to get the church's permission."

"That's wonderful, Ty. Why didn't you tell me?"

"Well, it's still in the talking stages now, honey."

Tameka didn't think Ty realized he'd called her honey, but the teens did. Tameka caught their smiles, and nudges to one another. Calvin was the only one that didn't look very happy about it.

By this time they'd finally reached the freeway exit to Halcyon. Percy in the other van and the cars in their party honked their horns in good-bye, and turned off in various directions, bearing their passengers home.

"Okay," Ty said to his passengers, looking briefly over his shoulder, "let's see, who do we have? Zayna, your house is closest, we'll drop you off first."

They made the rounds, taking each of the teens home. Once again, Calvin was last.

"Good night, Calvin. You were fabulous on the drums today."

"Thanks, Miss Morgan. Your solo was great, too. I knew you'd sing if we asked you to."

"Good night, Calvin," Ty said. "It's late. We'll wait until you get in."

"Hey, man, I can get in on my own." Calvin truculently replied. "I don't need no baby-sitter." He turned to Tameka, "You going straight home, Miss Morgan?"

"Why, yes, of course, Calvin. It's almost midnight. Where else would I go? Why do you ask?"

"Oh, I . . . I just thought maybe you all were going by Burger King or something."

"Are you hungry, honey?" Tameka kindly replied. "We can take you by the drive-through if you like."

"No . . . no, I'm okay. Well, uh, good night."

Despite Calvin's manly assertions, Ty did indeed keep the van right where it was until the boy was safely inside.

"You know what he was asking just now, don't you?" Tameka said as they pulled away from the curb. "This has gone on long enough. I think it's time I had a talk with Calvin, Ty."

"No, Tammi, don't," Ty put in. "I know you'd do it as gently as anyone could, but no matter how tactful you were, he'd be humiliated."

"But, Ty, this whole thing is affecting his relationship with you."

"Of course it is, Tammi. He sees me as his rival."

"Rival? Ty, Calvin's only sixteen. I'm twenty-three. Surely he understands it could never be."

"Since when has love ever been logical, Tammi? So a seven year age difference is hopeless, huh?" Ty chuckled. "I'm thirty. You gonna kick me to the curb?"

"No!" Tameka joined his laughter. "But I did think you were oh, twenty-six . . . twenty-seven."

"Why, thank you, ma'am." Ty studied his face in the rearview mirror, brushing back his hair with one hand. "Think I can get off shaving a few years from my résumé?"

Tameka laughed again. "And they say women are vain! Yes, you probably could. But my assessment wasn't based solely on your youthful countenance, sir. I had the impression you'd been out of college for only a few years."

"That's right, I have. But I have another title I rarely use. I'm actually the Reverend *Doctor* Barnett."

Tameka was pleasantly surprised—and impressed. "You are?"

"Yep. Ph.D., theology. I had a football scholarship to college. After two years, it was obvious I wasn't going to make it to the pros. I was good, but not good enough. Then my folks were killed. I kind of lost interest in everything after that, so I quit school. I wanted to travel, and I sure didn't have any money, so I joined the Marines."

He looked at Tameka meaningfully. "I wound up in the Gulf War." He didn't speak for a long moment. "Tammi, there's no way I can tell you what it was like. And then on top of the horror, there was the heat. That never relenting dry heat, that seems to suck your breath right out of your body. If there's a hell on earth, that was it. I think I was starting to go over the edge. Some of the guys had drugs. Marijuana, crack, cocaine, you name it."

"Drugs? How in the world could they get drugs?"

"Tammi, how do people in jail get drugs? I don't know.

But drugs seem to have a way of infiltrating almost everywhere, God help us.

"Anyway, I think I was on the verge of taking up on some of the offers." He caught Tameka's stunned reaction. "Yes, I was. I'm not proud of it, but I'd be lying if I said otherwise.

"Then I ran into this older guy, the chaplin. He was a Catholic priest named Dave Peterson. Somehow, I think Father Dave sensed I was in bad shape. He started always coming around, starting up conversations. We had some long, deep discussions about some real heavy stuff." Ty paused again. "He was a very wise man.

"When I got home, I kept thinking about those talks. About the things Father Dave said about life, about people, about God. My dad was a minister, so I was raised in the church. I had stopped going when they died. But then, I started back again, and well . . . here I am."

Tameka didn't speak. She was spellbound by this tale that told her so much about the makeup of this man.

"I'm sorry," Ty said after a pause. "I didn't mean to rattle on like that." He looked straight ahead. "I've never really told that whole story to anybody before."

Tammi leaned over and gently kissed his cheek. He gave her fragile half-smile in return.

"Tammi," Ty said after a beat. "I have to take the van back to the church, and get my car from the parking lot. Want to ride with me?" he looked at her hopefully. "Or would you rather I take you home now?"

Tameka arched one eyebrow, "What do you think?"

By the time they arrived at the church parking lot Percy had already come and gone, leaving the other van in its customary spot. Ty parked beside it, and came to the passenger side to open the door for Tameka. "Guess we missed Percy and Eddie Mae," she commented.

"Well, guess they kinda wanted a little privacy. They haven't had a chance to be alone all day, and neither have we," Ty added meaningfully.

"Be alone? Why would they want to be alone?" Tameka suddenly caught Ty's drift. "You mean . . ."

"For quite a little while now. You didn't know? Eddie Mae didn't tell you?" Ty asked as they crossed the parking lot to where the Roadmaster sat waiting.

"No, and Percy didn't either. I sensed something, but I thought it was just my imagination. You just wait until I see them!"

"Well, neither of them have made any official declarations, but it's kind of an open secret. I think they're concerned about appearances, too. After all, it's only been a little over a year since Percy lost his wife."

"Yes, I know," Tameka said as Ty opened the car door for her. "I was happy to see him so much like his old self when I got home. The last time I saw him, he was still taking it pretty hard."

"Now there's an age difference for you," Ty said after he had gone around to get behind the wheel. "I think they're concerned about that, too."

"Yes. Percy's got to be close to forty now." Tameka said as Ty pulled out of the parking lot. "And Eddie's only a year older than me."

"Well, I wish them Godspeed. They're good for each other . . ." he reached for Tameka's hand, "just like you and me."

Tameka didn't reply. She just slid closer, and put her head on Ty's shoulder.

"Are you hungry, sweetheart? Want to pick up on Calvin's idea, and stop for something to eat?" Ty asked solicitously.

"No, Ty, I'm fine. You?"

"No, that stop by Mickey D's on the way in will hold me until breakfast. But . . ."

"But what, honey?"

"I . . . I just don't want to take you home."

Tameka snuggled even closer to him. "I don't want to

go home." But by this time she had arrived home. Ty pulled the car into the driveway.

"This has been a truly glorious day, Tammi," Ty whispered. "I seem to be having more and more of those . . ." he put one arm around her shoulders, and cupped her face with his other hand, "since you came into my life."

The kiss began softly, gently, but then Ty put his other arm around Tameka's waist, and pulled her tightly to his chest. Her arms went around his neck, holding him closer still as she felt her body melt into his. Her lips parted with a low moan as his tongue touched hers, probing her mouth deeply, deliciously. A flame ignited deep within her as she ran her fingers though his thick, soft hair, and felt his hand leave her waist to caress her thigh.

"Oh, Tammi," Ty breathed against her ear, "you mean so much to me." He kissed her again, his lips trailing across her cheek down to the hollow of her throat. "You're so sweet, so wonderful in every way. I never thought I'd find you."

"Ty . . . sweetheart." Tameka was gasping with delight at the ecstacy of his touch. She cradled his head against her bosom, kissing his ear, lightly flicking it with her tongue.

"Oh, baby, you're driving me crazy." He kissed her lips once more, and Tameka felt herself totally surrender. Why deny it any longer? She was in love with him. And she wanted him as badly as he wanted her.

"Tameka, Tameka," Ty moaned her name over and over again as his lips slipped down and he buried his face in the cleft between her breasts. "I want you so much, baby," he whispered hoarsely, his words echoing her thoughts.

His hands found their way to her breasts, and gently cupped the quivering mounds in his big, powerful hands. Even through her clothing, her nipples made their jubilant presence known, rising to meet the bliss of his touch.

They shouldn't, Tameka knew. She should make him stop. Make him stop before things went too far. But she was powerless before the passion that inflamed her. The hard, muscular feel of his back as she held him tight, his fiery kisses, his melting caresses were more than she could resist. And it was even more. It was the man himself. She respected him. She admired him. She trusted him. She loved him.

Ty stopped suddenly, "Oh, Tammi, forgive me, baby. I . . . I didn't mean for things to get out of control like this."

Tameka caressed his cheek. "There's nothing to forgive."

"Tammi," Ty took her hands, and kissed them, one by one. "No, baby. Not this way. You deserve more. You deserve better than a quick, secret rendezvous in the backseat of a car. You deserve only the best a man can give." His eyes searched hers. "You weren't going to stop me, were you?"

Tameka met his gaze straightforwardly, "No."

"You should have. I could have . . . I almost . . . Why didn't you stop me, baby?"

As she looked into his eyes Tameka knew she couldn't lie to him. Her heart wouldn't let her lie to him. "Because I love you, Ty," she whispered.

Ty's eyes widened in wonder and disbelief, "What? What did you say, Tameka?"

"I said I love you, Ty."

"Do you mean it? Are you sure?"

Tameka laughed at his obvious rapture. "Yes, I'm sure." She leaned forward and cupped his face, planting a tender kiss on his lips. "Doesn't that feel like an I'm sure?"

Ty took her into his arms, "Yes, ma'am. It sure does." He held her close, his kiss thankful and protective. His arms tightened about her, "Oh, sweetheart. I didn't dare hope. It was just too much to ask for that you . . ."

"Hold it, mister," Tameka interrupted. "Aren't you forgetting something?"

Ty's face was puzzled for a second, and then a glimmer

of a smile crossed his lips. "Woman, you know I do. That goes without saying."

"Just the same, a girl does like hearing it," Tameka teased, running a finger across his full, tempting lips.

Ty drew back from her slightly, so that he could look into her eyes. And she saw there what he had, up to now, been trying so desperately to conceal. The total devotion, respect, yearning, and passion he held in his heart for her. His gaze blazed in its intensity. "I love you, Tameka Morgan, from the bottom of my soul. I think I have from the day we met. And you've just made me the happiest man on earth." His impassioned kiss was interrupted by the flash of headlights, and the roar of a car flying past.

"Now, who'd be zipping up the street at this time of night in this neighborhood?" Tameka wondered. "This street is hardly on the beaten path."

"Probably somebody who wanted to see what the happiest man on earth looks like," Ty replied, cuddling Tameka once more.

She looked up at him, the joy shining in her eyes, "And how ironic that he should have the happiest woman on earth by his side," she murmured in return. "But, look here, Reverend Doctor Barnett, if I'm not mistaken, you have a sermon to preach in about . . ." she looked at her watch, "six hours and forty-seven minutes. If you don't get some rest, you'll fall asleep in the pulpit."

They got out of the car, and Ty walked her to the door. Ty looked at the porch and screen door. "This is the spot where I first saw you," he whispered. "And where I first lost my heart. Good night, my love."

"Good night, darling."

Ty took her hands once again. "Don't worry, baby. Everything is going to work out. You'll see."

"I'm not worried, Ty. As long as I know you love me, that's all I need."

Ty wrapped Tameka up in his arms, his lingering kiss

telling her how much he hated to go more potently than words ever could.

Again they were interrupted by a bright flashing light, and the sound of a car whizzing past. "Who is that?" Tameka wondered.

"I think I know," Ty said, hesitantly, watching the rapidly retreating red taillights disappear down the quiet street. "I recognize the car." He looked solemnly down at Tameka, "I think it was Deirdre Slayton."

"Dee-Dee? Why would she keep driving back and forth past my house?"

"It's not you she's targeting," Ty told her. "It's me. She's been tailing me for months."

"What! Ty, are you sure? Have you confronted her with it?"

"Yes. At first I thought our 'accidental' meetings were just that—coincidence. But then I started to spot her out the corner of my eye at places she had no earthly business being, like basketball practice. When I confronted her with it, she denied the whole thing, even accused me of following her. Still, she sort of slowed down . . ." he looked at Tameka meaningfully, "until I started seeing you."

"Ty, honey, there are laws against that kind of thing. It's called stalking. And it's just as wrong for a woman stalk a man as the other way around."

"Yes, I know, love. But what can I do? Can't you see this six-foot-one, hundred-and-eighty-pound former football player going to the cops and filing a complaint about a woman stalking me? They'd probably laugh me out of the station house."

"Well, Jesse wouldn't, but I guess the other guys would," Tameka had to admit. "Then I'll go talk to her. I'll not have that heifer stalking my man!"

"No, you won't, my little spitfire," Ty laughed. "That would only make the situation worse. "And anyway, so far all she's done is look. 'Sticks and stones,' and all that. If words can never hurt me, looks sure can't. I just feel sorry for her."

"But, Ty, that's not normal behavior. Who knows what she's capable of? What about Pastor Hawkins? Have you told him?"

"Yes. He's the only other person who knows, except you." Ty smiled widely, "That's why he hustled her off so quickly at the picnic. He's talked to her, too, and told her if she didn't cut it out he'd talk to her mother."

"Well, did he?"

Ty chuckled once again. "Yes, he did. But Moms just got all puffed up, and told the Hawk he had to be mistaken. Her baby would never do anything like that. So we're back to square one. I've been hoping she'd just get tired of it and give up. Maybe it'll help that along . . ." he took Tameka in his arms, "now that I'm taken. But that's enough about Deirdre Slayton." Ty pulled Tameka close. "You and I have better things to do."

After a long, lingering good night, Tameka went inside, and stood in the doorway watching as Ty got into the car and pulled away, waving until he was out of sight. She gave a deep, contented sigh, turned off the downstairs light Mama had left on for her, and went upstairs, softly humming.

Tameka was surprised to see a light from under Mama's door. She knocked softly, "Mama?"

"Yes, baby, I'm up. Come on in, sweetheart."

Mama was seated in the stuffed armchair next to her bed, her glasses perched on the end of her nose, reading.

"Mama! What are you doing up so late?" A little smile crossed Tameka's lips. "I'm a big girl now. You weren't waiting up for me, were you?"

"No, honey. As long as you were with Ty, I knew you were in good hands." Tameka's smile naughtily broadened, as she reflected just how literally true that statement was. "Some rude rascal just called, asking for you. Woke me out of a sound sleep, ringing the phone off the hook.

When I told him you weren't in, he just hung up. Didn't even apologize."

"Him? It was a man?" Tameka sank down dejectedly on the bed. "I bet it was Danny. It would be just like him to not think about the time difference, and call here this time of night. And who else would call acting that way?"

"No, I don't think it was him. At least, it didn't sound like him. Then again, maybe it was. Whoever it was sounded kind of funny, like he was trying to disguise his voice."

"That doesn't sound like Danny," Tameka reflected, more to herself than to Mama. "He's too arrogant to even imagine that anyone wouldn't be happy to get a call from him."

"Enough about that. How was the concert?"

"It was wonderful, Mama! We won! We won first place!" Tameka went on to tell Mama all about the afternoon—discreetly leaving out the evening.

"Oh, baby, that's just fabulous. I'm so sorry I couldn't be there. But I'd promised to cater the Williams wedding long before I knew you'd be with the choir."

"It's all right, Mama, I understand. Percy taped the whole concert, so you can at least hear it. And it *was* fabulous."

Mama smiled knowingly, "And is the concert the reason your eyes are glowing?"

"Are they?" Tameka asked softly.

"Yes, they are. Girl, you're lit up like a firefly." Mama looked at the bedside clock. "Concert must have run mighty late."

"Well, after we got back to the city we had to drop all the kids off at home, and then Ty had to go to the church to drop off the van, and then . . ."

"Honey, I'm not asking for an explanation. You're a grown woman, and I know for certain you were raised right." Mama walked over, and sat down next to Tameka. "I'm just glad to see you so happy, child," she added, patting Tameka's hand. "Now we both better try to get a little sleep during what's left of the night. Aren't you planning on going to church tomorrow?"

"Yes, Mama, of course!" Tameka replied, as if shocked Mama could think otherwise.

Mama chuckled softly, "Somehow I thought you were."

Tameka hugged Mama, and gave her a kiss on the cheek, "Good night, Mama."

"Good night, baby."

Just as Tameka was about to close the door, Mama called to her, "Tammi?"

"Yes, Mama?"

"He's a good man, Tammi. I like him. Always have."

Tameka beamed. "Never could hide anything from you, could I?"

"Not much," Mama allowed.

Tameka blew her a kiss as she softly closed the door.

Just as Tameka had turned out the light, and was about to fall asleep, the telephone rang. Tameka snatched it up on the first ring. *Okay, Danny, or whoever you are. That's enough of this foolishness. I'll teach you to call my Mama's house with this nonsense in the middle of the night.* "Hello!" she practically shouted into the phone.

"Tammi? Baby, is that you?" It was Ty.

Tameka's whole demeanor changed in the blink of an eye. "Yes, honey, it's me. Where are you?"

"I'm home. I hope I didn't wake your mom. Is something the matter? You sounded strange just now."

"No, you didn't wake Mama. She's already awake. And the reason why is what caused me to answer the phone like I did." Tameka told Ty about the mystery call.

"It had to be that Dorsey, honey, calling to hassle you again. Just wait 'til the next time I see him!"

"Now, now. That's no way for a minister to talk on a Sunday morning."

"Yes, it is, for a man who don't take no stuff where his woman is concerned." Ty lowered his voice to a whisper, "You are my woman, aren't you, baby?"

"Yes, Ty, I am," Tameka purred into the receiver.

"That's why I called. I just wanted to hear you say so. Good night, my love."

"Good night, sweetheart."

The next few days were the most blissful of Tameka's life, spending them with Ty. They went for long drives in the countryside, down to the beach, and even drove to Atlanta for a jazz concert. Yet over her happiness was the shadow of the chaos she had left behind in L.A.

Tommy McDougall, the president of her record label called, wanting to know why she hadn't returned to the studio.

"What is it, Meeko? Are you unhappy with your contract? You're not due to renegotiate this year, but we don't want to lose you. Is it your royalty rate? Because I can talk to the board, and I'm sure we could . . ."

"No, Tommy, that's not the problem."

"I didn't think so. Look, honey, Dorsey really showed his ass at your last session. Yes, I heard about it. I've been waiting for you to tell me yourself."

"Tommy, I . . . I was just too embarrassed to mention it."

"There's nothing for you to be embarrassed about. Your only fault was being too green to know that guy's reputation before you hired him. I've never liked that barracuda, anyway, though I've been forced to do business with him. I have to hand him that. He does know talent when he sees it. Too bad he doesn't know how to treat them. That's why all his biggest clients have gotten away from him as soon as they were able to.

"Look, Meeko, this isn't the first time one of our talents has had to deal with a crazy manager. I'll put our entire legal staff at your disposal. You're valuable to us, and anyway . . ." Tameka could hear a smile come into his voice, "you're one of the few stars on our roster that I actually like. It'll be a pleasure to help you put the kibosh on that dirtbag.

"But you have to start the ball rolling. I'll give you any help or support you need, but it all starts with you. But don't wait too long, honey. Don't forget you and I have a contract. If you don't deal with Dorsey, and get back to the studio, I'll be forced to deal with you."

Tameka discussed the situation with Ty that evening, "I'm going to have to go back to L.A. soon, honey."

"Then I'm going with you."

"Ty, you can't. What about things here?"

"Baby, even preachers get to take a vacation. Just give me a few days to get things squared away."

"I can't ask that of you, Ty. This is my fight."

"Our fight, my beloved," he answered, holding her tight.

Chapter 7

Eddie Mae called early the following day. "What up, girl? What's on your agenda for today?"

"Just packing, Eddie. I've booked a flight for later this week."

"So you're really going back, huh?"

"Eddie, you know I have to go back. I've established a life there, a career. And I'm no quitter. You know that, too."

"I know, Tammi. But do you have to go now? I mean just when things were starting to get real with Ty, and . . ."

"I have to go, Eddie, and I don't want Ty to know until the last minute. He's determined to go with me, and I know the trouble that would cause him. I'm just going to have to talk him out of it, somehow."

"I understand, Tammi. But don't go this week. I need you."

"You need me? For what?"

"I want you to stand up with me." Eddie took a deep breath, "Percy and I are getting married Saturday."

"Aaah! Girl, you don't mean it! When did he propose?"

"Last night."

"Oh, Eddie, I'm so happy for you! But I don't know if I want to be one of your bridesmaids, after how you and Percy held out on telling me you two were 'sparkin,' as my grandma used to say."

"Oh, Tammi, I explained all that. We've just been taking things slow. He was still healing from losing Sophia, and I wanted to be sure he wasn't with me just on the rebound."

"Taking it slow? Sure doesn't seem like it, if he just proposed last night, and you're getting married in three days."

Eddie Mae giggled. "I think I have you and Ty to thank for that. I think you two inspired him. He told me he was tired of quote 'messin' around' unquote. After he asked me for probably the fiftieth time if I was sure he wasn't too old for me, he went down on one knee and popped the question. Now he doesn't want a long engagement.

"Anyway, I'm going to the beauty parlor today to get myself all gussied up for my wedding. My wedding! Want to go with me?"

Tameka looked at her reflection in the mirror across from her bed. She hadn't done much with her hair in the last month or so, and it would be a good idea to get it done before going back to L.A. Plus, she felt guilty about how little time she had spent with Eddie Mae since she'd been home. "Okay, girl, you're on."

"Hoped you'd say that. We've both got appointments for ten o'clock at Chez Funk."

"Chez *what?*"

"Chez Funk—you know—as in funky?"

"Now, look here, Eddie Mae McElroy, I don't want to go someplace and come out looking like a hoochie mama."

"The choice of name is unfortunate, I grant you, but they do the best hair in town. Meet me out front."

Tameka got to the beauty salon early, before Eddie arrived. She went in and up to the receptionist. "Good

morning. I have an appointment at ten o'clock. My name
is . . ."

"I know who you are," the girl snapped. She looked at
the appointment book. "You're seeing Sweet Pea. Have a
seat. He'll be free in a minute." The girl turned abruptly
and walked away.

*Well! And a jolly good day to you, too! Wonder who set her tail
on fire?* Tameka thought. Then she shrugged. *Oh, well. But
"Sweet Pea?"*

Tameka sat down in the small lobby, and picked up a
magazine, but the conversation of the women in the back
of the salon was far more interesting.

" . . . and then I told him to get his sorry behind out of
my house."

"Girl, I don't blame you. Damn, with your own sister!"

"That's okay, I've got boyfriend's payback—and I do
mean payback. I went and got the best divorce lawyer in
town. Men say 'it's cheaper to keep her,' but I say 'if you
play, you pay.' "

"Melanie, you getting a pedicure, too?"

"Yes, darlin'. Jerome likes me looking good from rooter
to tooter."

"Jerome? I thought your man's name was Rufus."

"Rufus? Honey, I tolerate *him* just to keep my car fixed."

"You out from under the dryer now, girl? Okay, tell us
what else they did."

"Oh, no, I can't. It's just too tacky." *That sounds like
somebody I know,* Tameka thought, *but I can't place the voice.*

"Oh, come on. Force yourself."

There was a general chorus of laughter.

"Well, since you insist." More laughter. "They had the

audacity to get busy in his car, right out in front of the house, and all the while her poor mother was upstairs asleep.''

"No! You're lying!"

"If I'm lying, I'm flying."

"Surely they were just kissing or something. You can't mean they were doing the nasty!"

"Capital N-a-s-t-y."

"Girl, please!"

"I saw it with my own eyes. Well, if they're going to stand right outside the church getting down, is any place sacred?"

Tameka's spine stiffened as the sound of laughter reached her ears. *I didn't hear that. I couldn't have heard that right.*

"And the saddest part of it all," the voice continued, "is that he's got the world-class nerve to call himself a minister."

There was no mistaking that. Nor any mistaking the identity of the speaker. Tameka recognized the voice now. Her legs felt leaden as she rose from her seat, and stumbled around the partition to the rear section of the shop.

Thirty or so women were scattered about the salon. Some were in beauticians' chairs with their hair in varying stages of production. Several more were under the dryers along the wall, and still more at manicurists' tables. But the largest knot was gathered around a woman in huge rollers in one of the chairs, her back to the entrance.

A round-faced woman with her hair wrapped in a towel was the first to see Tameka. Her chin almost hit her chest as her mouth flew open, but she made not a sound. One by one the rest of the room's occupants became aware of Tameka's approach, some jabbing their neighbors with an elbow. Slowly the rest of the room fell silent. By this point Tameka had reached the speaker's chair. But the woman in the chair forged on.

"The poor jerk will probably say he couldn't help himself, and he'll probably be right. She's got seduction down to an art form. I heard her own manager say she's screwed everybody in L.A.—including him!"

"Which makes him as big a liar as you are."

Dee-Dee whipped her chair around, to see what wench had the gall to give such a challenge. The blood drained from her face as she saw Tameka standing there, staring her down. But she gamely regathered her composure. "Well. Look what the cat drug in. Or perhaps in this case cathouse would be more appropriate."

Tameka's stare didn't waver. "Why are you doing this, Dee-Dee?"

Dee-Dee's eyes narrowed. "I already told you my name is Deirdre . . . or is your hearing as sparse as your morals?"

Tameka came a step closer. "There's nothing wrong with either. I heard every word of the lies you've been telling about me and Ty . . . *Dee-Dee.*"

Dee-Dee leaned back in the chair and crossed her legs. "Lies, huh? Are you going to stand there and deny your dirty little affair with Tyler Barnett, or that your own manager called you the biggest whore in L.A.?"

Tameka took a deep breath in preparation of refuting Dee-Dee's slanted rendition of the circumstances, but stopped. She looked around her at the greedy, glittering eyes, at the eager consumption of the live soap opera in their midst.

These people are nothing but vultures, she thought. *These are the kind of people who stop to gawk at accidents on the highway, the kind who just eat up those tawdry talk shows on TV.*

But as Tameka looked deeper she saw that wasn't universally true. *Some of these people are that way, but not all. Not even most.* Tameka saw here a look of compassionate support, there a look of anger, directed at Dee-Dee, not at her.

Tameka slowly released the breath she was holding. "No, I'm not going to deny it."

Dee-Dee was clearly caught off guard. "Because . . . . because you can't!" she cried out to cover her confusion.

"No. Because I don't have to," Tameka calmly came back. "I don't have to explain my actions, or Ty's, to you . . . or to anyone," she declared, sweeping the room with a determined gaze. Tameka turned back to Dee-Dee, "Let me ask *you* a question. How would you know what Ty and I were doing—how would you be there to see it—unless you've been following him around?"

Dee-Dee was silent, fidgeting uncomfortably in her seat. It was as if a lightbulb had gone on for the other women in the room. Yes, how else would Deirdre have known?

"I have only one other thing to say to you." Tameka went on. "You need desperately to get you some business."

"Some business?" Dee-Dee looked around the room as if to say "this woman is crazy." "What are you talking about?"

"You need to get you some business, Dee-Dee . . ." Tameka repeated, leaning forward to stare Dee-Dee dead in the eye, "so you can stay out of mine."

A chorus of oohs, gasps, and "no she didn'ts!" broke out all about the room, followed by stifled giggles. Some women didn't even try to hide it, laughing out loud.

"What the hell is going on in here?" It was Eddie Mae. Tameka had no idea how long she had been standing at the entrance listening, but it was apparently long enough to know Dee-Dee had been shooting off her mouth.

Eddie Mae marched over to where Tameka was standing next to Dee-Dee's chair. "How do you have the nerve to get on Tameka's case?" Eddie Mae fumed. "Let's talk about *your* recent history. How about you and that married lawyer you were living with in Atlanta—before he kicked you out?"

Deirdre began to sputter, "How dare you! That's a lie!"

"What part?" Eddie Mae shot back. "That you were shacked up with him—or that he kicked you out?"

"Both! I'd never live with a married man!"

"That's not what I heard," Eddie maintained with a skeptical smile.

"Oh, really! Then tell me what lying heifer told you that, so I can go slap her face! Who was she?"

Eddie crossed her arms as a wicked grin crossed her face, "Yo' mama."

Dee-Dee snatched off the hairdresser's apron covering her, and leapt up from the chair. "You bitch!" she screamed, going for Eddie Mae, but two beauticians caught her arms and held her back.

"Come on, Tameka," Eddie Mae said serenely, sticking her nose in the air. "Let's get out of here until they have the place aired out."

"You better go!" Dee-Dee shrieked. "And take that man-stealing slut with you!" Dee-Dee stopped struggling, and a frighteningly evil look consumed her face as she played her trump card. "Oh, have either of you ladies seen the morning paper?" She laughed sadistically. "You might find it enlightening."

Tameka was trembling as she and Eddie Mae stood on the sidewalk outside the salon. "What was that crack about the paper?" Eddie Mae asked Tameka. "Do you know what she was talking about?"

"No. I have no idea. I haven't read the paper today. Have you?"

"No. But something tells me we should. Come on." She headed for the grocery store just across the strip mall from the salon.

When they entered the door, everyone in the store seemed to pause, but instead of the greetings Tameka usually received, all they got were hard stares and averted eyes.

Eddie Mae went briskly to the newspaper vending machine at the front of the store, and got a paper. "I don't see anything," she said, flipping quickly through the pages. "There's nothing in here. Dee-Dee was just talking her usual bull ...'' Eddie Mae's voice trailed away, and her eyes widened as she stared at one page of the paper.

"Eddie? Eddie, what is it?" Tameka asked anxiously. Eddie Mae looked up at Tameka, sadness and sympathy filling her eyes. She silently handed the paper to Tameka.

"What is it?" Tameka searched the page. "I don't see any ..." then her eyes fell on the article's headline: "CABLE CHANNEL DROPS PLANS FOR PROGRAM FEATURING LOCAL MINISTER."

"Oh, no," Tameka breathed. Her head began to swim. She felt as though she might faint, and blindly groped with one hand for Eddie Mae's arm for support.

She struggled to read the article through her suddenly blurred vision.

A spokesman for local cable channel fifteen said today plans have been dropped for a program in the works that was to have featured local minister Dr. Tyler Barnett of the Third Avenue Church of Halcyon. The weekly program, which was tentatively entitled The Sweet Hour of Prayer, *would have had Dr. Barnett as its host and moderator. Plans had called for interviews with prominent guest ministers, and music by various choirs, centered around a sermon from Dr. Barnett.*

The spokesman had no comment as to the cause of the cancellation other than to say the channel's management felt Dr. Barnett's other recent commitments would limit his ability to host the program. Dr. Barnett could not be reached for comment.

Tameka swayed slightly as she stood with the paper in one hand dropped to her side. Eddie Mae put an arm around her waist to steady her. "Oh, Eddie," she finally whispered. "This is all my fault. They did this to him because of me."

"Tammi, don't talk foolish," Eddie Mae shook Tameka with the arm encircling her. "You haven't done anything wrong, and neither has Ty. We'll get to the bottom of this. Where's Ty now?"

"I . . . I don't know. I haven't talked to him today."

"Well, let's get out of here and go find him . . . and Percy. We can fight this crap if we all stick together, Tammi."

They turned to leave, and practically bumped into Calvin, who had just come in the door. Calvin looked at Tameka with an expression she had never seen from him before. "Good morning, Miss *Moore.*" He glanced at the paper, still clutched tightly in Tameka's hand. "Catching up on the latest in the entertainment world?" he asked with a hateful smile.

"Boy, what's wrong with you?" Eddie Mae snapped.

"Nothing's wrong with me," Calvin shot back. "I'm fine, now that I finally see thangs . . ." he stared Tameka up and down with contempt, "for what they really are."

"You shut your smart mouth!" Eddie Mae told him. "Calvin, surely you don't believe the gossip . . ." she snatched the paper from Tameka and shook it at Calvin, "or this!"

"I didn't believe it. I kept defending her to anyone who dared say a word against her, even my own mother!" Calvin's voice started to rise, and people had stopped in their tracks, staring at the trio near the door.

"But I can't ignore what I heard with my own ears." He turned to Tameka, his voice growing ever louder. "You thought I was asleep, like everybody else, didn't you?"

"Calvin, what are you talking about?" Eddie Mae insisted.

"I'm talking about her and him," Calvin spat the words out, moving in on Tameka, "just like everybody else in town. I'm talking about how I called her house the night of the concert. I called an hour after the two of them dropped me off. I called at one o'clock in the damn morning . . ." Calvin was shouting now. "And you weren't there!" he yelled into Tameka's face. "You weren't there!"

Tameka just stood there, too stunned to move, too hurt to speak.

"Where were you, huh?" Calvin raged on, circling Tameka. "At his house? At a motel?"

Eddie Mae stepped between Calvin and Tameka. "Boy, you better shut up, or I'm going to slap the taste out your mouth!"

Tameka could stand no more. She bolted wildly for the door. "Tammi! Tammi, come back! Tammi!" Eddie Mae futilely called after her. Tameka ran willy-nilly for the car, heedlessly bumping into people in her path. She jumped in and gunned the engine, nearly backing into a truck passing by.

No, please, God, no, Tameka pleaded. *Not to Ty. He doesn't deserve this. I don't mind for myself, but not him. Please don't let this happen to him.* This was the worst of her fears come home to roost. *I should never have let this happen. I should have stopped things before they even got started. Ty, my darling, my love. Forgive me. I can't change the past, but maybe I can help salvage your future—the only way I can.*

She savagely turned the wheel, and entered the freeway, pointing the car toward the airport.

Tameka leaned her head against the back of the seat, and looked out the window at the fluffy clouds sailing past. Mama would get the message she'd left on the answering machine and know she was all right, and where she'd left the car. She closed her eyes. *Ty? No, I won't call him. I've hurt him enough.* But she couldn't stop thinking about him, about his smile, the sound of his voice, the sweet ecstasy of his embrace. Suddenly something her father used to say entered her thoughts. *If you love something, set it free. If it's meant to be, it will come back to you.*

Tameka opened her eyes. "Miss?" she called to a passing flight attendant. "Could I have a pad of paper?"

"Certainly, Miss Moore," the woman replied. She

Get 4 **FREE** Arabesque Contemporary Romances Delivered to Your Doorstep and Join the Only New Book Club That Delivers These Bestselling African American Romances Directly to You Each Month!

No Obligation!

LOOK INSIDE FOR DETAILS ON HOW TO GET YOUR FREE GIFT.....

(worth almost $20.00!)

**WE INVITE YOU TO JOIN THE ONLY BOOK
CLUB THAT DELIVERS HEARTFELT ROMANCE
FEATURING AFRICAN AMERICAN HEROES AND
HEROINES IN STORIES THAT ARE RICH IN
PASSION AND CULTURAL SPICE...**

And Your First 4 Books Are FREE!

Arabesque is the newest contemporary romance line offered by
Pinnacle Books. Arabesque has been so successful that our
readers have asked us about direct home delivery. We
responded to your requests. You can start receiving four
bestselling Arabesque novels a month delivered right to your
door. Subscribe now and you'll get:

⋄ 4 FREE Arabesque romances as our introductory gift—a value
   of almost $20! (pay only $1 to help cover postage &
   handling)
⋄ 4 BRAND-NEW Arabesque romances
   delivered to your doorstep each month
   thereafter (usually arriving before
   they're available in bookstores!)
⋄ 20% off each title—a savings of
   almost $4.00 each month
⋄ FREE home delivery
⋄ A FREE monthly newsletter,
   Zebra/Pinnacle Romance News that
   features author profiles, book previews
   and more
⋄ No risks or obligations...in other words, you can cancel
   whenever you wish with no questions asked

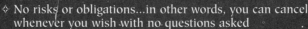

So subscribe to Arabesque today and see why these books are
winning awards and readers' hearts.

After you've enjoyed our FREE gift of 4 Arabesques, you'll begin
to receive monthly shipments of the newest Arabesque titles.
Each shipment will be yours to examine for 10 days. If you
decide to keep the books, you'll pay the preferred subscriber's
price of just $4.00 per title. That's $16 for all 4 books with
FREE home delivery! And if you want us to stop sending books,
just say the word...it's that simple.

*See why reviewers are raving about ARABESQUE
and order your FREE books today!*

WE HAVE 4 FREE BOOKS FOR YOU!

(If the certificate is missing below, write to:
Zebra Home Subscription Service, Inc.,
120 Brighton Road, P.O. Box 5214, Clifton, New Jersey 07015-5214)

FREE BOOK CERTIFICATE

Yes! Please send me 4 Arabesque Contemporary Romances without cost or obligation, billing me just $1 to help cover postage and handling. I understand that each month, I will be able to preview 4 brand-new Arabesque Contemporary Romances FREE for 10 days. Then, if I decide to keep them, I will pay the money-saving preferred subscriber's price of just $16.00 for all 4...that's a savings of almost $4 off the publisher's price with no additional charge for shipping and handling. I may return any shipment within 10 days and owe nothing, and I may cancel this subscription at any time. My 4 FREE books will be mine to keep in any case.

Name _____

Address _____ Apt. _____

City _____ State _____ Zip _____

Telephone ( ) _____

Signature _____ AR0998

(If under 18, parent or guardian must sign.)

Terms and prices subject to change. Orders subject to acceptance by Zebra Home Subscription Service, Inc. . Zebra Home Subscription Service, Inc. reserves the right to reject or cancel any subscription.

4 FREE
ARABESQUE
Contemporary
Romances
are reserved
for you!

(worth almost
$20.00)

see details
inside...

AFFIX
STAMP
HERE

ZEBRA HOME SUBSCRIPTION SERVICE, INC.

120 BRIGHTON ROAD

P.O. BOX 5214

CLIFTON, NEW JERSEY 07015-5214

returned a few minutes later with a pad of airline stationery. Tameka stared at the paper a long, long time. Anyone watching would have thought she was in a trance. The music came first, a melody formed from the intensity and rhythm of her love. The words quickly followed:

You're not here, my love. You're far away from
   me.
Yet in my heart you're ever present, for all eternity.
So although my heart is breaking as I leave to set
   you free,
We'll always be
Together.

I don't need to see your face to feel the sunshine
   of your smile
The warmth of your embrace wraps comfort
   'round me all the while
So even though we're torn apart by mile after
   lonely mile
We'll always smile
Together.

Do you feel me there? Yes, I feel you, too.
Do you know I fill my empty nights with thoughts
   of you?
Do you know that deep inside we've never really
   been apart,
'Cause when I want to see you, I just look inside
   my heart?

So I keep you with me, right beside me, everywhere
   I go.
People wonder why I smile this way, but they will
   never know
That your love within me, deep within me,
   flourishes and glows

But we'll always know,
Our love will grow.
And we'll always be
Together.

Tameka had dashed the lyrics down in a burst of passionate energy, the words flowing from her fingers in a blur
as the music flooded her mind. When she finished, she
just sat reading it over. The deepest sense of peace
descended upon her. Yes, it was true. It was all true. The
love between she and Ty had become a living, breathing
entity with a life all its own. It had been born from their
union, just like the child she had begun to dream of in
her heart of hearts. And that love cradled her, sustained
her, and put her frazzled mind to rest as she drifted off
to sleep.

"Miss Moore? Miss Moore?" The flight attendant
touched Tameka gently on the shoulder. "We'll be landing
shortly."

"Oh. Thank you," Tameka smiled groggily up at her.

The attendant bent to retrieve the pad that had fallen
to the floor at Tameka's feet. "You dropped this." The
woman glanced with interest at the writing as she handed
the pad to Tameka. "Is this a new song?"

"Yes. Yes, it is." Tameka held the pad against her bosom,
close to her heart. "I wrote it during the flight."

"Wow," the woman whispered in awe. "Can you tell me
the name of it? When I hear it I want to know it's the one
you wrote during my flight," the woman added proudly.

"Sure," Tameka looked down at the pad. "It's called
'Together.' "

"Oh," the woman said with a knowing smile. "Dedicated
to somebody special, huh?"

"Yes," Tameka smiled back at her. "Somebody very special."

Before leaving the plane, Tameka put on the dark glasses
she had in her purse, and tied her hair up in a scarf

supplied by her helpful attendant. Having no luggage, she headed straight for the exit, and thankfully made it to a taxi without being recognized.

"Where to, lady?" the driver asked.

Tameka gave him the address of her Beverly Hills condo.

The guy whistled. "The high rent district, huh? Uh, I hate to ask you this, my sister, but that's quite a hike from here. Black is beautiful, but business is business." He peered closely at Tameka in the rear view mirror. "You got the fare?"

Tameka took off the scarf and the glasses, and peered back at him. "Yes, I got it."

The guy's mouth fell open. "Well, cut my legs off and call me Shorty Long! It's . . . it's you!"

Tameka had to laugh at his amazement. "Yes . . . it's me."

"Hey, Miss Moore, sorry about the fare business. No offense intended."

Tameka smiled, "And none taken, my brother. Let's go."

The receptionist's desk was vacant when Tameka walked into Danny's office later that afternoon. She had changed from the casual clothes she wore home to a black Dior suit and heels. She meant business, and she wanted to look like it.

Tameka went up to Danny's office door, and was just about to knock when it opened, and a woman, a girl really, came out. The girl didn't see Tameka at first, she was too busy straightening her skirt and buttoning her blouse with one hand as she closed the office door with the other.

She turned, almost bumping into Tameka. "Oh! Ah, can I help . . . Meeko Moore! I'm sorry. Good afternoon, Miss Moore. I knew you were one of the agency's clients, but I was just so surprised to see you. I've only been here six weeks. It's wonderful to meet you. I love your music," the girl stammered on, running a hand over her disheveled hair. "Dan . . . er, Mr. Dorsey didn't tell me you had an appointment this afternoon."

"I don't have an appointment," Tameka said kindly, feeling sorry for this poor girl who was subjected to God knew what humiliations to keep her job. "But I'd like to see Mr. Dorsey, if he's free."

"Yes, yes, of course. I'll let him know you're here." She slipped back into the office, and was out again in a matter of moments. "You can go right in, Miss Moore."

"Thank you." Tameka stopped with her hand on the doorknob, "Honey, your blouse is buttoned crooked." The shame on the girl's face pierced Tameka's heart.

Danny was seated at his desk. He leaned back in his chair, and put his feet up on his desk. "The Prodigal Daughter returns. No need to stand on my account," he gestured magnanimously to a chair. "You can sit in my presence. I'm not a king—or Don King—yet." He laughed, finding this extremely amusing. Tameka just stood looking at him. "Well, what's the problem? Go, ahead, sit down."

"No, thanks. I won't be here long."

"Oh, Meeko, don't be like that. We've had arguments before. So the best man won. Don't be a sore loser."

"Yes, Danny. The best man won." Tameka was silent a moment as she reflected just how true that was. The best man *had* won. One of the two best men she had ever known. And her bond with that man had shown her just how strong her convictions were. How wrong it would be to let this man before her continue to have any say over the course of her life.

She closed her eyes, and felt Ty's goodness, his wisdom, his strength. *"So I keep you with me, right beside me, everywhere I go."* He was here.

"Meeko!" Tameka realized Danny had been calling her name. "What's up with you, girl? You sick or something?"

Tameka blinked. "No, I'm fine." She opened her purse.

"Danny, this is for you." She handed him the legal size envelope.

"For me?" He flipped the envelope over, checking it out back and front. "What is it?"

"It's a letter bearing my signature severing our business relationship."

"It's . . . it's a what!"

"I said 'It's a letter bearing my signature severing our business relationship.' In other words, Danny . . . you're fired."

Danny dropped the envelope on his desk as though it was a snake. "What! Have you lost your mind? You . . . you can't fire me!"

"I just did," Tameka said quietly.

Danny gave her an evil grin, but Tameka saw beads of sweat forming on his brow. "It's not that easy, baby girl. We . . . we have a contract, remember?"

"Yes, we do. A contract either of us can terminate if the other party violates any part of it. You violated the part that mandates you obtain my approval of all performance material."

"Now, look, Meeko, this has gone far enough. Yes, maybe technically you can do this, but get real." He leaned forward menacingly, "Girl, don't you know the damage I can do your career if I put my mind to it?"

"Yes, Danny, I do. But before you do anything rash . . ." Tameka laid a card on his desk, "Maybe your attorney should give this man a call."

Danny glanced casually at the card, "So who's this?"

"Simon Lansky. *My* attorney."

Danny flipped the card off his desk. "Who are you trying to fool? That ain't your attorney. I know your attorney. I hired your attorney."

"Oh, that attorney? I fired him, too." Tameka pointed at the card. "This man is my attorney now. You're not the only one with friends in high places, Danny. If you'll look closely, you'll see my attorney is head of the legal department for my record label.''

A look crossed Danny's face Tameka had never seen before—abject fear. He knew when he was outflanked.

Danny pounded his fist down on the desk as he shot up from his chair, "That damn Tommy McDougall! Damn him!" Danny looked up at Tameka. As long as she had known him she'd never seen him look so demonic. In spite of her resolve, Tameka drew back a step.

"So you went and got 'The Man' on your side. I bet your holy roller preacher man put you up to this, didn't he?

"My personal life is none of your business, Danny."

"Yeah, that's it." Danny started around the desk. "I bet the two of you did a bunch of holy rollin'—in his bed! Did the good reverend lay one of his special after midnight baptisms on you, baby?''

Why, he's jealous, Tameka realized with shock. He was still coming toward her. "Stop right there, Danny. You don't think I'd be silly enough to come up here alone, do you? There's a burley gentleman Tommy introduced me to right outside in the corridor. All I have to do is scream."

Danny slowly sat back down. "I'm leaving now, Danny." Tameka went to the door. "If I were you, I wouldn't leave this office until my friend and I are gone."

Danny didn't get up, but the glare he gave Tameka was ugly to see. "This isn't over, Meeko," he growled.

"Oh, yes, it is, Danny. Good-bye." Tameka started out the door, then paused. "Oh, and by the way, my name ain't Meeko, it's Tameka . . . but you can call me Miss Morgan . . . 'cause you're nasty."

Tameka started to breeze through the outer office, then stopped, looking thoughtfully at the receptionist, who was typing away at a computer keyboard. Tameka went over to her. "Excuse me."

The girl stopped, but didn't look up. "Yes, Miss Moore?"

"What's your name?"

The girl looked up then, her surprise apparent. "It's Melantha, Melantha Gordon." She gave Tameka a shaky smile, "But everybody calls me Milo. I hate Melantha."

"You do? It's a beautiful name. Do you know what it means?"

Melantha nodded her head, "It means 'dark flower.' "

"That's right. And that's what you are. How old are you, Milo?"

"I . . . I just turned eighteen last month."

Tameka looked at Melantha keenly, "Do you like your job, Milo?"

The girl's lower lip trembled as tears filled her eyes. "No, ma'am," she answered softly.

Tameka opened her purse, and took out her checkbook. She scribbled quickly before tearing out the check and handing it to Melantha. "This should help you out until you find another job. If it runs out first, or you can't find a job, give me a call." Tameka tapped the check with her pen. "That's my home number."

Melantha looked up, and the tears that were in her eyes now flowed down her cheeks. But her lips weren't trembling anymore. Now they were smiling. "Oh, Miss . . . Miss . . ."

"You're welcome. Now get your purse. Let's get out of here."

Just as they were going into the corridor, Danny's voice came over the intercom. "Milo, what time is my appointment at the Hilton? . . . Milo? . . . Milo? . . ."

Chapter 8

Tameka unlocked her front door, and turned to the huge, kind man who'd accompanied her to Danny's office. "Thank you, Sandy," she offered her hand.

"No problem." Sandy's huge paw swallowed her hand. "Mr. McDougall told us to take good care of you. If that guy gives you any trouble, you just give us a call at that number I gave you." He touched the brim of his hat, and was gone.

Tameka closed the door behind her, taking care to throw the dead bolt, and then hit the security alarm pad next to the door. The glowing red light showed her the alarm had been activated. She slowly climbed the stairs to her bedroom, peeling off her jacket as she went.

Tameka went directly to the answering machine, next to her bed. The message light was flashing wildly. She listened to the frantic messages, then sat down on the bed, kicking off her heels as she punched out the number.

"Hello?"

"Hello, Mama. It's me."

"Tameka? Oh, thank Jesus! Tammi, where are you, baby? Are you all right?"

"Yes, Mama, I'm fine. I'm at home."

"I've been worried to death about you!" Mama scolded.

"I'm sorry. I didn't want you to worry. I called before I got on the plane. Didn't you get my message?"

"Yes, I got it. Eddie Mae came by looking for you, and we went out to the airport, but your flight had already taken off. Oh, Tammi, how could you do this, baby?"

"Mama, I had to leave. I guess I was a little hysterical, and I didn't have to move as abruptly as I did, but the fact remains that I had to leave. There were things I needed to do here, and . . . and I'd already done far too much there."

"Tammi, Eddie Mae told me about the things that happened this morning. Oh, honey, I'm so sorry. Those malicious heifers! I got so mad I almost lost my Christianity."

"Margaret Taylor Morgan, I'm surprised at you!" Tameka was amused—and touched—by her always genteel mother's feisty defense of her baby. "Mama, who's that talking in the background?"

"I think half the town is here: Jesse, Eddie Mae and Percy, Reverend Hawkins, all the kids from the choir, and a lot of other people from the church. And all of them are angry as red ants."

"Ty's not there?" Tameka asked softly.

Mama paused before answering slowly, "No, honey, he's not. We've all been looking for him, but no one's seen him all day."

That explained why none of the many message on her machine had been from Ty. He didn't have the number there. There had been no reason to give it to him. Of course it was unlisted, but if Ty had wanted it, he could have gotten it from Mama.

"Tammi? Tammi, are you still there?" brought her back from her contemplation.

"Yes, Mama."

"We were hoping you'd have heard from him."

"No, he hasn't called. I don't think he has the number."

Mama was silent again for a moment. "Honey, I know there's a good explanation."

Tameka didn't reply.

"Running away never solved anything, child." Mama said quietly.

"This may be the exception that proves the rule, Mama. I couldn't stay there and shame you, and ruin Ty's chance at . . ."

"Girl, you haven't ruined anything! Don't you know that? A small group of jealous, mean-spirited people put out a bunch of lies, that's what happened!"

"But Ty's chance for a television ministry was . . ."

"Tammi, did you know Dee-Dee Slayton's uncle was the general manager of the cable station?"

"No. No, I didn't."

"Well, the whole town knows it now. He's the one who took it upon himself to cancel Ty's program. The board of directors of the station knew nothing about it. But they know it now. The station was flooded with calls after that article appeared in the paper. And when I say her uncle was the manager, I do mean was. The board didn't appreciate him using their station for his niece's petty revenge."

Tameka gave a huge sigh of relief. "You mean Ty's program is still on?"

"Yes, honey. After all this uproar they probably wish they could get it on tonight!" Mama lowered her voice, "But that's not the important thing. The important thing is that Ty loves you."

"Then where is he, Mama?"

"I don't know, baby, but I know that if you love somebody, you've got to have faith. You've got to believe in them, no matter what. Do you love him?"

"Yes, I do."

"Then have faith, girl. Hang on, and have faith."

"I'll try, Mama. I'll try."

"Eddie Mae wants to talk to you, honey. Hold on."

"Tammi?"

"Hi, Eddie."

"Girl, how could you pull a bonehead stunt like this? Your mother and I almost killed ourselves trying to catch you at the airport after we got your message."

"Eddie, I can't take a bawling out right now, girlfriend. This has been the longest day of my life."

"I'm sorry, Tammi. But I love you like a sister, and if you can't count on a sister to tell you off when you need it, well, hell, what's the world coming to?"

In spite of herself Tameka burst out laughing. And her laughter almost became uncontrollable when she heard Mama call out in the background, "Don't you cuss in my house, Eddie Mae McElroy!"

"That's more like it," Eddie said with satisfaction. "If the day ever comes when I can't make you laugh, Tammi, I'll turn in my license."

"Eddie, you are a major idiot," Tameka said, wiping her eyes, "and I love you for it."

"All kidding aside, Tammi . . . when are you coming home?"

"Eddie, I am home. I live here now, remember?"

"You know what I mean, girl."

"Eddie, I . . ."

"I've been calling Ty's house all day leaving messages, after we found out you had gone. And you really haven't heard from him?"

"No, I haven't."

"Look, as soon as I see him, I'll make sure he has the number, and tell him to call you."

"No, Eddie. Please don't. If he's going to call me, it has to be because he wants to. He knows either you or Mama could give him the number."

"Okay, Tammi, we'll play it your way. But I know it's going to be all right. I've got a good feeling about this one."

"Eddie, I'm so sorry I'm going to miss your wedding. Kiss Percy for me, okay?"

"Honey, all the kissing I do on that man is strictly for myself! Uh, Tammi, Calvin's here. He feels just terrible about this morning. He wants to talk to you. Is it all right?"

"Yes, it's okay. I'll talk to him."

"Miss Morgan?"

"Hello, Calvin."

"Miss Morgan . . . Oh, God, I'm sorry! I'm so sorry! I was just so . . . so jealous. I know it's stupid, but I was. I just couldn't control it." Calvin sounded on the verge of incoherence. "When I called your house that night, and your moms said you weren't there, I could just imagine you with Rev. T, and . . . and I can't explain it. It just drove me crazy."

"Calvin . . ."

"The next day I was so mad I told my moms, and she got on the phone, and called half the people in town!" He was crying now.

So that's what happened. With both Calvin's mother and Dee-Dee spreading that poison, no wonder things got out of control.

"And then I saw that article in the paper, and I . . ."

"Calvin . . . Calvin!"

"Y . . . yes, Miss Morgan."

"Calvin, what you said to me was wrong, and unfair. But I still care about you, and I forgive you."

"Miss Morgan . . ."

"Calvin . . ." Tameka paused to make sure he was listening. "I said I forgive you. As far as I'm concerned, it's over, forgotten, okay?"

"Okay, Miss Morgan."

"Now there are two more things you have to do. You have to go somewhere still and quiet, and pray to the Lord to forgive you." Tameka smiled. "Don't worry about that one. If you're sincere, He will. The second thing is harder. Honey, you're going to have to forgive yourself. That's the only way you can put it behind you. Understand?"

"Yes, I understand."

"Will you do it?"

"Yes." Tameka could tell that he'd stopped crying.

"Good. And don't let any of the other boys tease you about crying. It takes a real man to cry, and a real man to apologize when he's wrong. Good night, Calvin. Can you put my mother back on now?"

After telling Mama about firing Danny, and saying good night, Tameka finally hung up the phone. She looked around her. The clothes she'd worn home from Georgia were still in the chair where she'd left them when she came home to change and call Tommy. She'd have to let the cleaning service know she was back. She lay back on the bed, and against her will started thinking about Ty.

No, that won't do. I'm exhausted. I'll take a shower, and go to bed. That way I won't have to think about him. She sighed. *I just hope I don't dream about him. That would be more than I could bear.*

The phone's ringing was so unexpected, Tameka jumped. Ty! She eagerly snatched up the receiver, "Hello?"

"Meeko, it's me. Listen, I've been thinking this over, and . . ."

"Danny, we don't have anything to talk about."

"Yes, we do. Just give me a . . ."

"Danny, I'm hanging up now, okay?"

"Girl, would you just listen? I . . ."

"Good night, Danny." Tameka hung up.

Before she could stand up, the phone rang again. Tameka's inclination was not to answer it, but the thought that it might be Ty persuaded her.

"Hello?"

"Now, don't hang up, I . . ."

Tameka hung up.

The phone promptly rang again. Tameka regretted not turning the answering machine back on. She sat there watching the telephone, counting the rings. It rang forty-three times before he finally gave up.

I'm not going through this all night! She put the phone system on no ring, and turned the answering machine on again. That way if her mother, or Eddie, or . . . Ty called, the machine would pick it up. She'd check her messages in the morning.

After her shower, Tameka put on her favorite pair of silk pajamas, got under the covers, and switched off the light. After about twenty minutes, she switched it on again. Exhausted as she was, she just couldn't sleep. Her eye fell on the pad containing her new song, on her dresser.

Tameka got out of bed, and went over to pick up the pad. Just reading it over again made her feel closer to Ty. The peaceful feeling she had after writing it returned, the melody as strong as ever in her mind.

I don't think I could ever forget the music, no matter what, but since I can't go to sleep anyway, why not go downstairs, and put it on tape.

Slipping into the loafers she wore home earlier that day, Tameka put the pad under her arm, and went downstairs to her studio. Going to her piano, she turned on the reel to reel tape recorder next to it, and settled the microphone into its stand on top of the piano. Tameka put the pad on the music rack and sat down on the piano bench.

The music flowed from her fingers. She did the song once through to make sure it was the way she wanted it, then set the tape on record. Just as she was about to start, the doorbell rang.

Who in the world could that be? Tameka thought. A small voice inside her popped up to say *Maybe it's Ty!* But then another voice answered. *It couldn't be. He doesn't have your address here any more than he has your telephone number.*

Still, she went to the door, hoping against hope that by some miracle it would be him. Just as she reached the door someone started pounding, and a voice called out, "Meeko! It's me! I know you're in there. Open up!"

Tameka started not to even answer him, and then decided if she didn't he'd probably try to pound on the door all night, and then she'd have to call the police.

"Danny, what are you doing here?" Tameka asked wearily through the door.

"Meeko, Meeko, baby, I just want to talk to you."

"I said everything I have to say to you this afternoon."

"Look, can't we just talk?"

"No, we can't. I'm finished talking, Danny. Like I told you earlier, my lawyer will contact your lawyer. I think it's best if we just let them handle things from now on."

"But . . ."

"Good night, Danny." Tameka turned and walked away from the door, going back into the studio. She was trembling, but kept her resolve. *It's going to be tough,* she told herself, *but somehow I'll get through these next few days. Eventually it will penetrate even Danny's thick skull that I mean what say.* Against her will the thought surfaced, *Ty. If only Ty were here . . .*

Danny was still ringing the doorbell like a crazy man, and then started pounding on the door again. "Open this door, girl! Do you hear me? I said open this door!" Tameka stood immobile in the entryway. Conduct this extreme was unusual for even Danny. But then, the situation was one Danny wasn't used to. It didn't happen often. He liked to do the discarding. He didn't care for being on the receiving end of the heave-ho.

Danny's entreaties continued. Tameka wasn't worried about him breaking in. She'd had a special security door put in when she bought the house by the same company that had installed the alarm system. And her closest neighbors were so far away she doubted they could hear anything, even with Danny shouting at the top of his lungs. Still, she couldn't have him acting a fool outside her door all night. Just as Tameka was starting to worry, to wonder if she should call the police, the pounding stopped.

Good. And good riddance, Tameka thought, going back

into the studio. Still, she couldn't deny how shaken she was. She sat down at the piano again, her longing for Ty stronger than ever. *Well, at least I made the right decision,* she told herself. *It just couldn't work. Ty knows that as well as I do. That's why he hasn't called. He knows it's best to simply cherish the short time we had, and just let it go.*

Tameka felt the tears starting to return. She quickly moved to turned the tape recorder back on again, and found she'd never turned it off—again. *Will I never remember to turn this thing off when I'm interrupted,* she chided herself. She rewound the tape to the beginning, put the machine on record, and sat down once again. And once again, her thoughts turned to Ty.

I can't be with you, my love, she thought, *but this song is for you. It will be a keepsake of our love. And now and forever, whenever we hear it, we'll remember.*

Tameka closed her eyes and began the song once again, the bitter-sweet memory of being in Ty's arms bringing a delicate smile to her lips—and tears to her eyes.

"Hey, now, I like that. Is that dedicated to me, baby?"

Tameka was so deep into the music's spell, and so secure of her solitude, that it took a second for the voice to register on her consciousness. When it did, Tameka turned her head so quickly she pulled a muscle in her neck. She leapt from the piano bench, eyes narrowed. "How did you get in here?" she hissed at Danny.

He tossed a key in the air, and caught it with a casual flick of his wrist. "Like I told you before, sweet thang, I got connections. Have you forgotten who recommended your alarm company? The owner and I go way back." He tossed the key again. "All it took was a call."

Tameka was so angry she was shaking. "Well, first thing tomorrow morning, I'll be making a call—to my attorney. He'll be adding another name to his caseload. I hope your friend's got lots of money. He's going to need it."

"See, Meeko, I knew you'd get all pissed off about it," Danny said with reproach in his tone, as though his unauthorized entry was Tameka's fault, not his own. "That's why I tried to get in the polite way."

"The polite way?" Tameka exploded. "You mean the legal way, don't you?"

"Don't be like that, baby." Danny stumbled a bit as he came toward her. "We've been together almost three years now, We've done a lot for each other. Okay, I admit it . . ." Danny flung his arms open wide, losing his balance and almost falling in the process, "you've done as much for me as I've done for you. There. Is that what you've been wanting me to say? Okay, I'll admit it. You're the most successful client I've got."

"Had," Tameka succinctly replied.

"Look, woman, I'm trying to make it right with you. You know my feelings for you go beyond just our business arrangement. I've never wanted a woman like I want you. I'm trying to apologize here. And believe me, darlin' . . ." he stumbled again, "that's something that don't happen very often, so listen up."

Now Tameka realized what was wrong with Danny. He was drunk. Anger left her as fear took its place. As he stood there swaying before her, Tameka could see out into the entryway, where in his intoxication Danny had left the front door wide open. Danny was capable of major nastiness when sober. Tameka didn't plan on sticking around to see what he could do when drunk.

I can't let him see that I'm afraid. If he knows I'm afraid, I don't stand a chance. Tameka choked back her fear, and said in what she hoped was a convincingly calm voice, "Danny, it's late, and we're both tired. Maybe I was hasty." She tried to get past him. "Let's sleep on it, and we'll talk it over again tomorrow, okay?"

"Yeah . . . sleep on it." Danny's eyes began to glitter, "Now that's what I'm talking about." He again came at her, blocking her exit. "You've held out on me long enough, baby girl. It's time to pay the piper."

"Danny . . ." Tameka was almost faint with fright, "now, listen, this isn't going to solve anything, and . . ."

"Oh, but it will, honey." He was almost drooling. "It'll resolve almost three years' worth of frustration." His face scowled in an ugly grimace. "I bet if I was that mealy-mouthed preacher you wouldn't be so quick to show me the door. Here you've been giving me the cold shoulder all this time, only to fall into his arms at a crook of his finger. Well, he's not the only one who knows how to pass the collection plate." Danny's laugh sent a chill down Tameka's spine as they continued to circle the room. " 'Cause, baby, tonight I'm going to do some collecting of my own!"

Tameka lunged, hoping to get past, and with Danny slowed down by the liquor, almost made it. But he managed to stick out his foot, tripping her. She fell hard to the floor, and before she could get to her feet, he was on top of her. She could smell the dank, whiskey stench of his breath as he covered her lips with slobbering kisses.

"Danny! Danny, stop this! Are you crazy? Let me go!" Tameka struggled desperately to get away, but small as she was, had no chance of escaping.

Danny held both her wrists down above her head with one hand, ripping her top open with the other. "Baby, you can make this easy on yourself or not," he panted, tugging at the waistband of her pants. "Either way, I plan to enjoy the hell out of myself, so you might as well relax."

Tameka got one hand free, and slapped him with all her might. Danny was momentarily stunned, and his grip relaxed just long enough for Tameka to roll away from him. She quickly scrambled to her knees in preparation to sprinting for the door, but he caught one ankle, pulling her back down.

Danny flipped her onto her back and slapped her. "Okay, bitch, you want it rough? You *got* it rough! Thought you were slick rescuing my secretary from big, bad Danny Dorsey, didn't you?" He pinned her arms down with his knees. "That didn't make no never mind. Girls like Milo are a dime a dozen. I had another one there before the day was out. And Milo wasn't all that, anyway. While you on the other hand . . ." He squeezed Tameka's buttocks, "Baby, I got a feeling you're going to be something special."

Tameka began to feel light-headed. Danny's face above her seemed out of focus. "You're mine, and you're going to stay mine," he growled huskily as his knees forced her legs apart.

"No!" Tameka's scream was so forceful it left her throat raw. "Please! Don't do this! Danny! Stop! Please stop!" All she heard in reply was the sound of his laughter.

"Leave her alone, you bastard!" a third voice bellowed.

Suddenly, she was free. Danny's smothering weight was gone so quickly she was left gasping. And there before her stood Ty. Tameka was sure she was hallucinating. That the reality of what was happening to her was so unbearable she had blocked it out, and replaced it with the image of the one person she wanted to be with at that moment more than anyone else in the world.

But then he fell to his knees by her side, and pulled her into his arms, "Tameka! Sweetheart, are you all right?"

This was no dream. He was really there. Tameka threw her arms around him, trembling with relief and thankfulness. "Ty . . . Ty . . ." All she could do was cling to him, whispering his name over and over.

Danny was dazed by Ty's initial blow, but was staggering to his feet. He looked wildly about the room for a weapon, his eye settling on the heavy metal holder for Tameka's piano microphone. He grabbed the stand, flinging the microphone to the floor. The loud electronic whine warned Ty just in time. He ducked just as the stand whizzed by his head, missing him by mere inches. Ty shot to his feet, catching Danny with a commanding uppercut to the jaw. Danny crumpled to the floor as if shot.

Ty leaned over him. Danny was out cold. By this time

Tameka had gotten to her feet, and stood wobbling precariously, using one hand to hold her torn clothing together across her bosom. Ty went to her, and helped her to the sofa. "Baby, are you hurt?"

"No, Ty. I'm still a little woozy, but I'm all right . . ." she touched his cheek, "now."

Ty gently kissed her, softly, gently. "Tameka, thank God I got here when I did." He wrapped both arms around Tameka, as if to protect her from all harm. "As I approached the house, I saw the car in the driveway, but I thought it was probably yours. As the taxi pulled away I saw the door was wide open, and then I heard you scream. What happened? Did he break in?"

Tameka told him the whole sad story, including her firing of Danny that afternoon. "But Ty, how did you get here? How did you know how to find me?"

"I went shopping early this morning, and when I got home, there was a message from Eddie Mae telling me you'd gone. I packed a few things, and hustled out to the airport. I tried to call your mother from there, but I kept getting busy signals. I got on the first flight I could. I tried calling your mother again as soon as I landed. This time I got through. Then I called you, but all I got was your answering machine, so I hopped a taxi, and headed this way."

Tameka laid her head on his shoulder, "I've never been happier to see anyone in my life."

Ty held her closer, "Tammi, we've got to call the police. Where's your phone?"

"If we call the police this will be all over every newspaper in the country. They'll be a trial, and we'll have to testify. Can't you see the headlines: Minister in Love Nest Brawl with Pop Star Lover, film at eleven."

"I don't care about that, baby."

"Ty, I can't bear putting you through that. Honey, I can't bear going through it myself. I just want to forget the whole obscene episode, not have to relive it over and over again."

Danny groaned and stirred around a bit.

"Are you sure that's how you want it?" Ty asked.

"Yes, honey, I'm sure."

Ty left the sofa and stood over Danny. Danny rubbed his jaw as he looked up at Ty, "I might have known you'd show up sooner or later, lover boy."

Ty reached down, and snatched Danny up by the lapels of his jacket like he was a rag doll. Ty shook him violently, and pulled Danny's face to within inches from his own. "Good thing for you it was sooner. I'd keep my smart mouth in check, if I were you. I just caught you in the act of assaulting my woman. If you had done what you intended to do, God forgive me, I might have killed you."

Ty pushed Danny in the direction of the front door so forcefully Danny stumbled and fell. Ty picked him up again by the scruff of the neck. "Get up, you sorry excuse for a man. I'm going to cut you a favor. I'm going to let you leave here under your own power, rather than in a police car, or the back of a meat wagon, like you deserve. So let's get moving."

Tightening his grip on Danny's collar, Ty grabbed his belt and bum-rushed Danny to the door. Danny's feet were barely touching floor. He looked like a puppet.

Ty took him out the door, and then gave him another hard shove. Danny went sprawling on the lawn. "You should be sober enough to drive now." Ty told him. "Get out of here before I change my mind." Ty turned to go back into the house.

Tameka had followed them to door, and shouted the warning a second too late. "Ty! Look out!"

Ty started to turn, but Danny was already upon him. The two of them fell forward, Ty face down on the lawn, Danny on his back. Tameka screamed as Danny grabbed Ty's hair, viciously pulled his head back, and began slamming his face into the ground. Danny pulled Ty's head back once more, but then Ty pushed mightily against the ground, rolling over on his back, causing Danny to topple off.

In the maneuver Ty's jacket had come half off, limiting the movement of his arms. Ty dropped it to the ground just as Danny charged him again. But this time Ty was ready. He punched Danny hard to the stomach. Danny doubled over, his breath rushing out in a loud *ooof.* Ty went at him for a follow up-punch, but Danny, still bent over with one hand to his stomach, held up his other hand in surrender.

"Okay, man. Enough. I'm going." This time Ty stood in the doorway with Tameka and watched as Danny lurched to his car and drove away.

"Ty, baby, are you all right?" Ty had a cut running through his left eyebrow, and it was bleeding freely. The blood was running into the corner of his eye, and had already stained the front of his shirt.

"Yes, honey. It hardly even hurts." He grinned at Tameka, "I must have cut it on a stone or something while your former manager was using my head for a basketball. It's nothing."

"Nothing! We've got to stop that bleeding. Come with me."

She took his hand and led him up the stairs to the bathroom adjoining her bedroom. Ty sat on the counter, while Tameka got out cotton swabs and disinfectant. As Tameka straightened, Ty frowned deeply, and grasped her chin, turning her face, staring at it in the bright bathroom light.

"What's the matter?" Tameka wondered.

"That monster's hand print is on your cheek." Tameka was touched to her soul. Ty had choked the words out, as if the sight of her injury caused him deep anguish.

"Honey, it's okay. It's just a little numb."

Ty leaned forward and gently kissed the red outline on

her cheek. "I would not suffer the winds of heaven to caress your face too roughly," he whispered.

Tameka smiled tenderly. "You ain't slick, buddy. I know that quote. That's Shakespeare."

Ty kissed her hand, "Yep." He looked up into her eyes, his adoration shining like a beacon. "He wrote it just for the way I feel about you."

"L . . . let me get you bandaged up before you bleed to death." Tameka said unsteadily. She washed the cut and held cold compresses against it until the bleeding stopped.

"Ow!" Ty squirmed as Tameka dabbed the wound with the stinging medication. "Woman, please! The cure is worse than the curse! Lighten up!"

"Hold still," Tameka giggled, dimples flashing. "I'm almost finished. Not half an hour ago you were my knight in shining armor, coming to my rescue in combat, and now you're complaining about a little tingle?"

Ty grinned back at her, "Oh, so I'm not your hero anymore, huh?"

Tameka stopped smiling, and leaned forward to tenderly kiss the wound he'd sustained in her defense. "You'll always be my hero, Ty," she whispered, looking lovingly into his eyes.

Ty put his arms around Tameka, pulling her between his legs to his chest, "Then why did you leave me, baby?" He kissed her passionately, running his fingers through her hair. "Don't you know how I felt when I heard you were gone? My first thought, my only thought, was to find you." He kissed her again. "Baby, don't you know we belong together?"

"Ty, your being with me was hurting your ministry. And your ministry is more important than me. It's more important than us."

"Tameka," Ty pulled her closer still, his gaze blazing in its intensity, "did it ever occur to you that God may intend for you to be a part of my ministry? Because, even now, you're a part of me; a part of my life, a part of my heart.''

Tameka looked into Ty's eyes, and knew without a shadow of doubt that she belonged to this man—now and always. She didn't know what was going to happen with her singing, or with Ty's ministry, but suddenly, she had no worries. Because she knew, from deep in her soul, that God blessed her union with this man. And she knew somehow she would go on singing. Ty would continue to minister. Because that was what each had been called to do. Just as they were called to be together.

Ty took both her hands in his, ''Honey, about my shopping trip this morning . . .''

Ty looked at her from across the room. He could feel his visual exploration of her body wash over her like a wave. The intensity of his gaze drew her closer, and closer still, until she was standing directly in front of him. She could hear the crisp crackle of his shirt as he took the one step forward necessary for them to touch. For a moment they just stood that way. Ty's thighs touching hers, aligned with hers, rubbing against hers. And Tameka could feel the fierce hardness of his manhood, as it rose and stiffened in tribute to her magnetism. Ty's eyes bore down into hers, seeming to delve deep into her soul. Their noses were mere centimeters apart.

Then slowly, his arms embraced her. Tameka could feel the fluttery motion of the powerful sinews in his arms as they tightened about her waist. Her arms rose as though under a spell and encompassed his neck, as she rose on her toes to thrust her body closer to his. Tameka felt her toes leave the earth as Ty lifted her entirely, drawing her up, so deeply into his grasp that her eyes were level with his.

And from those eyes radiated bottomless devotion. There was no sham, no pretense in his gaze. There was no shield or barrier there either. Ty was baring his heart, his soul, his very being to Tameka, willingly, totally, joyfully.

"I love you, Tameka," he whispered.

Tameka felt Ty's hands behind her knees as he lifted her higher still, until she was cradled in his arms. His full, soft lips were moist as they covered her mouth, her cheeks, her neck. His earthy, wandering kisses continued as he slowly carried Tameka to the bed, laying her gently on the spread.

Ty sank down beside her, his hands caressing her back, until the hand moved languidly down her thigh to the hem of her skirt. And then his hand was under her skirt, softly stroking her inner thighs.

Ty kissed Tameka again, his tongue entering her mouth, its tip massaging the inside of her cheeks, her teeth, sucking her tongue, as his other hand began to unbutton her blouse. The blouse fell open as the last button was undone, and Ty buried his face in the hollow between her breasts, kissing, licking, and gently nipping each trembling mound with his teeth. His hands were beneath her, cupping and squeezing her buttocks. His hands moved up her back until they were under her blouse, at her bra. Ty continued to nuzzle her breasts as he undid the bra hooks one by one. Tameka felt suddenly unfettered as the bra popped open.

Then Ty clutched the fabric between the cups in his teeth, drawing the bra down to her waist, exposing her quivering nipples. Her nipples were so inflamed that the kiss of the open air was cool to the touch, causing them to crinkle and swell even more. Tameka gasped with delight when Ty suddenly dipped his head, and drew her right nipple into his mouth, his lips formed a ring of fire as they entrapped the swollen bud. His tongue lapped her nipple, causing her to moan.

As Ty hands cupped her face and he again smothered her lips with kisses, Tameka's hands fluttered between them, unclasping and then unzipping his fly. Ty moaned this time as her cool, slender fingers slid from his waist to his back, inside his shorts, her hands stroking and caressing his naked haunches.

Then it was time. They could wait no longer. The balance of their clothing flew all about the bed as they undressed each other in eager anticipation.

Ty kissed her again as his hands slid between her firm, silky thighs. His fingers thrilled her, ignited her. And then it wasn't his fingers. Ty lay down fully on top of her, only partially supporting his weight with his elbows—only just enough not to hurt her . . . only just enough. Tameka felt the manly heft of him. The hard, powerful contours of his body, his soft, smooth, warm, deep sienna skin, the scent of his musky maleness making her head swim.

"I love you, Tameka," he repeated, his lips touching her ear, his breath warm and moist on its inside. His manhood, hard and blunt, was knocking for entry.

Tameka put her arms about Ty's back, and pulled him closer. "I love you, Ty," she breathed, feeling her body open to him.

As he entered her, Ty felt a small tremor run through Tameka's body as an ember of pain flashed across her eyes. Disconcerted, he began to draw away. Tameka held him that much closer, wrapping her legs tightly around his. "No. Stay. I love you, Ty," she repeated. "And you could never hurt me, because you love me, too. I want to be yours in every way. Will you let me? Will you teach me, my love?" she whispered, drawing his lips down to hers.

"Baby," Ty said much, much later, his arms still about her, feeling the beat of her heart against his chest, "why didn't you tell me? Did I hurt you? If I had only known! I could have been . . ."

"Been what?" Tameka lovingly challenged. "More gentle? More tender?" She snuggled closer to him. "Impossible, my love."

"Oh, but, honey . . . I'm so sorry . . . I should have asked . . . I should have assumed. . . ."

"Well, why would you? It's been my secret. Who would ever guess that a single, young, black, relatively attractive female pop recording artist living alone in L.A. would be a . . ."

"I should have," Ty whispered, "because the single, young, black, exquisitely beautiful female pop recording artist living alone in L.A. . . ." he kissed her forehead, "is you."

"Well, it's too late now, fella," Tameka punched him playfully in the shoulder. "Now that you've broken me in, you gotta keep me."

Ty started laughing, and Tameka joined him, until their eyes suddenly met, and the smiles lifted from their faces. As their arms enveloped each other, they sailed off once again to that private island all their own.

Chapter 9

"Miss Moore? I heard you were on this flight. Remember me?"

"Yes, of course. How are you? I didn't see you when we boarded."

"I'm serving coach this trip. What a coincidence we should both be on the same flight again so soon. But then, this is one of my regular runs."

Tameka turned to Ty, "My friend here was the first to see our song. In fact, it's due to her kindness that I had paper to write it down!" She looked up at the flight attendant, "I'm sorry, I never asked your name."

"It's Tameka. Tameka Rivers." She was puzzled by their sudden chuckles. "Did I say something?"

"No, I'm sorry. It's just that my name is Tameka, too."

"It is? But I thought . . ."

"That's just my stage name. Tameka is my real name." She looked at Ty, "Well, one of them, anyway. Miss Rivers, this is Reverend Tyler Barnett."

Ty started to rise, but had forgotten about his seat belt. "Pleased to meet you, Miss Rivers," he said, shaking

Tameka's offered hand. "Forgive me for not standing," he gestured to the belt, "under the circumstances."

"Not a problem," the attendant laughed. "But please call me Tameka."

"And we're Tammi and Ty," Tameka told her.

"I hope I'm not being nosy," Tameka began, "But you said 'our' song, and you told me before it was inspired by somebody special. Was Ty the . . ." She looked closer at them, and her face beamed, "Oh, I see." She leaned toward Tameka, "Tammi, you are a very lucky woman."

Tameka looked into Ty's eyes, and squeezed the hand holding hers, "I know."

"Ty," Tameka said suddenly, "I think Jesse likes Mama."

"Well, of course he likes her," Ty said.

"No, honey. I mean I think he *likes* her. And I think she likes him, too."

"How would you feel about that?"

"At first it felt kind of strange. I've called him Uncle Jesse for as long as I can remember. But he isn't any blood relation." She paused a long moment, blinking. "Ty, I just thought of something. Jesse never married. I always wondered why. He's a sweet, smart, kind, handsome man with a good job, and an IRA, who owns his own home, free and clear. The sisters at church have been after him for years. And I'd bet my bottom dollar he's not gay."

"And . . ." Ty waved his hand as if to say "what's your point?"

"And," Tameka went on in a whisper, "what if the reason Jesse never married is that all these years . . ." she looked at Ty in contemplation, "he's been in love with Mama?"

"Well, I don't know," Ty said rubbing his chin. "But I do know he's been in love with her ever since I got here."

Tameka stared at him, "Why didn't you tell me?

Ty shrugged, "You didn't ask."

Tameka just gave him a look before going on, "I think I like the idea. Daddy's been gone five years now. Mama keeps up a good front, but I know she's been lonely.

"I hated to leave her to go to L.A. In fact, the only way I did go is because she called me into her room to talk to me about it one night. And one thing she said convinced me. She told me, 'Tammi, he'd tell you to go.' " Tameka gave Ty a sad smile, "And I knew she was right."

"She's a special lady." Ty smiled tenderly, "And she knows how to raise 'em."

Tameka smiled back, "You're not bad yourself."

Ty touched her knee, "Glad you think so."

"I hope that . . . oh!" Tameka turned up the volume on the radio, "I love James Ingram!"

"I like him, too, but I usually like him with a little less *volume,*" Ty raised his voice to be heard.

"I'm sorry," Tameka said, turning the volume down— a little. "I'm a musician, honey. I can't help it."

"Oh, yeah?" he grinned at her wickedly, "Wanna join me in a duet tonight?"

"Sir!" Tameka was scandalized.

"That's not what you said last night."

Tameka's smile faded. "Last night I didn't know there was a membership meeting this evening."

"I'm sorry, baby. I should have told you. The truth is, I plain forgot. I didn't check my calendar until this morning. I was too sleepy last night when we got in."

"You mean too ready to go to bed."

"Same thing."

"Not with you it isn't." Tameka paused. "Ty, I know you have to go, but do you really think I should?"

"Are you a member of this church?" he asked, eyes on the road.

"Yes."

"Then I think you should go. But it's your decision. I'll take you home, if you want me to." Ty looked at Tameka,

"Really, baby, it's your decision. Either way you decide, I got your back."

Tameka looked at him, then nodded decisively, "I'm going."

Ty nodded, "Good." He looked over at her fondly. "Honey, stop fidgeting." Ty couldn't help laughing. "Anybody would think you're going to a hanging, not a church meeting."

"I hope those words don't prove to be prophetic."

Ty laughed, "My goodness, girl. Calm down!"

"I mean, who knows what's going to happen at this meeting? After Mama had her purse stolen at church last week, I guess anything's possible."

Ty grew serious, "Yes, that I definitely don't like. If you can't feel secure in your own church, were can you feel safe? I hope we can get to the bottom of that and find out who did it."

"So do I. She's been fretting over it ever since. See? That's what I mean. This situation is just so unpredictable that . . ."

"Baby, if you keep it up, you're going to make *me* nervous."

"Come on, now, 'fess up, aren't you at least a little bit nervous?"

"Nope. Why should I be? I'm the assistant pastor of this church. I belong at that meeting." He looked at Tameka meaningfully, "And you belong there, too. By my side."

"But Ty, after all the talk and those ugly scenes at the hair salon and the grocery store . . . Not to mention that business about the newspaper article. And I think there's probably a slight chance somebody noticed you weren't at church on Sunday, since you were scheduled to preach the sermon."

"That's no problem. I called in sick."

"You what? Ty, you can't call in sick."

"Well, I did. I called the Hawk on Saturday, and he told everybody I was sick."

Tameka was aghast, "Ty, he didn't. How could you ask the Ha ... Pastor Hawkins to tell a whopper like that?"

"It wasn't a whopper. I was sick. Sick and tired of you dragging me into your bed every fifteen minutes."

Tameka laughed, and snuggled a little closer, "Well, you sure didn't act like it, hot stuff!"

"You better stop talking dirty now," Ty said with a roguish smile, pulling into the church parking lot. "We're here."

"Me talking dirty?" She jabbed him with an elbow. "Why, you ... I'll show you talking dirty!"

"Shhh!" Ty winked and whispered, "Good—but save it for later!"

Heads turned when they entered the parking lot. Ty opened the door for Tameka, and offered his arm. As they strolled to the entrance, Ty cordially greeted those standing about the church chatting in casual groups. The responses ran the gamut from warm smiles, friendly smiles, uncertain smiles, frosty smiles, no smiles, turned backs, and a few clueless folks who were wondering what was going on.

Their reception was about the same inside. The meeting was taking place in the church multipurpose room. Tables and chairs had been set at the front of the room for the church officers and elders facing the balance of the room, where chairs had been placed auditorium style.

Folks were starting to filter in in earnest now. Tameka and Ty went to the front of the room to greet Pastor Hawkins. He shook Ty's hand warmly, and bent to give Tameka a kiss. Mama was already there, seated in the front row. She waved, and Tameka went to join her while Ty took a seat at one of the head tables, after greeting the rest of the church officers.

Mama reached over, and took Tameka's hand, "Hello, baby."

"Hi, Mama." Tameka kissed her cheek.

The hand Mama held was trembling. Mama patted it

with her other hand. Several people made a point of coming over to speak to Tameka, especially parents of the teens in the choir. Several others made a point of staying away. Dee-Dee Slayton and her mother were nowhere in sight.

Eddie Mae and Percy came in just as Pastor Hawkins was about to call the meeting to order, taking a seat next to Mama and Tameka. Tameka leaned over to kiss and greet them both.

"Eddie! I thought you two were on your honeymoon!"

"No, honey. When we found out you were coming back so soon we decided to postpone it to this Saturday, so you and Ty could stand up with us."

"Oh, Eddie, that's so sweet of you. But I never would have expected you to do that. To delay your wedding just for me . . ."

"Well, don't get too sentimental about it. I also found out my dress won't be ready until this week!"

Tameka smothered a laugh, "I should have known!" Tameka turned to Mama, "Why didn't you tell me?"

Mama shrugged, "Eddie Mae wanted to tell you herself."

Eddie nodded to the head table, "How's Ty?"

"As usual, steady as a rock. Me? I'm kinda jittery."

"Mrs. Morgan, any news about your purse?" Percy asked.

"No, nothing so far. I can't understand it! I came to my regular usher board meeting on Saturday morning, and left my purse in the pew while I was up, and it just disappeared. There were a couple of other meetings going on then, so God knows who took it.

"Fortunately, I had left my credit cards and checkbook at home. I only had about forty dollars on me, so it wasn't much of a financial loss. But the inconvenience! A lot of my personal records were in that purse, and some business records, too."

At the front table, Pastor Hawkins began banging the gravel. "Can we come to order?" Those still standing around the room found their way to seats. Pastor Hawkins waited for the hubbub to die down, banged the gavel once more, and declared, "I now call the monthly business meeting of the Third Avenue Church to order. Will the secretary read the minutes of the last meeting?"

Mrs. Dale, the secretary, read the minutes in her usual dry drone. There was no discussion of the minutes, and the church membership motioned, seconded, and voted they be accepted as read.

"Any old business?" the Pastor asked. Several matters ranging from changes to the church day-care center to building the new addition were discussed and voted on or tabled as appropriate.

"Any further old business?"

Thelma Fuller rose shyly.

"The chair recognizes Sister Fuller."

"I . . . I don't know if this correctly falls under old business," Thelma began, "but, well, I guess everybody here knows our Young People's choir took first place at the Atlanta Gospelfest." There was a lively chorus of applause, whistles, cheers, and "Amens".

"Well, a lot of us parents got together . . . well, all of the parents, actually, and got a little thank you for Sister Morgan."

Tameka couldn't have been more caught off guard, or more touched.

"It's not much," she reached into her purse, and pulled out a small trophy. "It's a replica of the one the kids won. We weren't sure if she'd be here tonight, but . . . Tammi?"

Tameka stood slowly and turn to face Thelma.

"Tammi, you put in a lot of hours, and a lot of hard work, and a lot of . . . love into helping our children." Thelma walked to the front of the room to where Tameka stood. "We . . . we just want you to know how much we appreciate it." She humbly handed Tameka the statue.

Tameka blinked back the tears. "Thank you Thelma," she said hoarsely. "Thank you all. It's beautiful. I'll treasure it always."

Calvin was the first one to pop up, with the rest of the

choir dead on his heels. Almost all of the rest of the assembly stood for the ovation, but not quite all. But Tameka's didn't even notice. Her eyes were riveted to Ty's as he stood applauding, the quiet pride on his face there for all to see.

"Amen." The pastor intoned, as the ovation died down. "Is there any more old business?" There was not. Any new business?" the Pastor asked. Ty started to rise, when a voice bellowed from the back of the room.

"Yes! I have urgent new business. I move that Tyler Barnett be removed as assistant pastor of this church!"

Every head turned to the speaker. But Tameka knew who it was before she looked. This wasn't the first time this voice had come out of nowhere to bring her heartache.

Dee-Dee stood straight and stiff, eyes hard and cold, staring directly at Ty.

A buzz of chatter arose from the assembly. Pastor Hawkins gaveled them to silence, and surveyed Dee-Dee calmly. "That is a most unexpected and, if I may say, surprising motion, Sister Slayton. Normally a motion of such gravity would be brought by myself or one of the elders, and only then after much discussion."

"With all due respect, Pastor Hawkins, I think you and the other church officers, as well as a number of the general membership, may have been duped by this man into believing he is something he is not. I confess I myself fell under his spell for a short while. But now I know him for what he is: a liar, a hypocrite, and an promiscuous womanizer."

All eyes now turned to Ty, who sat to all appearances unruffled, straightforwardly returning Dee-Dee's stare. But Tameka, who knew him intimately, knew the subtle signs; the moving muscle in his jaw, the flat line of his mouth. She knew he was mightily ticked off indeed. And so was she.

Tameka started to rise, but Mama put a firm hand to her arm. "Ty can handle it, honey."

"But, Mama, I'm not going to let that hussy stand there and . . ."

"Hush, girl. Pastor Hawkins has the floor."

"Those are serious accusations indeed, Sister Slayton," the Pastor said gravely. "I hope you're prepared to back them up." He turned to Ty. "Reverend Barnett, under the circumstances, I think it only appropriate to offer you an opportunity to comment at this point."

Ty stood slowly, buttoning his jacket, "Pastor, I'm not a perfect man, nor would I ever claim to be. But I can honestly say I know of no behavior on my part that would disqualify me to serve as assistant pastor of this church."

"I hope you're not going to pretend you haven't spent the past few days at Tameka Morgan's house in L.A.," Dee-Dee declared. At that point the entire room turned to stare at Tameka. She returned their scrutiny just as forthrightly as did Ty.

"If you plan on denying it," Dee-Dee continued, "you can save your breath . . . and your lies! I've got proof!" She began furiously rummaging in her huge sack of a purse, spilling papers and credit cards all about the floor.

"Here!" she cried triumphantly, brandishing above her head what appeared to be a bundle of photographs. "Here's the proof right here!" She quickly strode up to the front of the room. and slapped the pictures down on a table. There was a sharp gasp from the assembled group. "I'd like to see you try to explain this away!"

The elders gingerly picked up the pictures, passing them around to the rest of the group. They were pictures of Tameka and Ty, entering and exiting Tameka's house, having dinner on her terrace, walking in her garden, arm in arm.

"Reverend Barnett?" Pastor Hawkins prompted, looking up from one of the pictures.

"Where did you get these pictures?" Ty demanded of Dee-Dee.

"It doesn't matter where I got them. All that matters is

what they show. But before you start trying to claim they're fakes or something, I'll tell you where I got them. I took them!"

"You took them!" Ty exclaimed incredulously. He came from behind the table. "Do you mean to tell me you flew all the way out to L.A. just to spy on me and Tammi?"

"You're damn right I did!" Dee-Dee was so out of control by this point she didn't even heed her language . . . or where she was using it. "I followed you out to the airport, and when I heard that tramp had left town . . ." At the word *tramp* Tameka had to restrain Mama from leaping up. "I knew where you where going," Dee-Dee ranted on. "So the next day I took a little flight out to L.A. myself. Somebody had to expose you for the deceitful charlatan you are!"

Tameka rose from her seat at that declaration. "How could you stake out my house?" Tameka challenged Dee-Dee. "You don't even know where I live . . ." A light ignited in Tameka's eyes. "Wait a minute. Mama's purse . . . You stole Mama's purse!"

"I had to get at her address book some way. And I didn't steal anything." Dee-Dee reached into her huge handbag and pulled out Mama's much smaller one, tossing it down on the table with a triumphant flourish. "She can have it back now," Dee-Dee smugly folded her arms. "I got what I wanted."

"You've gotten more than you bargained for today, Deirdre," Ty said quietly. He moved forward slowly, putting his hands in his pockets. "First of all, I never denied spending the weekend with Tameka."

"Then it's true?" one of the elders asked with dismay.

"Yes, it's true," Ty replied. He turned to face Dee-Dee. "You notice anything different about me?"

"No, I don't see anything different about you," Dee-Dee spat out. "What happened to you usually doesn't show any outward signs—unless I get close enough to see if there are any bites on your neck!"

Ty slowly took his hands out of his pockets. "You don't have to get that close to see what's changed." He held up his left hand, palm inward. The band encircling the third finger caught the light, flashing gold fire. A huge collective gasp filled the room. "My wife has one just like it," Ty finished simply.

Tameka stepped forward, and quietly took Ty's hand. He looked lovingly into her eyes as he gently raised her hand to his lips. A gold band exactly like the one Ty wore did indeed encircle her left ring finger.

They turned in unison to face the assembly. Ty said softly, "We were married the night I arrived in L.A." He looked tenderly down into Tameka's eyes, putting his arm around her waist. "Weren't we, Mrs. Barnett?"

Tameka's face glowed as she gazed into her husband's eyes, "Indeed we were, Reverend Doctor Barnett."

One tremendous roar arose. People were rushing the couple to offer congratulations and good wishes. Tameka was kissed and hugged to the point where her hair was mussed, and her cheeks covered with lipstick smears. Ty had his hand pumped and back slapped to the point where both were almost sore.

Many a chagrined face was seen about the room, and there were more than a few who wished they had kept their mouths shut. Some looked truly anguished, and examined their hearts over the pain their thoughtlessly spoken words may have brought this young couple, whose only crime was to fall in love.

"Order! Let's have some order in here! The meeting is still in session." Pastor Hawkins was banging away with the gravel, but with a huge, happy grin on his face. It took several minutes to restore order, but eventually people found their way back to their seats.

"It's very understandable that you would want to offer your congratulations to this fine young couple," the pastor began. "My number one assistant called me over the weekend to tell me of their marriage, and I gather there is a wedding reception in the works." He beamed down at Tameka, "Is that correct, Sister Barnett?" Tameka nodded happily.

The pastor looked around the room for a long moment with a stern, but at the same time mournful, gaze. "I know it's not Sunday, but I think the time is right for a bit of preaching. Everyone in this room knows there's been a lot of gossip about Reverend Barnett and his new bride over the past several weeks. I've not taken any official notice of it up to this point because that's usually the best way to deal with gossip, ignore it.

"But this is an unusual and disturbing example of the harm loose talk can do. Here we have two very gifted and dedicated people who both show great promise in their chosen fields. These two people love each other. What's wrong with that? And it was only through the strength of that love they managed to survive. They've hurt no one, yet they've endured much suffering because of the reckless talk of many of you present. Don't worry—I'm not going to point you out. You know who you are.

"I only want to add one thing. The next time you feel the urge to pass on some juicy gossip, or someone comes up wanting to tell you some, think of Ty and Tameka—and get a life!"

There was a general burst of laughter and applause, and many sprung out of their seats to give the pastor a standing ovation. Unfortunately, human nature being what it is, a few of those doing the loudest cheering were the biggest gossips in the room.

Still, the pastor's words didn't just fall on deaf ears. A good many present made private resolutions to do just what the pastor had suggested.

"All right, then, on to the business at hand. We have a motion on the floor. Sister Slayton, in light of the information you now have, do you wish to withdraw your motion?"

There was no response. Not surprisingly, Dee-Dee had fled.

"Since the motion has not been withdrawn, parliamentary procedure requires that we carry forward with it. The motion before us is that Tyler Barnett be removed as assistant pastor of this church. Is there discussion?" Silence. "Do I have a second?" Silence again.

"Well, I'm going to second it myself," the pastor said, "because I think we owe it to Ty to have a vote recorded. The motion has been made and seconded. Those in favor?" Not so much as a sneeze. "Those opposed?

The room rang with a resounding *no*. "Motion denied!" the pastor pronounced, banging the gravel so hard the head flew off it and skidded across the floor.

"Is there any other new business?"

Mrs. Dale, the church secretary, stood. The pastor looked at her in amazement. Other than her monotonous reading of the minutes, she never said a word at church meetings. "The chair recognizes Sister Dale."

"I'm not one to point an accusing finger, Brother Pastor, as you said. But I have a problem with a church member stealing from a fellow member, and repeatedly bearing false witness against others. I know we are to forgive, but forgiveness must be asked before it can be given. I don't feel I would be doing my duty as an officer of this church unless I moved that the board re-exam the membership of Deirdre Slayton."

Not surprisingly, the motion carried. Both Ty and Tameka elected to abstain from the voting.

"Is there any other new business?" Pastor Hawkins said for the second time, this time looking directly at Ty.

Ty stood. "The chair recognizes Number . . . I mean Reverend Barnett."

"Thank you, pastor. Church, I've been invited to host a cable television program on channel fifteen." Ty smiled. "Due to recent developments, I think most of you know the basic details. The board has reviewed the proposal, and given their approval. I feel that through this ministry we can reach many more people than would be possible by any other means. I promise you my participation will in no way compromise or diminish my service to this church. I ask for your approval of the project."

"Is there discussion?"

Sister Rakestraw stood, and adjusted her string of minks.

"The chair recognizes Sister Rakestraw."

"Well, I don't know much about it, but I don't much go for the idea."

Ty was recognized. "What about the program bothers you, Sister Rakestraw?" he asked.

The sister thought about it for a second, then responded, "I ain't got cable."

Sister Rakestraw didn't see what was so funny. Once the burst of laughter subsided, Ty very solemnly promised, "Sister, I'll tape it for you."

Sister Rakestraw nodded, "Well, it's all right, then." Having said her piece, she reclaimed her seat.

"Any further discussion?" There was none. "Do I hear a motion?"

Mama stood, "I move that my son-in-law be approved to participate in the project as outlined."

Percy popped up. "Second."

The motion carried unanimously.

"We would normally hear reports from the various departments at this time, but since the hour is late, do I hear a motion?"

Reggie Fuller was recognized. "Since this meeting has lasted longer than the Israelites wandered in the desert, I move we hear the reports next time. Let's eat!"

"Brother Fuller has motioned—in his own unique way—that we table the reports and adjourn."

This motion also carried unanimously. Having demolished his gravel, Pastor Hawkins banged his fist on the table. "We are adjourned!"

The meeting was followed by the usual social hour with beverages and light snacks. Since it was summer, there was also ice cream. Tammi and Ty were surprised and touched when Mama produced a beautiful three tiered wedding cake.

"So that's what you've been doing all day," Tameka said as she hugged her.

"Mighty fine cake, Margaret," the pastor said to Mama, helping himself to another piece. He turned to Ty, "You know, Number One, I'm a little hurt you two didn't wait to get back here so I could have married you. What was the rush?"

Ty just gave him a look.

"Oh. Never mind," the pastor said.

Since the gathering had turned into a sort of impromptu reception for Ty and Tameka, they felt obligated to stay until the end, greeting all the folks who wanted to give them their personal good wishes.

Tameka saw Jesse enter the room, and quickly went over to him. "Oh, Uncle Jesse, I was wondering where you were!"

"Things got a little hectic at the station house, Tammi," Jesse told her. Tameka wondered what the problem was. He seemed distracted.

"Well," she beamed up at him, "have you heard the news?" Tameka held up her hand, showing him her wedding ring.

Jesse looked at her tenderly, and it seemed to Tameka, very sadly. She was touched. *Bless his heart. He looks like he's about to cry.* "Yes, honey. Your mother told me," he finally responded.

"I wish you could have been there so you could have given me away," Tameka said softly. When he seemed to wince at her words, Tameka was surprised. *My goodness, I know how much he cares for me, but I never thought he'd get this emotional over missing my wedding!* Tameka brightened. "Aren't you going to kiss the bride?"

Jesse leaned down and gently planted a kiss on her forehead, looking despondently into her eyes. *This isn't like*

Uncle Jesse, Tameka reflected once more. *What's wrong with him?*

"Where's Ty, Tammi?"

"He's right up front," Tameka smiled again at just the thought of her new husband. She took Jesse's hand, "Come on," she urged, leading him forward.

Ty saw them approaching, and turned with a smile. "Sheriff James," Tameka said with a lighthearted laugh, "may I present my husband, Tyler Barnett?"

Ty laughed as well, going along with his wife's playful manner. "Pleased to meet you, Sheriff James," he said, grabbing Jesse's hand, and giving it a hearty shake. "Or should I just holler 'Uncle'?"

Jesse looked tremendously discomfited. He cleared his throat, "Tyler Barnett . . ."

"Oh, enough kidding around, man. Loosen up! We're family now!" Ty laughed again.

Jesse didn't laugh. His eyes looked tortured. "Tyler Barnett . . ." he began once more.

"Jesse, what's wrong?" Mama asked anxiously.

Jesse looked at her. He seemed to sag, "Margaret . . ." he couldn't find the words to finish.

Jesse turned back to Ty, "I'm sorry, Ty," he whispered. He straightened. "Tyler Barnett," he said yet again, this time in his normal voice, "Y . . . you're under arrest for . . ."

The few people remaining began to laugh. "Under arrest? For marrying your problem child?" Ty put in. He put an arm around Tameka, and kissed her. "If that's a criminal offense," he said, looking lovingly at his bride, "I hope I get life."

Everyone was smiling except Jesse—and Mama. "Jesse . . ." she began again, touching his arm.

"Ty . . ." Jesse said, reaching for the handcuffs in his belt. The laughter only increased.

"Sheriff, give it a rest," Percy chuckled. "If you don't cut it out, somebody around here is liable to think you're serious!"

"He is serious," Mama said, staring at Jesse with horrified certainty.

The smile dropped from Tameka's face as she looked in rising panic from Jesse to Mama and back to Jesse again. "Uncle Jesse?"

"Tyler, this breaks my heart," Jesse said sadly, "but you *are* under arrest."

The room fell silent. Ty looked at Jesse as though he'd never seen him before. "Under arrest? Jesse, if this is your idea of a joke, it's not very funny. Under arrest? For what?"

Jesse sighed mightily, "We just got an extradition order from California. You're under arrest for the attempted murder of somebody named Danny Dorsey."

Tameka was so suddenly lightheaded she lost her balance, lurching heavily into Ty. She would have fallen had he not put an arm around her. Ty half dragged her to a nearby chair, while Eddie Mae ran for some water. Jesse stood stiffly by, clearly forlorn.

Ty went on one knee by Tameka's side, gently holding the paper cup Eddie Mae had handed him to Tameka's lips. "Honey? Honey?" he called softly.

"I'm all right, sweetheart," she breathed after a few moments. She looked up at Jesse in supplication. "Uncle Jesse, this has got to be some kind of hideous mistake. You know Ty. He could never attempt to kill anyone."

Ty stood while helping Tameka to her feet as well. He looked Jesse in the eye, "Jesse, you know this is totally bogus, don't you?" he said firmly.

Jesse was miserable, "Son, I know you as a person, and I have my own opinion of you as a person. But I'm not here as Jesse James right now. I'm here as the sheriff of Barnum County. And as the sheriff of Barnum County I have to place you under arrest." He reached for the handcuffs again. "Though I wish to God I didn't," he finished softly, more to himself than to them.

Ty looked at Jesse a long moment, then said quietly, "I understand."

"No!" Tameka screamed. "Uncle Jesse, you know who Danny Dorsey is. He is . . . he was my manager. Remember? I've told you about him," she babbled desperately. "Remember how I told you what a sleaze he was? Well, this is nothing but another one of his low-down tricks! Uncle Jesse, you've got to believe me!"

Jesse looked at Tameka compassionately, "I do believe you, sugar. And if this is some sort of put-up job, I'll do anything in my power to help get Ty out of this mess. But for now, I've got to take him in."

Reverend Hawkins stepped forward. "Sheriff, Tyler Barnett is an ethical man. He's not going to run off anywhere. Do you have to arrest him? If it will help, I'll personally vouch for his appearance in court."

"No, Pastor. For this offense, there's no leeway. I have to take him into custody." Jesse put Ty's hands behind his back.

"All right, then . . ." The pastor reached out, and put his hand over the handcuffs, "but I really don't think those are necessary . . ." he looked at Jesse, "do you?"

Jesse looked at the Pastor, then put the handcuffs back on his belt. "Okay, Ty. Let's go."

Tameka clutched Ty's arm. "No! You can't do this! Please, Uncle Jesse!"

Jesse's eyes were deep wells of sadness, "Tammi, I have no choice."

"Then I'm going with him!"

"No, Tammi. No, you're not," Ty said firmly.

"Ty, I . . ."

"Listen, baby. I'm innocent, you know that. We don't have anything to fear." He put his finger under her chin, tipping her face to look into his eyes, " 'Yea, though I walk through the valley of the shadow of death, Thou art with me . . . ,' remember that?"

Tameka nodded, the tears flowing down her cheeks.

"Then keep remembering it. Keep repeating it. You gotta be strong now, honey. I'm counting on you to be strong, to make me proud. Now look, get my telephone book. It's at home in my desk. Call Lincoln Palmer. He was my roommate in college. He's an attorney. And tell Linc I want him to tell my sister. He lives in Chicago, too, and he's known her for years. He can go over and tell her in person. That would be best. Oh . . ." Ty reached into his pocket. "Here are my keys. You'll need them for the house and the car."

"But, Ty . . ."

"Just call him, Tammi. And try not to worry. And pray." He kissed her tenderly, then smiled sadly, "Some honeymoon, huh? I love you, Mrs. Barnett."

Tameka stood straight and proud. This courageous, upright man was her husband. He had said he needed her strength. He was going to have it. "I love you, too," she said regally, giving him a confident smile.

Jesse turned to Mama, "Margaret . . ."

Mama just leaned forward and lightly kissed his cheek, patting his chest with her hand. Then she turned, and kissed Ty's cheek as well, looking into his eyes. "The Lord will provide, my son," she whispered. Ty quickly squeezed her hand.

Then Ty and Jesse walked to the door side by side, and out into the gathering dusk.

Chapter 10

"May I speak to Lincoln Palmer?"

"Yes? This is Lincoln Palmer."

"Hi. This is Tameka Morgan . . . I mean Tameka Barnett."

"Yes?"

"I'm married to Tyler Barnett."

"Huh?"

"I'm married to Tyler Barnett?"

"Look, who is this?"

"I'm Tyler Barnett's wife. Your friend Tyler Barnett?"

"Reverend Tyler Barnett?"

Tameka was getting frustrated. "Yes, Reverend Tyler Barnett."

"Look, lady, I don't know how you got my number, or what you're trying to pull, but my friend Reverend Tyler Barnett doesn't *have* a wife."

"He does now. Look, you may know me better as Meeko Moore."

"Oh, right. And I'm Toni Braxton. I *know* I'm hanging up now."

"No, don't!" Tameka pleaded. "Listen, did Ty ever tell you Meeko Moore's mother is one of his church members?"

"Yes . . ." Palmer admitted cautiously.

"Then is it so far-fetched to believe we met, and fell in love, and got married?"

Palmer was silent a long time, then he said, "And did Ty hit the lottery, too?"

"Look," Tameka said, really getting frazzled, "what is it going to take for you to believe me?"

He paused another moment. "Sing 'Follow Your Heart.' "

Tameka started to speak, then took at deep breath and began to sing instead. After the first verse she stopped, and said, "Well?"

Silence.

"Mr. Palmer?"

"Well, I will be dipped in shit."

In spite of her agitation and despair, Tameka had to suppress a laugh.

"You really are Meeko Moore," he whispered. "Nobody could imitate that voice. And you're married to Ty?"

"Yes," Tameka said, grateful he finally believed her.

"That lucky son of a b . . . biscuit eater!"

Tameka did have to laugh out loud at that one.

"But why isn't Ty calling himself?" Palmer's voice showed alarm.

Tameka stopped laughing, and her eyes brimmed with tears. "He . . . he's in jail."

"What! Now look, darlin', I've been silly enough to believe you're Meeko Moore, but ain't no way I'm gonna believe Ty Barnett is in jail!"

"Mr. Palmer . . . Lincoln, Ty's in trouble and we need your help. Please, just give me five minutes to explain."

As concisely as she could, Tameka covered the events since she and Ty met, up to and including his arrest that afternoon. It took considerably longer than five minutes, but Lincoln didn't interrupt, other than to ask a question every now and again.

After she finished, Lincoln said, "I'll be on the next flight down. Do you think Ty is in danger?"

Tameka was confused, "Danger? I don't understand what you mean. He's in jail, but as far as I know he's not in any danger."

Palmer chuckled sadly, "You've led a sheltered life, haven't you? Unfortunately, in this country one of the most dangerous places for a black man to be is in jail. I can't hear the words *southern sheriff* without seeing fire hoses, billy clubs, and police dogs."

Tameka recalled the terrifying grainy black-and-white films of atrocities that occurred in southern towns before she was born. She remembered her mother's haunting narratives of being spit on during civil rights marches when she was a child.

"I understand now. But this southern sheriff is a black man, and an old family friend. He doesn't allow the mistreatment of any of his prisoners, black or white. Ty's in no danger."

"Good. Meeko, when are they flying Ty back to L.A.?"

"Please call me Tammi. Tomorrow morning is what they're telling me."

"And you're flying out there tomorrow as well?"

"Nothing could keep me away."

"Okay, look, no use me coming down there, then. Tell Ty I said not to say anything to anyone. I mean nothing to nobody. Got it?"

"Right, Lincoln."

"Linc. I'll fax the sheriff's office there and the D.A. in Los Angeles a memo informing them I'm Ty's attorney of record. Now here are my pager and cell phone numbers, write them down." He gave them to her. "Both numbers have nationwide coverage, so get in touch with me right away if anything happens. All right?"

"All right. Linc, I can't thank you enough. I . . ."

"Tammi, I love Tyler Barnett like a brother. I'm heading over to Randy's house now. Hang in there, honey. We'll slip our friend a get-out-of-jail-free card asap. Try to get some sleep. I'll see the two of you tomorrow in L.A."

It was far after visiting hours, but Jesse didn't have the heart to tell Tameka she couldn't come down to the jail to see Ty. Jesse came to pick her up personally. Tameka woke up Mama, who had fallen asleep on the sofa after coming back to Ty's house with her. There was an awkward moment when Mama scooted over next to Jesse to make room for Tameka in the front seat. Then they both started to speak at the same time.

"Tammi . . ."

"Uncle Jesse . . ."

Both fell silent. After a moment, Jesse reached over Mama's lap to take Tameka's hand. Tameka leaned over Mama, and kissed his cheek. No one said another word until they arrived at the station.

Ty was still in a holding pen, since he was to be extradited the following morning. The walls were of a sickly yellow tile, and there was a frosty gray concrete floor. The only nonhuman objects in the cell were two long wooden benches and a pay phone. The only human objects were a man lying on one of the benches with his back to Tameka . . . and Ty.

Ty was sitting on the other bench. He had taken off his jacket and his tie, and was sitting with his elbows on his knees, his face buried in his hands. Tameka's throat constricted when she saw the man she loved in that bare, bitter cage. But she took a deep breath, and lifted her chin, knowing it would only hurt Ty that much more to see her cry.

Ty looked up at her approach. Seeing Tameka, he rose from the bench, and rushed up to the bars. "Tammi! Baby, what are you doing here? You don't belong here. I . . . I don't want you here. I don't want you to see me like this."

"Ty," Tameka said softly, "you knew I was coming. You know there was no way I wouldn't."

"Tammi . . ."

"Ty, my father used to say if you want to see if a situation is fair, turn it around. If our roles were reversed, if I were the one in there . . . wouldn't you come to see me?"

Ty gave her his slow smile, "Your father was a wise man."

She reached through the bars for his hand. "I know. That's why I waited until I found myself a wise man to get married. Honey, I talked to Lincoln Palmer."

Ty grinned, "He's something else, isn't he?"

Tameka grinned back, "That's putting it mildly. He said he would met us in L.A. tomorrow, and in the meantime for you to say nothing—to anyone. He was very emphatic about that."

"That won't be hard. Except for them bringing me an indigestible meal a couple of hours ago, I haven't seen anyone—but him," Ty jerked his thumb at the man on the bench, who was now snoring.

Ty's fingers tightened on Tameka's hand, "But, honey, I don't know if your going to L.A. is the best idea. Maybe you should stay here with your mom, and . . ."

"Tyler Barnett, you stop that foolish talk this instant!" Tameka's eyes were flashing. "I'm not some sweet young thing that has be shielded from the ugly side of life. I'm your wife. I took you for better or worse. We didn't know then the worse would come so soon, but since it has, bring it on!" Tameka kissed the back of his hand, and held it to her cheek, looking deeply into his eyes, " 'Wither thou goest, I will go. And where you lodgest, I will lodge . . .' "

Ty blinked quickly as his eyes misted over. " 'Who can find a virtuous woman? For her price is far above rubies. The heart of her husband doth safety trust in her, so that he shall have no need of spoil.' Tammi, I vowed I would never marry unless I found a woman who made me feel that way." He raised her other hand to his lips. "Thank God, I have."

Tameka's tears flowed now, but they were tears of gladness. Gladness that even now, in their darkest hour, their love's light shone brighter than ever.

Ty winked at her, "You know, it's quite an asset for a preacher's wife to be able to quote scripture from memory."

"Book of Ruth, chapter one, verse sixteen," Tameka sniffed.

"I agree with everything you said, except one. You are young . . ." he leaned forward, "and you are *very* sweet." Their lips met. Tameka yearned to feel his arms around her.

"Ooo-wee! Who the hell is that?" The guy on the bench, who was obviously high on something, had awakened, and was staring at Tameka like she was a pork chop. "Move over, my brother," he said, pulling himself up to a wobbly stance, and wiping his mouth with the back of his hand. "I wanna get in on some of that!"

"You're not going to get in on anything but a fist if you don't shut your stupid mouth and sit down," Ty coolly told him. "This lady is my wife, so you keep a civil tongue in your head around her."

The guy muttered something under his breath, but promptly sat down, nonetheless. "Stupid, huh? I'm stupid?" He lay back down, and rolled over to face the wall again. "Least if I had a woman like that at home," he remarked sluggishly, "I wouldn't be stupid enough to get myself arrested!" He almost immediately started snoring again.

Ty and Tameka couldn't help but laugh at this tirade, then Ty looked at Tameka sadly, "You know, he has a point."

"Honey, there's only one reason you're in there—the evilness of Danny Dorsey. Oh, Ty, if only I had let you call the police that night! Then none of this would have ever happened."

"Tammi, I'm as much to blame as you. I didn't try very

hard to convince you, now did I? And I knew it was the right thing to do—for a lot of reasons. Suppose that maniac tries to rape another woman? This is a case of pay me now, or pay me later. We didn't deal with him then, so we're going to have to deal with him now.''

Jesse stuck his head in the door, "Tammi, I'm sorry. You're going to have to leave now, honey.''

"All right, Uncle Jesse. I'll be right there.''

"Jesse," Ty called to him, "I know you bent a couple of rules to let Tammi come. I appreciate it, man.''

Jesse just gave them an unhappy smile as he left.

"Okay, babe. I'll see you at some point tomorrow then," Ty said as brightly as he could manage. As he leaned forward once more to kiss her, Tameka felt the tears stinging the inside of her eyelids, but held them back.

Tameka gave him the brightest smile she could muster. "See you then, sweetheart," she said softly. She turned quickly, and strode for the door, turning just as she reached it.

Ty was still at the bars, holding on to them with one hand while he waved good-bye with the other. The stark loneliness of his surroundings crushed her. Not trusting herself to speak, she smiled, waved, and went out the door, collapsing in tears into Jesse's arms as soon as the door closed behind her.

Jesse just stood there, holding her and stroking her hair until the tears subsided. He handed her his handkerchief. "I'm sorry," Tameka sniffed as she dried her eyes.

"No need," Jesse croaked in a raspy voice. "It's good to get it all out sometimes, Little One.''

Tameka smiled up at him through her tears, "Little One? Uncle Jesse, it's been a long time since you called me that.''

"I guess so, darlin' " he hugged her once more. "Too long.''

"I'm okay now," Tameka said, standing straight. "Uncle

Jesse, do you know anything at all about the case against Ty?"

"Not much, Tammi. He's accused of trying to kill this Danny Dorsey. I called the LAPD, and they told me Dorsey had been shot."

"Shot!"

"Yes. It happened on Sunday night. He's claiming Ty came over to his place to confront him about some legal entanglements between you and Dorsey, and Ty got hot, pulled out a gun, and shot him."

"Ty doesn't even have a gun! And neither do I."

"They haven't found the weapon yet, Tammi."

"Anybody who knows Ty—or Danny—knows how preposterous that story is. They couldn't have much of a case. Danny probably paid somebody off to get it this far."

Eddie Mae and Percy were there. "Come on, Tammi. "I'm spending the night with you at your mom's tonight."

"I'm not spending the night at Mama's. I'm spending the night at home."

"At home? Tammi, what are you talking about?"

"At home," Tammi repeated, looking at Eddie Mae. "My home. The home I share with my husband."

"Tammi . . ."

"Just like my home in L.A. is now his, his home in Halcyon is mine." Tameka's eyes were starting to glaze. "I want to go home, and sleep in the bed I slept in with my man last night."

"All right, Tammi, Jesse can take your mother home, and Percy can drop us off at your place."

"No, Eddie. I know you're doing it because you love me, my sister," she touched Eddie Mae's arm, "but tonight I need to be alone."

Eddie Mae didn't argue with her. She just looked Tameka in the eye. "You sure that's how you want it? Are you going to be okay?"

Tameka smiled, "Yes, I'm sure."

Outside, Jesse opened the squad car door for Mama. "Tammi, all you have to do is call," Mama told her.

Tammi hugged her, and got into the car with Eddie Mae and Percy. Nobody said anything for a while. Then Percy asked, "How is he, Tammi?"

"Sad. But okay."

"Tammi, Eddie Mae and I want to go with you tomorrow."

"That's sweet of you. Both of you. But you don't need to. Mama is going, and we'll have Ty's . . . Ty's attorney." The reality of it hit her all over again, but she this time she won the struggle to stay composed.

"We don't mind," Eddie said. "Really."

"I know. Thanks. But it's okay."

Eddie Mae and Percy watched from the curb as Tameka went up the short walkway to the small two bedroom ranch house. She waved from the doorway as the two pulled away.

The twelve people came filing back into the courtroom. They were moving stiffly, mechanically, like Michael Jackson doing the robot. They turned as one. They sat as one. The judge looked down from an enormous podium that had to be ten feet high.

"Has the jury reached a verdict?" the judge intoned. It was Jesse. The word verdict *echoed over and over.*

"We have, Your Honor," the jury said as one.

"The prisoner will please rise," Judge James demanded. Ty stood, head unbowed, eyes unafraid.

"The chairman will please read the verdict."

The chairman stood. At first Tameka couldn't see his face. Then she realized his head was on backward. She was looking at the back of his head, although his body was facing her. Slowly the head began to turn, just like in The Exorcist. *The head spun faster and faster on each revolution, but even from the beginning was too fast for Tameka to see.*

Then, suddenly, it stopped with a nasty snap. *It was*

Danny. He began to laugh, his laugh filling the court room, bouncing off the walls. Tameka turned. Every other juror, all eleven of them, was Danny.

"We the jury," Danny smirked, "find the defendant, Tyler Barnett, guilty as all hell." He began to laugh again. As they led Ty away Danny's laughter began to swell and swell. It hurt Tameka's ears.

She was trying to get to Ty, but her feet felt mired, as if in deep mud. Ty was reaching for her, but they were only getting further apart. "No!" Tameka screamed . . .

"No!" Tameka awoke, soaked from the perspiration that covered her body. The phone was ringing. "Hello?" she said groggily, still seeing the demons of her nightmare before her.

"Hello, sweet thang," hissed the voice she had just heard in her subconscious hallucination. For a moment she wasn't sure she was really awake. She sat up.

"W . . . who is this?" Tameka whispered, dreading the answer.

"Come on, baby. You know who this is. You need to tell your old man to get his number unlisted, now that he's married to a big star. Or did you think I wouldn't find out so soon? I told you I've got contacts."

"What do you want?"

His spectral laughter came across the line. "Well now, girl, I think you *know* what I want. See what happens when you give it to somebody else? I saw you first. Hell, I would have even married you, if that's what it took. But no, you had to get with that Bible-carrying wuss." He laughed again. "Well, don't look like he'll be getting any no time soon."

"Please," Tameka petitioned, "please don't do this. I don't know who shot you, but you know it wasn't Ty."

"Sure. I know it, and you know it, and altar boy knows

it. Even your precious God knows it. But nobody else does—and nobody else is ever going to find out."

"You can't . . ."

"Yes, I can, I am, and I will. Oh, and by the way, don't waste your time trying to get phone records to prove I made this call. I'm at a phone booth."

"But . . ."

"And you know what else, sweetness? One of these old days while hubby is buried behind bars, I'm coming for you, and I'm going to get what I was after when he so rudely interrupted us. Pleasant dreams." Tameka was left listening to the dial tone.

Tameka pushed the off button, and sat there, staring at the cordless phone, trying to separate shadow from reality. When the phone rang again, she was so startled she dropped it as if it were a serpent. *I'm not going to answer it. No matter if he lets it ring all night, I'm not going to answer it.* But Ty had left the answering machine on, and coming from the other bedroom down the hall, which Ty had converted into an office, Tameka could hear the message was being left by a woman.

She scrambled to pick the telephone up from the floor. "Hello?"

"Hello? Is this Mee . . . I mean, is this Tameka?"

"Yes," Tameka said breathlessly.

"This is Ty's sister, Randy. And you're really Meeko Moore, and Ty's . . . wife?"

"Yes, Randy. We were married Friday. Ty's told me a lot about you. It's good to hear from you."

"Well, Tameka, to be honest, he hasn't told me much of anything about you. He told me he had met Meeko Moore about a month or so ago, but other than that . . . Well, when Linc Palmer came over this evening, I was speechless."

"I can imagine."

"And glad as I was that the person who told me was

Linc . . . and in person . . . still, I've been waiting to hear from you."

Tameka started to get angry. *Well, excuse me, I've been a trifle busy. My husband of less than a week is cooling his heels in jail tonight for something he didn't do!* her thoughts screamed. But she caught herself before words to that effect came out her mouth. She thought of her father's rule. If she had a dear brother (she was sure Ty had to be a dear brother), who had out of nowhere some married some pop star, and then gotten jailed for trying to kill the star's manager . . . well, Tameka could just imagine how things might look to Randy.

Just as Ty's home was now hers, his family was now hers, as well. After she thought it through, she said, "I'm sorry. You're right. I should have called you as soon as I got home." Tameka paused. "I went to see Ty."

"How is he?"

"Randy, you know him. He's being Ty; strong and confident and calm, and . . . Oh, Randy," Tameka choked out, seeing him again behind bars, waving good-bye. "I . . . I'm sorry," she said after a moment.

"I understand, Tameka," she said, sounding as if she really did. "I'm coming out to L.A. tomorrow with Linc."

"You are? Wonderful. I know Ty will be glad to see you, and so will I. Is your brother coming, too?"

"No, Chad took a summer course, and he's got a final in two days. But he wants to. It took all I had to convince him Ty wouldn't want him to screw up this class."

She's right. Ty wouldn't. Tameka thought.

"So I'll see you in L.A.?", she continued, asking as if she wasn't sure Tameka would be there.

"Yes. Yes, of course I'll be there," Tameka said, a little bit too forcefully.

"I wish the circumstances were different, but I'm looking forward to meeting you," Randy said. But she didn't sound like it.

"Same, here," Tameka said. She felt uncomfortable, but didn't know why.

They said their good-byes, and Tameka lay down in bed, looking up at the ceiling, trying not to be afraid.

The phone was ringing again. Tameka was amazed to see it was daylight. She'd had no sensation of falling asleep. It was as though she closed her eyes one second, and the next second it was hours later. And she didn't feel the least bit rested. Was it Danny again? She didn't care. She wasn't going to spend the rest of her life in fear because of him. "Hello?" she boldly answered.

"Hello, Tameka? This is Jesse, honey. Are you all right? Did I wake you?"

Tameka's blood ran cold. "What's wrong, Uncle Jesse?" she asked abruptly.

"Who said anything was wrong?"

"Uncle Jesse, I've known you twenty-three years. You can't fool me. Now, what's wrong?"

"Well, honey, it's not that anything's *wrong;* it's just unexpected, that's all."

"What's unexpected?"

"The LAPD came for Ty already."

Tameka looked at the bedside clock. It was only 7:05. "You mean they're there now?"

Jesse hesitated, "No, Tammi. I just got a call from the station. They left for the airport about half an hour ago."

"What? You mean Ty's already gone?"

"Yes, Tammi. I'm afraid so."

"It's okay, Uncle Jesse. I know there was nothing you could do. Look, I gotta call Mama, so we can try to arrange an early flight."

"She's right here, Tammi," Jesse said, apparently handing Mama the phone.

She's right there? Tammi thought. She'd assumed Jesse was calling from home. What would Mama be doing there that time of morning?

"Tammi?" Mama's voice came on the line.

"Mama? Where are you?"

"Why, I'm at home, baby."

Then what is Jesse doing there? flashed through her mind.

"Mama, I didn't make any airline reservations last night. I should have but . . ."

"I've already done it, dear. Our flight leaves at eleven o'clock. Uncle Jesse will take us to the airport."

"Thank you, Mama," Tameka said gratefully. "And thank Uncle Jesse for me, too. I know he did all he could."

"We'll be by for you at ten." Mama paused, "Or do you want us to come earlier? I can come over right now if you want, honey."

"No, Mama. I'm fine. I'd just better get up, and get to packing. See you at ten."

Hanging up, Tameka looked mournfully over at the luggage against the wall. She wouldn't have much packing to do. She and Ty hadn't really unpacked from their trip home. *I'll need to take his suitcase, too. He doesn't even have a change of clothes with him.* The thought almost caused her to break down again, but she caught herself, and quickly went into the bathroom for a shower.

She set the water for cool, and stood under it, trying to clear her mind and her racing thoughts. *There's got to be some way. Some way to establish that Ty is innocent. If only Danny had pulled this stunt the night we flew to Vegas to get married. Then the airline and hotel records would prove Ty couldn't have done it. But we went back to my place Saturday. And we spent all of the rest of the time alone until we came back here Monday night. If only someone had seen us, could testify that . . ."*

Tameka jumped out of the shower, and grabbing a towel, ran to the bedroom, getting the sheets wet as she sat on the bed, reaching for the telephone directory. She picked up the telephone, and punched out the number.

"Hello?" a sleepy voice replied. Tameka knew that voice, sleepy or no.

"Hello?" another voice said, also sleepily, before Tameka could speak.

"It's okay, Mama. I've got it."

Tameka could hear the other party hang up.

"Hello?" Dee-Dee said again.

"Hello, Dee-Dee."

Dee-Dee paused, "Who is this?" she asked warily, but Tameka would have bet that she knew.

"This is Tameka."

"I thought so," Dee-Dee hissed. "How dare you call my house, and at the crack of dawn, at that! What do you want?"

"I need to talk to you."

Dee-Dee gave an icy laugh. "I can't imagine anything you and I have to talk about, Mrs. Barnett. And where's the mister this early in the morning? Surely you newlywed lovebirds have better things to do than make harassing phone calls."

"It's Ty I need to talk to you about, Dee-Dee. He needs your help."

"He needs *my* help? This oughta be rich. Go ahead, I'm listening."

"I need to see you in person. Can I come by?"

Dee-Dee paused, then said, "Sure, why not? When?"

"Now."

"Now? Are you nuts? It's only . . ." she paused, apparently checking a clock. "It's only seven-forty."

"I know, but this is urgent."

Dee-Dee paused again. "All right, come ahead. But don't ring the doorbell. You'll wake my mother. I'll be watching for you."

"I'll be there in twenty minutes."

Tameka hung up the phone, dried herself off, and pulled on jeans and a T-shirt. Thrusting her feet into some sandals, she grabbed her purse and Ty's keys, and ran out the door.

Sitting in Maybeline, Tameka was glad her father had

taught her how to drive a standard shift. As she put her foot on the clutch, being in the car without Ty brought her anguish home again in a wave. But she steeled herself. Tears wouldn't do now. Ty's future was in the balance. She needed all her strength—and wits—for the task ahead.

When Tameka pulled into Dee-Dee's driveway, she could see a curtain pulled aside in the front window, and someone peeking out. As she was going up the front steps, the door opened.

Dee-Dee made no greeting, she just stood aside for Tameka to enter. She was wearing a red terry-cloth robe and—Tameka had to look twice to make sure her eyes weren't deceiving her—purple Barney slippers.

Dee-Dee looked Tameka over dryly and sniffed. Then she turned and started walking away. "Let's talk in the kitchen," she threw over her shoulder, not even looking around.

Tameka followed her into the kitchen. Tameka remembered the two of them, along with Eddie Mae and some other girls, making chocolate-chip cookies in this kitchen when they were about twelve or so.

Dee-Dee went to the coffeemaker on the counter as Tameka just stood there. "Well, you might as well sit down," Dee-Dee graciously said, pouring a cup of coffee. "You want some?" she asked.

"Yes. Thank you."

"What do you take?"

"Cream, one teaspoon of sugar."

"Only one?" Dee-Dee snickered, adding the condiments. "Watching that dynamite figure, huh?" She poured a second cup, and brought both over to the table. "I like mine the way I like my men—black and strong," she laughed bitterly. "All right, what's so urgent?"

"Dee-Dee . . ." Tameka began.

"I told I don't use Dee-Dee no more!"

Tameka forced herself to stay cool. "All right. Look, it's about Ty. He . . . he was arrested yesterday."

"Arrested! Ty Barnett? Please! What kind of ignorant joke is this?"

"It's no joke, De . . . Deirdre. He was arrested yesterday."

"You're serious, aren't you?" Dee-Dee said, looking closely into Tameka's face.

"Yes."

"Ty arrested! For what?"

"For . . . for attempted murder."

"What! Now, look, Tameka, I don't know what you think you're . . ."

"It's true. Please just listen to me." Tameka proceeded to tell her about Ty's arrest, including his extradition that morning.

"It's got to be true," Dee-Dee said, more to herself than to Tameka. "You couldn't make up a fantastic tale like that."

"Deirdre, this is what I need to know . . ." Tameka leaned forward eagerly. "Danny was shot on Sunday. Were you watching my house Sunday night?"

Tameka's intent dawned in Dee-Dee's face. She leaned back, putting one elbow on the back of the chair. "Sunday . . . let's see . . . that was the night you two had dinner out on the back terrace, wasn't it?"

"That's right!" Tameka said excitedly. "So you know neither of us left my house that night?"

"Right. I sat in my rental car watching all night long," Dee-Dee said bitterly. "Neither of you left the house."

"Oh, thank God," Tameka breathed. "You can testify that Ty couldn't have shot Danny that night!"

"Wrong."

Tameka was caught off guard. " 'Wrong'? What do you mean? I don't understand."

Dee-Dee looked thoughtful. "Well, I guess technically your statement is correct. I could testify that Ty didn't do it." She gave Tameka a twisted smile. "But I won't."

A look of horror crossed Tameka's face as Dee-Dee's words sank in. "You can't mean that."

Dee-Dee took another sip of her coffee. "Oh, but I do."

"But, Dee-Dee, you don't understand." Tameka's panic made her forget, and call Dee-Dee by the name she'd called her all her life. "Ty's freedom is at stake."

Dee-Dee slammed her coffee cup down so hard the hot liquid splashed across her hand. She didn't even seem to feel it. "No, *you* don't understand! So Ty's freedom is at stake, huh? What do I care, since he would just be free to be with you? I loved Ty. He would have come my way sooner or later—I know he would have—if you hadn't shown up."

Tameka couldn't believe her ears.

"And after Ty humiliated me at the meeting yesterday," Dee-Dee argued on, "you expect me to make a fool of myself in court just so he can come running back to your arms? Fat chance!"

Tameka knew getting angry was the worse thing she could do now, but she was at the end of her tether. Her eyes narrowed. "Ty didn't humiliate you. You humiliated yourself."

"Oh, thank you for the play-by-play analysis," Dee-Dee sneered. "And I bet you think I don't know you and Ty are behind the move to get me expelled from the church, huh?"

"Ty and I had nothing to do with that, Dee-Dee. Somebody else made that motion. Ty and I didn't even vote."

"I said don't call me Dee-Dee!" she screamed, jumping up to slap Tameka's coffee cup off the table. The cup plummeted to the floor and shattered. "Now you get your married ass out of my house! And tell your jailbird husband I said I hope he rots there!"

Tameka leapt up. Dee-Dee seemed so out of control she wouldn't have been surprised if Dee-Dee had slapped her. But she had to try one last time. "You say you love Ty. If that's true, how can you stand by, and see him convicted of a crime he didn't commit?"

"Your hearing's not too good, is it? I said I loved Ty—

past tense. Every last bit of love I had for him drained out of me last night, when I found out he'd up and married you! And guess what replaced it?" She laughed grotesquely. "Guess that old song is right. There *is* a thin line between love and hate!"

She came at Tameka menacingly, "And I guess you didn't hear what else I said. I said get out of my house, or I'll throw you out—in chunks!"

Tameka started for the door, Dee-Dee on her heels shrieking, "Get out! Get out now!"

As Tameka reached the door, Mrs. Slayton came to the top of the stairs. "Dee-Dee! Dee-Dee, what on earth is all that . . ." Her voice trailed away as she saw Tameka. She looked down at Tameka coldly, "Tameka, what are you doing here? Haven't you and Tyler Barnett done enough?"

Tameka ignored her. "Dee-Dee, please. You've got to tell them . . ."

"I ain't got to do nothing but get you out of my house! And I guess I have to do it myself. Since the police chief is screwing your Mama, it wouldn't do much good to call him!"

"Dee-Dee!" Mrs. Slayton gasped, shocked. "What kind of talking is that you're doing, girl? And what did Tameka mean? You've got to tell who what?"

"Nothing, Mama," Dee-Dee said, slipping into the fake good girl act she'd used on her mother so successfully for so many years. "Tameka was just leaving." She looked at Tameka, her eyes wild with malice, "Weren't you?" Tameka saw where the spilled coffee had raised blisters on Dee-Dee's hand, and still she seemed not to feel it.

Faced with a malevolence too deep for her to conquer, or to even comprehend, Tameka left without another word.

Chapter 11

Tameka and Mama walked down the ramp from the plane to the gate lobby. She was glad Tameka Rivers, the friendly flight attendant, had not been on this flight. She couldn't have taken the further reminder that Ty had been by her side the last time she'd flown.

"Linc should be here to meet us, Mama. I called my attorney from the record company, and he said he'd be here, too."

Just then a bright light shone in Tameka's eyes. "Miss Moore, when is your husband going to be indicted?" a voice yelled. As her vision cleared, Tameka saw the lobby was teaming with reporters. They jostled the two women trying to get away.

"Who's the lady, Miss Moore?"

"Can we see your wedding ring? Why didn't you have a big wedding?"

"Has your husband been in trouble with the law before?"

"He's a doctor? Where does he practice?"

"*We* heard he was a minister. Is that true?"

"Are you pregnant, Meeko?"

Tameka was about a second from screaming when a commanding voice said, "All right, folks. Miss Moore and her mother have had a long flight. She'll have a statement for you later, but for now she just wants to get home."

Tameka looked up at the very tall, very dark-skinned, very handsome man at her elbow. "Linc?" she whispered.

He smiled and nodded. He took Tameka and her mother each by an elbow, and began leading them away.

"Who are you, sir?" a reporter called out as the pack followed.

"I'm Reverend Barnett's attorney."

"Who's Reverend Barnett?" asked another.

Linc looked at the reporter like he was crazy. "Miss Moore's husband," Linc replied patiently, as though he was talking to a child.

"Oh . . . so he *is* a minister. What church . . ."

Tameka had noticed a number of large men closing in around them. Some of the men neatly cut Tameka and her party off from the following reporters, while others continued with them as they made for the door.

Just outside the door was a black stretch limo. Linc led the women to it, and opened the door.

Tameka bent to get inside. "Tommy!" She scrambled in quickly. Mama and Linc followed. The limo immediately left the curb.

"My guys will get your luggage," Tommy said.

A slender man with salt-and-pepper hair leaned forward, offering his hand. "Hello, Meeko. We've talked on the phone several times, but never met face to face. I'm Simon Lansky." Simon was the attorney Tommy had lined up to help her terminate Danny's contract.

"Yes," Linc said. "And Simon and Tommy have put a lot of resources at our disposal, Tammi."

"That's right, Meeko," Tommy told her. "I don't know your new husband, but I do know you. Any man that you would marry couldn't have done the things he's accused of. My record label has a lot of clout, and it's all at your beck-and-call." Tommy grinned devilishly. "And it's going to be a pleasure putting that dirtbag Dorsey in check."

Tameka introduced her mother to the men. Lincoln Palmer was about Ty's age, and dressed in a sharp navy blue suit, with a tie and pocket kerchief of brightly colored kenté cloth. He was Michael Jordan bald, and had a single gold stud in one ear. His light brown eyes were startling for one so dark-complected, but Tameka was sure they were naturally so. Linc wasn't the kind of man to truck with the vanity of colored contacts. He didn't need any artifice to add to the impact of either his demeanor or his looks. This man eluded an air of self-possessed confidence. He was just the kind of friend she would have expected of Ty.

"Linc, the media has gotten hold of this already?" Tameka asked in dismay.

He sighed. "I'm afraid so, Tammi. The facts are just starting to come out, with some having more information than others. But they're all onto the story, and not about to let a little thing like accuracy stop them from getting a by-line." He handed her a newspaper that was lying on the seat beside him.

"MINISTER LURED TO MURDER BY LIAISON WITH POP STAR" screamed up at Tameka from the top of the article.

> *Tyler Barnett of Halcyon, GA, was today extradited to Los Angeles County to answer charges of the attempted murder of Daniel Dorsey, well-known local theatrical agent. Mr. Dorsey was shot Sunday night in what was allegedly an attempt on his life by Barnett.*
>
> *Mr. Dorsey is the agent for recent Grammy award winning singer, Meeko Moore, and Dorsey claims Barnett, who was having an affair with the singer, had influenced her to discharge Dorsey in favor of Barnett as her manager.*
>
> *"The poor innocent kid," Dorsey stated. "This guy comes*

along, and sees a meal ticket, and she fell for his line. When I wouldn't bow out without a struggle, he decided to take me out permanently."

In an even stranger twist, despite first reports that Barnett is a physician, it has since developed that he is instead an ordained minister. There are unconfirmed reports that Barnett and Moore may have married in a secret ceremony.

Neither Miss Moore nor counsel for Barnett could be contacted by press time.

Tameka was livid. "How can they get away with printing this . . . this filth?" she stormed.

"I'll tell you how, Meeko," Simon sadly volunteered. "As a recording artist you're legally considered to be a 'public person'. Basically, that means since you make your living in the public eye, statements about you in the media are far less subject to slander and libel laws than people who are legally 'private persons.' "

"Are you saying that since I'm an entertainer the press can say anything they want about me?"

"No, but they have a lot more leeway. Which unfortunately many push to the extreme, secure that most celebrities won't sue for fear of losing a long, ugly, expensive court case. Not to mention focusing even more attention on the very comments they found objectionable in the first place."

Tameka shook her head, "How did they find out about this so soon?"

"Many reporters, especially in L.A. and New York, regularly search recent public records—birth, marriage, divorce . . ."

"But I thought those records were confidential," Mama put in.

"Some are, some aren't," Simon told her. "For example, death records. These are open to the public in most localities. But even those records that are confidential seem to find their way into the media's hands." He looked at Tameka, "Especially if the subject of one is a celebrity."

"You mean somebody discovered our marriage records? But I married under my real name, Tameka Morgan."

Simon shook his head, "And you think they don't know your real name? It hasn't exactly been kept a secret. My guess is somebody stumbled across the marriage records and started snooping. Your husband's arrest would have naturally drawn attention because Dorsey is your manager."

"Was my manager," Tameka couldn't help rectifying.

"Oh, right. Sorry. Anyway, my guess is somebody else picked up on you being shown as your husband's next of kin on his arrest record." He looked to Tameka again. "You were, weren't you?"

"Yes. I'm sure Ty would have given me as his next of kin."

"Okay. So some snooping got started on that end as well, with both the investigations having one common thread—you. From there it was just a matter of time until the two pieces of information crossed."

Tameka smothered her anger and frustration with the press situation. That wasn't the subject foremost on her mind, anyway.

"Linc," Tameka asked, "have you seen Ty, yet?"

"No, Tammi. My flight arrived just before yours."

"Where's Randy? I talked to her last night, and she said she was flying in from Chicago with you."

"She did," Linc replied somewhat uneasily. "She . . . ah, went on ahead."

"Why didn't she wait for Tammi?" Mama asked sharply. Tameka hadn't wanted to make an issue of it, but was wondering the same thing herself.

"Well, I guess she was just anxious to see Ty," Linc said discreetly. "These are visitors' hours now."

Mama was not appeased. "I still don't see why she

couldn't have waited. She couldn't want to see him more than Tammi does."

Tammi heartily agreed, but didn't want to escalate the matter.

"Well, anyway," Linc continued, in an attempt to table the question, "these gentlemen ..." he gestured to Tommy and Simon, "were here to meet me, so the three of us have been talking, planning a strategy. Tommy's people have found out a good deal about the charges against Ty. That's giving me a decent start."

Linc nodded to Simon, "I'm a top-notch criminal attorney, but I know very little about the in-and-outs and legalities of the entertainment world."

"Whereas I'm not much on criminal law—except drug charges—and my entire practice is entertainment law," Simon continued.

"So, together, we make a formidable team," Linc concluded. "I'm not going to tell you not to worry, Tammi, but I will tell you I'd go to jail myself before I'd let them put this trumped up sh ..." he glanced over at Mama, "er, stuff over on Ty. I'm heading on down to the jail now to speak to him, right after we take you and your mother home."

"I'm not going home. I'm going with you to see Ty."

"Tammi, they won't let you in during my consultation with him as his attorney."

"Then when can I see him? I'm not leaving until I get to see him," Tameka said, and Linc saw she meant business.

"Okay, Tammi, I'll see what I can do. I don't see any reason you can't see him during normal visitors hours."

Tameka turned to Mama, "We'll run you home first, Mama."

"Not on your life," Mama said firmly. "He's your husband, but he's my son-in-law, and my pastor. I'm going, too."

Tameka just patted her hand gratefully.

The pack of reporters was present at the courthouse as

well. Their presence had conscripted a large number of rubbernecking onlookers, who wanted to know what was going on. Tameka's exit from the car initiated the onset of a lively commotion. "Look! It's Meeko Moore!," "Miss Moore, I love your stuff," and, "Hey, Meeko, can I get your autograph?" were added to the probing questions from the reporters. Tameka and Mama were shielded by Linc, Simon, and Tommy's boys, as best they could.

Linc spoke briefly to the desk sergeant, then told Tammi. "Simon and I are going in to confer with Ty now. Unless you'd like to see him first, Tammi."

Tameka started to say yes, then answered, "No, Linc. the sooner you and Simon start working on Ty's defense, the sooner he can get out of here. No, I'll wait and see him after you talk to him."

"Well, then, they said there's a waiting room here for you ladies." Linc motioned them to the side, as the bodyguards took up posts outside.

There were only three or four other people in the waiting room, all of them women. One or two seemed to show a glimmer of recognition when they looked at Tameka, but none spoke, and went back to their own private deliberations. Tameka could empathize, since she now knew all too well how it felt to wait outside while your man was in jail.

"Linc, you're sure I can see Ty after you're finished?" Tameka asked anxiously.

"Yes, Tammi, I've set it up. Now just wait here. We'll be out as soon as we can." He and Simon started off down the corridor.

"Linc?" Tameka called after him.

Linc turned.

"Let him know I'm here, okay?"

Linc gave her a gentle smile. "I will, honey, but somehow I have the feeling he already knows."

"Tammi," Mama said softly, "you haven't had a bite to

eat all day. I saw a sign for a cafeteria. You want to go for a bite?''

"No, Mama. I couldn't eat a thing." She saw the concern on Mama's face, and smiled. "I'll eat when we get to my house. I promise." Then Tameka's own face grew concerned, "Mama, have you eaten today? You know with your diabetes you can't be missing meals." Mama's silence gave Tameka her answer. "Mama, you go on down, and get something."

"I don't want to leave you here alone, Tammi."

Tameka smiled. "Now who's going to bother me when I'm surrounded by police? I'm fine. You go ahead."

"All right." Mama stood. "I won't be long."

Tameka kept going over things in her mind, unable to relax, to do anything but think of the man beyond the door ahead, where her heart lay.

It's going to be all right. Danny can't have a case. Ty didn't do it, so how could anyone prove that he did? But she was still uneasy. There had to be something more than was obvious on the surface. She couldn't believe the police would have issued a warrant for Ty's arrest merely based on a wild story from Danny. There had to be something else. Something they were not aware of.

A tall, shapely woman came into the room. Tameka knew immediately that she had to be Ty's sister, Randy. She had Ty's eyes, and his mouth, and Tameka thought she might have had his smile had she been smiling.

But she most certainly was not smiling. Her face was a motley of confusion, anger, sadness, and fear as she looked around the room. She spotted Tameka and approached. "Hello, Tameka, I'm . . ."

"Yes, I know," Tameka said, rising. "I'd know those eyes anywhere." She reached to give Randy a hug, but Randy quickly took a seat instead.

"Have you seen Ty yet?" Tameka and Randy both asked at the same time.

Randy smiled little at that, and it was indeed Ty's smile.

"No. I went by the hotel first to drop off my luggage. Then when I got here, I had to fight my way past that mob outside to even get to the door." Tameka picked up a hint of an accusatory tone in her voice at that statement.

"Then at first the police wouldn't believe I was Ty's sister. I bet they thought I was some reporter trying to get an exclusive. They took me off to another room, and checked out my I.D. By the time that was finished, they told me Linc had arrived, and Ty was meeting with him."

Despite the fact that Randy would not have faced such roadblocks, at least not alone, had she waited for them, Tameka's heart went out to her. She reached over and took Randy's hand, "You've had quite a morning."

Randy looked startled at first, but then smiled again, "Well, I would imagine yours hasn't been all that great, either." She looked closely into Tameka's face. "You look tired," she remarked frankly.

"I didn't sleep well last night," Tameka confided.

"You know, you're not what I expected." Randy commented out of nowhere.

"Really?" Tameka came back, the dimples making an appearance. "You're exactly what I expected; a tall, beautiful woman who looks like my husband."

Randy grinned, "You mean your husband looks like me. I'm the oldest. I had this face before he did. Gosh, hearing you say 'my husband! . . .' I came down to see Ty about six months ago, and he didn't even have a girlfriend. Although the women at the church seemed to be in his face every time we turned around, especially this one."

"You mean De . . . Deirdre Slayton?"

"Yes, that was the one. I didn't much like her. Do you know her?"

"Yes, we grew up together," Tameka replied simply, not going into details.

"You have my sympathies. She seems so nice on the surface, but underneath . . . I don't know. I just didn't trust her."

"Your instincts are good." Tameka said pithily.

"They usually are," Randy said matter-of-factly. "And I came here all prepared to not like you."

Her feelings were no surprise, but her words were. Tameka had already gotten the impression Randy had major reservations about her marriage to Ty, especially since it had led to the situation at hand. And Tameka guessed she could see how it might look from Randy's point of view. But she was surprised at Randy admitting it so openly. "You were?"

"Yes, I was," Randy replied. "Tameka, I'm not one to beat around the bush. I say what's on my mind, and let the chips fall where they may. I came here all prepared to find some Hollywood floozy who didn't really care about anything but getting her nails done and getting high. But you're not like that, are you?"

Tameka had to smile at her new sister-in-law's blunt assessment. "No, I'm not."

"I should have known. I know Ty. He would never marry a woman like that." Randy paused. "You really love him. Don't you?"

Tameka turned to look her dead in the eye. "Yes. I do."

Randy nodded, "I picked up on that from the way you say 'my husband.'"

Mama came back then, and Tameka introduced the two of them. She sensed Mama appraising Randy and her blunt, forthright manner. There wasn't anything soft and fuzzy about Randy. But from their short conversation, Tameka had picked up that she was a perceptive, thoughtful woman, who was honest enough to admit when she was wrong. Tameka had no problem with her directness. She could deal with outspoken people as long as they could assess themselves as honestly as they assessed others. Randy was apparently one of that number.

Shortly after that, Linc and Simon came back. Tameka didn't like the solemn looks on their faces. "Linc, what's the matter?" she asked with great concern. "Is Ty all right?" Her look turned to horror as she remembered Linc's words to her the night before—Ty wasn't in Uncle Jesse's jail now. "Linc, is . . ."

"No, Tammi. Ty's not hurt in anyway. He's being treated well. It's just that there are some factors in this case we're going to have to deal with."

"What factors, Linc?"

"We shouldn't discuss that here, Tammi. Come on, Ty's waiting to see you. I'll take you back there." When Mama and Randy started to follow, Linc said, "Sorry, ladies, just one visitor at a time."

Linc accompanied Tameka as she was registered, went through a metal detector, and had her purse searched. Linc couldn't go beyond that point with her, even though he was Ty's attorney. "I'll wait for you right here, Tammi," he told her.

The guard led Tameka into a small room that had a thick glass partition running along a counter across middle of the room. There were chairs at the counter on each side, with mini-dividers separating each chair from its neighbor.

"Have a seat at window seven, Miss Moore. He'll be out shortly."

"Mrs. Barnett."

"Huh?"

"It's not Miss Moore. It's Mrs. Barnett."

"Oh, okay," the guy shrugged.

As soon as Tameka was seated, a door on the other side opened, and Ty entered. Linc was right—he had told Tameka Ty wouldn't yet need the change of clothing she had brought for him. He was dressed in an orange denim jumpsuit with "PRISONER" stamped across the back in big black letters. Tameka could see a guard remaining at the door, looking through the glass insert, watching them.

But still, her heart lifted to see Ty, to see for herself that he was all right. He brightened when he saw her, and came rushing to the window to take his seat.

There were speaker holes in the glass, so they were able

to hear each other. But at least in Georgia they had been able to touch. Here they could only look into each other's eyes with wistful longing.

"Hello, baby," Ty said softly. "Did you have a good flight out?"

"Yes, honey. You?"

"It was okay." He looked closely at her face. "You look tired." A ghost of his old smile crossed his lips. "Beautiful, but tired."

"You, too."

He really smiled that time. "Oh, so I'm beautiful now, huh?" he teased.

Tameka didn't smile. "You've always been beautiful, Ty. You're the most beautiful man I've ever known."

That got to him. Tameka could see him visibly crumple. *I'm doing him more harm than good this way. I should be trying to lift his spirits, to give him some hope, rather than saying stuff like that to make it even harder.*

"Tommy McDougall from the record company has put his entire legal staff at our disposal, Ty," Tameka said brightly.

"Yes, so Linc told me. I'll have to thank him personally when . . . when I get out."

The way Ty lingered over that "when" made Tameka's blood turn to ice. It was almost as if he was saying *"if* I get out," which was totally unacceptable.

"Yes. And we'll have a huge party to celebrate," Tameka said, with fabricated gaiety. Ty gave her a knowing look. "Can't fool you, can I?" Tameka said ruefully.

He smiled again, "No. But I love you for trying to."

"Randy and Mama want to say hello to you, Ty."

"Tammi, don't let that gruff manner of Randy's put you off. She's as lovable as they come under that facade. She was only twenty-two and just out nursing school when our parents were killed. I was twenty and away at college. Chad was only thirteen. Randy finished raising him practically alone."

"I won't have any problems with Randy, Ty. She and I have one major thing in common—we both love you." Tameka paused, then asked, "Is Randy short for Miranda?"

"Nope, but she'd like folks to think that. Her real name is Randolph."

"Uh, excuse me?"

"My folks had a thing about preserving family surnames. Randolph was my mother's maiden name. Tyler came from one grandmother, Chadwick from the other." Some of his usual lively manner came back as Ty described this part of her new family's history to his bride. "But don't call her Randolph unless you want to make her really mad," he finished with a chuckle.

A guard came in the door on the visitor side. "Miss . . . Mrs. Barnett, your attorney said to tell you visitors' hours are over in half an hour."

"Thank you," Tameka told him.

"I'd better go now if Mama and Randy are going to have any time at all," Tameka reluctantly told Ty.

"That's okay, honey. You never really go away. I've got you here," he whispered, tapping his chest. "Tammi, before you go, sing our song for me, will you?"

Tameka wished he hadn't asked. She wasn't sure she could get through the song. But there was no way she'd refuse. As she sang, she was amazed to feel the same peace descend on her as when she wrote it. When she finished, rather than being distressed, she felt uplifted. She knew they both were.

Having managed to leave him on a high note, Tameka didn't want to spoil it. They touched their hands briefly to both sides of the glass in farewell, and Tameka quickly left.

Randy and Mama went back to the cell area together. Since time was so short, Mama would wait with the guard while Randy went in, to save time. Simon excused himself, saying he had a court date, but would see them at Tameka's that evening. Tameka was glad for this opportunity to speak privately with Linc.

"All right, Linc. I want to hear now what that long face is all about."

"Tameka, let's wait until later, I . . ."

"Nobody can hear us here, Linc, " she insisted.

He looked at her intensely, "Okay, Tammi. Here it is. The indictment is set for ten o'clock tomorrow. We don't have much of a case. All I've really got is your testimony and Ty's."

"Well, so? All Danny's got is his word. And believe me, that's not worth the dirt under the bottom of your shoe."

"Yeah, I can believe that. From what Ty told me, I'd like to get a piece of that chump myself. But Dorsey's got a little more than just his word. He has been shot, although it's just a shoulder wound. Somebody had to shoot him."

"I'm sure there are a lot of people who'd love to shoot Danny. Right now, I'm one of them," Tameka said shortly.

"You don't mean that, Tammi. But Dorsey's been shot. And it's obvious he's recently had a good butt whippin' from all the bruises Ty admits to laying on him."

"But that was at my house, not Danny's, after he broke in on me, and tried to . . ."

"I know, Tammi." He looked at her sternly, "You two should have called me then. And then called the police."

"I know, Linc," Tameka said miserably.

"Sorry, hon. I didn't mean to rub it in. We all make mistakes, and how were the two of you to know it would turn into this fiasco? But the fact that Dorsey's attack wasn't reported, and that there's no sign of forced entry at your place isn't helping our defense one bit . . . And then there's the jacket."

"What jacket?"

"You didn't know? Ty's sport jacket was found at Dorsey's home. The jacket was torn, and the bloodstains on it are Dorsey's blood type."

"So that's what happened to Ty's jacket!" Tameka

exclaimed, remembering the jacket Ty had left on the lawn after his fight with Danny. "We didn't even think about it until we got back from Vegas. Then I figured some guy with the landscaping service must have thrown it away. But Danny must have . . ."

"That's right, Tammi. That's what we figure. Dorsey came back for it. So, while the case against Ty is weak and circumstantial, it was enough to get Ty arrested, and I'm afraid, enough to get him indicted. But I don't think a jury will convict on evidence that lame, so take heart."

"Linc, you mean this will actually have to go to trial? Ty might be in jail for months!"

"Yes, Tammi," Linc said sadly. "I'm afraid that's a possibility. But in that event, I'll do everything I can to get the trial date moved to as early as possible. There is one other possibility. Ty told me about this crazy woman at your church, the one who followed him here . . ."

"I tried that, Linc. No dice." Tameka told him about her last encounter with Dee-Dee. "But couldn't you force her to testify, as a hostile witness or whatever you call it?"

Linc gave her small smile, "Yes, that's what we call it. And it seems like the word *hostile* was invented just to classify her." He turned serious. "Yes, I could subpoena her, and she'd have to appear. But I can't make her tell the truth, and from what you've told me, the lies she might tell could only make Ty's case worse. That heifer might even testify she saw Ty leave that night with fire in his eyes, and a gun in his hand!"

"I wouldn't put it past her. But did Ty tell you about the pictures she took?" Linc nodded. "Don't they help?" Tameka wanted to know.

"Not without her testimony to back them up. There's nothing about them that proves *when* they were taken."

Mama and Randy came back then. Mama had obviously been crying, and Randy looked to be on the verge of tears. "Let's go, ladies," Linc said, putting his arm around Randy. "All three of you look about done in, and I've got a lot of work to do before tomorrow morning. McDougall has placed a car and driver at our disposal for the duration. He should be right outside. He can take me and Randy to our hotel, and take you two home."

"Linc, I've got three empty bedrooms. You and Randy are staying at my place."

"You're sure, Tammi?" Linc asked. "It would make things a lot easier logistically."

"I wouldn't have it any other way. In fact, I think I'm a little ticked you two didn't assume you were staying with me. I did, although I guess I should have said so. Randy, Ty is your brother, and Linc, you said Ty was like a brother to you. You two are family. And you're staying in our home."

The limo was indeed waiting, along with Tommy's guards, and after fighting though the crowd once more, they made a stop for Randy's luggage, and went to Tameka's. Mama had, of course, been there before, but Linc and Randy were impressed with Tameka's large, beautifully decorated home.

"You even have a music room," Linc said with admiration, peeking in at the white grand piano.

"Yes," Tameka said shakily. "That's where . . . where . . ."

"Oh. That's right. Don't think about that now, Tammi," he said, putting an arm around her shoulders and leading her away.

After showing everyone to their rooms, Tameka went to her bedroom. Deciding to take a shower before dinner, she opened her closet for a robe. What greeted her was one of Ty's shirts, hanging where he'd left it. She remembered how she'd playfully moved all her clothes to one side of the huge closet, and told him the other was his side. Matching her giddy mood, he'd deliberately left this one shirt behind, "to hold my place," he teased her.

The sight of that lonely shirt hanging in the closet so woebegone did to Tameka what the day's other travails had not. She broke down in sobs, sitting on the side of the bed, burying her face in the soft folds of the fabric that still held the scent of Ty's cologne.

She found herself lying on the bed. Someone had come in, taken off her shoes, and covered her with a blanket. Mama. Looking at the clock, she realized she'd been asleep for more than an hour. The short nap had refreshed her. After she'd showered and changed, Tameka left to visit Mama's room. But Mama wasn't in her room. Tameka knew that the second she walked out of her bedroom. The house was alive with the smell of good southern cooking. So Tameka headed to the kitchen instead.

Mama wasn't alone. Both Randy and Linc were there, having themselves changed clothes. They were sitting at the table with Mama.

"I was wondering how much longer you could hold out, Tammi," Linc said, going to the stove and getting himself another heaping helping of collard greens. "Have mercy! The smell of this food woke me out of a sound sleep. I could hear these greens calling my name, 'Lincoln!, Lincoln!' "

Tameka laughed at his foolishness. "My mama's the best cook in the state!" she said proudly, getting a plate out of the cupboard.

"You want to make that the world?" Randy put in. From the looks of her plate, the mac and cheese were her favorite. "Get your own!" she said to Linc, smacking the back of his hand as he tried to make off with one of her chicken wings.

The nap seemed to have helped Tameka's appetite. Having not eaten all day, she was ravenous. "Now it's the corn bread that does me in," Tameka told them, helping herself. "I could make a meal out of it alone."

Tameka settled next to Mama at the table. "I knew you would come down to eat sooner or later, baby, but you needed your rest so bad, I didn't want to wake you. Feeling better now?"

"Yes, Mama." Tameka patted her hand. "And thank you for coming in to cover me."

Mama was puzzled. "I didn't cover you, honey. When I peeked in, you already had a blanket over you. I thought you did it yourself."

Nobody said a word, but Randy gave Tameka a bashful smile.

After the meal, the three of them shooed Mama, the only one who hadn't had a nap, up to bed, while they cleared the table, and loaded the dishwasher.

"Tammi, I want to tape your statement as to the events as they occurred, starting with the meeting when you fired Dorsey. I taped Ty's statement this afternoon, in fact I fell asleep listening to it. We have one thing in our favor. We know Dorsey's lying. There's got to be something he's forgotten, something that'll knock a hole in his story." Linc looked resolute, "And I'm going to find it."

"What about the key Dorsey used to get in here that night?" Randy asked. Apparently Mama and Linc had filled her in on the details of the case. "Has anyone checked with the security company that he told Tammi helped him get it?" Tammi looked at Randy with respect. She hadn't thought of that.

But Linc had. He shook his head sorrowfully. "Good thinking, Randy, but Simon's people have already checked into that. The company's owner said he hasn't talked to Dorsey since he did some work for him several years ago. Of course he's lying, to cover up his own misconduct. He knows he'd lose his contracting license if he admitted it. But we haven't completely given up on that line. They're checking with locksmiths to see if we can find somewhere Dorsey took the code the guy gave him, to have a key made."

"But that's a real long shot, isn't it?" Tameka asked with dismay.

"Yes, it is," Linc admitted, "but we're leaving no stone unturned." He reached into the briefcase at his feet, took out a tape recorder, and turned it on.

"Okay, Tammi. I need you to give me the whole story.

Everything you can remember, what everybody did, what everybody said, even what may seem like the most insignificant detail.''

It hurt Tameka to even think about the events of that horrible day, let alone deliberately try to recall every lurid detail.

But for Ty's sake, she'd endure ten times more. She closed her eyes, trying to picture Danny's office, and began.

Chapter 12

Tameka awoke at 7:30. Ty. Her husband was her first thought. Her first act was slip out of bed to her knees. *Heavenly Father, I thank Thee for allowing me to see another day, and for the man Thou hast brought into my life as my husband and helpmate. Please deliver Thy servant Tyler Barnett in his hour of need. And please give Ty and me the strength to meet whatever awaits us in the day ahead.*

Having placed her troubles in the most powerful hands in the universe, Tameka wandered downstairs in her robe and slippers for coffee, humming "Take Your Burdens to the Lord (And Leave Them There)". The house was quiet. She was apparently the first one up. She heard the ringing of the phone, but it suddenly stopped. Tameka was amazed it wasn't ringing off the hook. She'd put it on no ring last night, and there were a ton of messages when she awoke to check them that morning. Many were from friends and family, but most were from the media. An unlisted number didn't seem to be much of a deterrent for the determined.

Well, I guess if they can find ways to unearth personal records, getting an unlisted number couldn't be much of a challenge. But it might at least slow them down for a while if I get the number changed she thought. But still, she had returned it to ring mode, thinking an important call concerning Ty was a possibility.

The phone rang again, and was again cut off just as quickly. *Boy, either Mama, Linc, or Randy are really on the case with that phone,* she thought gratefully.

Linc was at the kitchen table with a cup of coffee and had papers spread all over the table. He didn't look up as Tameka approached, and as she drew closer she saw why. He had a headset on, and was listening to it intensely. He didn't glance up until she nearly in front of him. He grinned at Tameka, taking off the headset. "Mornin'."

"Good morning. I see you've been up for a while," Tameka said, helping herself to coffee. The papers weren't the only reason for Tameka's statement. Linc was wearing a jogging suit, and from the looks of it, not just for show. The sweatshirt was soaked all around the neck, and under the arms.

"Yeah," Linc said, wiping his face and his head with the towel around his neck. "Gotta have my morning jog. Clears my head, and Lord knows I need a clear head today." He held up a hand to Tameka. "I wouldn't get too close. I haven't had my shower yet."

Tameka grinned as she sat down at the table. "I think I can take it. What are you listening to so zealously?"

"You."

"My Lord, if my music makes you frown like that, I'd better see a vocal coach."

"As if you needed one. It's not your music, Mrs. Barnett. I'm listening to the tape you made for me last night. I've been listening to you and Ty all night. There's something . . . something I can't quite put my finger on that's bothering me. And whatever it is is in both Ty's tape and yours. So I've been going over each tape again and again, from the point where Ty entered that night. It's here, I'm just missing it, but it's here."

"What's here?" Mama said entering the room. As usual, Mama was fully dressed, nylons and all.

"Good morning, Mama." Tameka kissed her cheek.

"Mornin', Mrs. Morgan," Linc started to rise as she entered, until Mama waved for him to keep his seat. "I was just telling Tameka something is bugging me about the tapes she and Ty did for me covering the confrontation with Dorsey."

The phone rang again, then stopped. *Randy's really quick on the draw,* Tameka thought.

"What is it about the tapes, Lincoln?" Mama asked with great interest.

"I . . . I don't know yet, ma'am. It's something small, but significant. I just can't put my finger on it."

"Put your finger on what?" Randy came into the room, dressed in a robe, like Tameka.

"Something about the thing with Dorsey that just doesn't fit."

"Linc's been listening to the tapes all night, Randy," Tameka informed her.

Randy came up to Linc, and put her hand gently on his shoulder. "You needed your sleep last night, mister," she said fondly. "You always were like this, even back when you and Ty were still undergraduates." Randy went to the counter and poured herself a cup of coffee. "But don't worry, whatever it is, you'll get it. I've never known you not to get anything you really went after, Lincoln Palmer."

"Well, even I miss out on that every once in a while," Linc replied, looking pensively at Randy. Randy, busy with her coffee didn't see him, but Mama and Tameka did, and exchanged a look.

The phone rang again, then stopped. "Wait a minute," Tameka said suddenly. I thought one of you was picking up the phone, but we're all in here now. What's going on? Is it out of order?"

"Tammi, I'm sure that's your secretary handling the calls," Linc said. "And doing a mighty fine job, if you ask me. She's been here since seven o'clock. That ringing almost drove me crazy until you cut it off last night.

"My secretary? Linc, I don't have a secretary."

Linc suddenly looked alarmed, "Then who's that in your office?"

The four of them ran to Tameka's office, next to the studio, with Linc in the lead, and Tameka right behind. They could hear a voice as they approached, "No, Miss Moore has no comment at this time. She's home with her family, and would just like some privacy. Sure, I'll take your number, but I can't promise when or if she'll be able to return your call."

Tameka's party ran into the room. There, behind Tameka's desk, sat Milo—Melantha Gordon—the young girl Tameka had freed from Danny's sexually harassing clutches.

Milo gave them a big smile as they stood there staring at her. "Yes, certainly I'll tell her. Good-bye," Melantha said into the telephone before she hung up. "Good morning, Miss Moore," she smiled at Tameka.

"Melantha . . . Milo . . . what are you doing here?"

"You know this person, Tameka?" Linc asked.

"Yes, I know her. She used to be Danny's secretary."

"What!" Randy charged Milo, "You've got a lot of nerve, you little hussy, trying to come in here to spy for your no-good boss! I'll show you . . ."

Milo's smile faded quickly as she jumped up from the desk, and drew back in confusion. "No, hold on, Randy!" Tameka told her sister-in-law, as she stepped between the two women. "I said she used to be Danny's secretary. She's not anymore, and she left because of his mistreatment. Believe me, she has no reason to do any favors for Danny Dorsey."

"Well, okay," Randy said, stepping back, "if you say so, Tammi. But what is she doing here?"

"That's a good question," Tameka said, looking at Milo. "Honey, just what are you doing here?"

"I'm answering the phone," Milo said simply.

"She drove up as I was leaving for my run," Linc told them. "When I asked who she was, she said she was your secretary, Tammi, so I let her in. And was I glad. By the time I got back, some reporters were camped on the steps, and she was in the process of sending them on their way. I joined in with a threat to sue if they didn't get off your property, but if not for her, they would have disturbed the whole household. And you say she's not your secretary?"

Milo came up to Tameka, and smiled, "You told me to come see you if I needed a job," she smiled, then turned serious. "Miss Moore, you were there for me when I needed help. I read about all this in the paper, and I figured maybe I could return the favor."

Tameka was bowled over by Milo's caring thoughtfulness. She couldn't speak just then, so she just reached out, and gave Milo a hug. "Thank you, dear," Tameka finally choked out. "I do need you, and you're doing a wonderful job." She released Milo, and smiled, "Would you like some breakfast?"

"No, ma'am. Thanks, but I've already eaten."

"Well, since the office is in such good hands, let's go get some breakfast. I'm starving." She started out, then turned back to Milo, "Oh, by the way, you're hired."

Milo gave her a grateful grin as she picked up the ringing phone yet again.

As they went back into the kitchen, Linc leaned over to whisper, "Tameka, I told you I don't think clearly before my run. I should have been more cautious about who I let in here. She could have a reporter, or really been one of Dorsey's snoops—or worse. I'm sorry."

"Not to worry, Linc. No harm done. In fact, Milo will be a tremendous help in dealing with the media."

"But are you sure you can trust her?"

"Yes, I'm sure." She briefly filled him in on why she was so sure.

"That Dorsey has got to be stopped," Linc said forcefully. "He's a disgrace to black men everywhere."

"He will be, Linc. I'm sure of that now."

"You're mighty confident."

"Yes, I am. This morning I got on my knees and talked to my Agent."

A large crowd of reporters had gathered outside of the house by the time they left for court a little before nine. Tommy McDougall had been true to his word, sending the limo for them, complete with two hefty gentlemen to help smooth the way. Tameka recognized one of them. "Hi Sandy," she said once they were underway. "Good to see you again."

"Good to see you again, too, Miss Moore. I'm sorry for your trouble. That guy just doesn't know when to quit, does he?"

"What's he talking about, Tammi?" Linc wanted to know.

Tameka explained how Sandy had gone with her on her visit to Danny's office. Linc was extremely interested. "Did you overhear what they said, man?" he asked Sandy eagerly.

"No, I'm sorry, I didn't. I was in the corridor. Close enough to hear Miss Moore if she called out for help, but not close enough to hear a normal conversation behind closed doors. Wish I could help. That dude is bad news."

"Linc," Tameka said slowly, "Sandy couldn't hear us, but Milo may have."

"Of course!" Linc immediately picked up his cell phone, and called Milo back at Tameka's house. "Great!" he said, hanging up. "She did overhear the conversation. It's not much, but she can at least testify as to Dorsey's character—or lack of same—and to the threats he made when Tameka fired him. That's something."

"So is Milo coming down to court now?" Mama asked.

"I won't need her until this afternoon. The D.A.'s office will present their case first, and then we'll probably break for lunch. I'll put Tammi and Ty on first, and then Milo. She'll need help getting into the courtroom, so we can send the car and our friends . . ." he indicated Sandy and his partner, "back for her."

Of course, the press was waiting for them at the court-house, as well as Simon Lansky. Linc gave a brief statement: "Reverend Barnett is completely and totally innocent of the charges against him. The D.A.'s case is so flimsy as to be ludicrous, which we intend to prove." He refused questions, and led his party into the courthouse, with the assistance of Sandy et al.

Simon waited with the women in a small conference room right off the courtroom while Linc took Ty the suit Tameka had brought for him. In a short while Linc was back—with Ty. Two guards accompanied them. Tameka's throat tightened when she saw Ty was in handcuffs. But when they reached the conference room door, one of the guards unlocked the handcuffs and removed them. Ty gratefully rubbed both wrists as he came into the room with Linc.

Ty immediately went to Tameka. They didn't speak, but just stood looking at each other a moment. Then Ty took Tameka into his arms, the first time they had been able to embrace since the awful day of his arrest.

"Hi, baby," he whispered into her ear. He kissed her tenderly.

"Hello, Ty," Tameka looked up at him with a sunny smile. Just being in his arms again made her feel better than she had in days.

Ty embraced Randy and Mama as well, and shook hands with Simon. They all sat down, the Barnetts holding hands, while Linc and Simon went over what would happen in the courtroom.

"Again, this is not a trial," Simon told them. "This is an indictment, which is basically a review of the charges and evidence against Ty, and his first real opportunity to show the evidence does not warrant the case going to trial.

It's a private session with a judge and a twelve person grand jury. They'll be evaluating the evidence and make the determination as to if a bill of indictment is to be issued. While the general public is not permitted, interested parties can sit through the proceeding."

"And while it isn't a trial," Linc picked up the explanation, "it is a courtroom, and regular courtroom procedure will be followed. The assistant D.A. and I can cross-exam each other's witnesses, and make objections. Any questions?"

"Lincoln?" Mama said softly.

"Yes, Mrs. Morgan?"

"I have only one question. Would you join us in prayer?"

Linc blinked rapidly. "It would be my honor."

They all stood and joined hands. "Precious Lord," Mama began. "We thank Thee for Thy many blessings. My son-in-law, Tyler Barnett, is a good and virtuous man. Please keep Thy arms of protection about him. Impart Thy strength to Tyler, and to my child, and bless their union. Please touch the tongue and mind of Lincoln Palmer, and show him the path Thou would have him take. These things we ask in Jesus' name, and for His sake. Amen."

"Amen," they all echoed.

It was time.

They entered the courtroom. Simon, Linc, and Ty were seated at a table to the left of the judge's bench. The women took a seat on the bench directly behind. Two men, one old, one young; one black, one white, were seated at the table to the right.

Just then, the door opened, and in swaggered Danny, with his right arm in a sling. On his other arm was a voluptuous young woman in a tight orange dress. When Danny saw Tameka, he grinned, and blew her a kiss. She trembled with anger, as Randy reached out to take her hand. Randy shot Danny a look so venomous, even he was taken aback. After all, Randy was taller than he was. With a little less swagger in his walk, he and the woman took a seat on the other side of the courtroom.

Ty had turned dark at Danny's entrance, and started to rise. Linc had taken tight hold of Ty's arm, and was whispering animatedly in his ear.

"All rise!" the court clerk cried. The judge entered from her chambers, and was seated at the bench. She was a sixtyish woman with completely white hair pulled into a bun. She reminded Tameka of her fifth grade music teacher. Tameka took this as a good omen. She liked that teacher.

"Court is now in session, the Honorable Virginia Applebaum presiding."

"The clerk will read the charges," Judge Applebaum said, looking over the top of her glasses.

"This is case number 126621, the State vs. Tyler Barnett. The charge is attempted murder."

"Is the state ready?" the judge asked.

The two assistant district attorneys stood. "Yes, Your Honor," said the older black man. "Malcolm Baker for the state, assisted by Jack Milewski," he indicated the other man.

"Is the defense ready?"

Linc and Simon stood. "Yes, Your Honor. Lincoln Palmer for the defense, assisted by Simon Lansky."

"The defendant will rise." Ty stood, straight and proud. "Dr. Barnett, how do you plead?"

"I plead not guilty, Your Honor," Ty firmly replied. A snicker was heard from Danny's direction. Ty scowled, but didn't lower himself to look.

"The jury has been selected?"

All four lawyers affirmed that it had.

"The clerk will seat the jury."

The clerk went to door, and motioned in the twelve men and women of all ages and races. They were evenly divided, six men, six women. They filed into the jury box, and were seated.

"Ladies and gentlemen of the jury, I am Judge Virginia Applebaum. The case you are to hear is not a trial. This is a grand jury indictment hearing. The difference, simply put, is that you are not here to determine the guilt or innocence of the defendant. He is, by law, innocent until proven guilty. Your task is merely to ascertain if the evidence is sufficient for the case to be brought to trial, for his guilt or innocence to be legally determined. Do you have any questions?"

There were none. At the judge's direction, the jury was sworn in, the attorneys introduced, and the charges reread.

"Mr. Baker, you may call your first witness."

"The state calls Erma Lee."

The woman with Danny stood and took the stand. Linc turned around to Tameka, mouthing, "Who is she?" Tameka just shrugged.

"Please state your name," Baker said.

"Erma Sue Lee."

"Miss Lee, where are you employed?"

"I work at the Daniel Dorsey Agency. I'm Danny's secretary."

"Danny being the owner, Mr. Dorsey?"

Erma looked at Baker like he was a fool. "Yeah. That's what I said."

"Mr. Dorsey is a talent agent?"

"Yes."

"Was the singer known as Meeko Moore one of his clients?"

"Yes."

"On Friday past, July 24th, did you have occasion to overhear a conversation between Mr. Dorsey and Miss Moore?"

Tameka gasped audibly at this question, and leaned forward to whisper in Linc's ear.

"Yes." Erma seemed bored.

"Please give us the gist of that conversation."

Erma's face screwed into a frown. "The what?"

Baker sighed. "Please tell us what they said."

"Oh. Well, she told Danny now that she was a big star, she didn't need him anymore. She told him her man said he would manage her from now on."

"Her man?"

"Right. Him, the guy over there, Barnett." She pointed to the defense table.

"And how did Mr. Dorsey reply?"

"He told her the guy was just playin' her, and she should stick with him."

"Did Miss Moore respond to that?"

"She sure as hell did. Told Danny her old man would jack him up good."

The judge interrupted, "Miss Lee, what does that mean . . . 'jack him up?' "

"It mean to beat him up, hurt him, kill him, Your Honors."

"Thank you. You may proceed, Mr. Baker."

"No further questions, Your Honor."

"You may cross examine."

Linc and Simon had been whispering feverishly. Simon stood. "Miss Lee, how long have you worked for Mr. Dorsey?"

"Oh, about a week now."

"Isn't it true you just started working for him on the day in question, July 24th?"

Erma squirmed in her seat a little, "Well, so what? That ain't got nothing to do with my hearing."

The judge interrupted again, "Is that a 'yes,' Miss Lee?"

Erma looked away, "Yeah."

"And isn't it also true that you did not begin working for Mr. Dorsey until late in the afternoon, when he called your temporary agency?"

Erma glared at Simon. "So?"

The judge didn't bother to clarify this time.

"So, isn't it true you never overheard a conversation between Mr. Dorscy and Miss Moore, because Miss Moore had already come and gone before you came on duty?"

Erma stared desperately at Danny. He looked straight ahead, ignoring her stare. "No," Erma finally said. "No, I heard what I said I did."

Simon was silent a moment, then he said, "Miss Lee, you pointed to Tyler Barnett, identifying him. Have you seen him before today?"

"Yeah, sure. I told you he came to the office with Miss Moore."

Danny buried his head in his hands.

"No, I don't believe you did say that, but since you say it now, would you mind describing him?"

Erma paused, staring at the defense table. Tameka could almost hear Erma going "eeny-meeny-miney-moe" in her mind.

"The witness will please answer the question," the judge said.

"He . . . he's that bald guy over there with the earring," Erma finally blurted out. The left side of the room broke out in huge smiles. The right side of the room groaned.

"Miss Lee," Simon said, "would it surprise you to learn that the man you just identified is Lincoln Palmer, a well-known defense attorney from Chicago? The man next to him is Tyler Barnett."

Erma's eyes darted around for a way out, "Well, so I made a mistake. It's dark in here, and they look so much alike."

"Oh, really? Did you think Dr. Barnett had shaved all his hair off since last week?"

Baker was on his feet. "Objection!"

"Sustained. The jury will disregard that last question."

"No further questions, " Simon said.

"You may step down," the judge told Erma.

Erma flounced off the stand, glaring at Simon. She went to take her former seat next to Danny, but something in his face and bearing made her instead turn, and go out the door. She never did come back.

"The state calls Officer John Timmons."

Officer Timmons testified as to the call from Danny Dorsey on the night of July 24th. He described how he and his partner had found Mr. Dorsey shot upon arrival at his home, the living room in shambles. Ty's jacket was introduced into evidence, with the officer verifying it was found at the scene.

"We have no questions for this witness, Your Honor," Linc said after the state's questioning was complete.

"The state calls Daniel Dorsey."

Danny was a pitiful sight as he lurched from his seat, and limped heavily to the witness stand. As he was painfully seating himself, he bumped against the witness microphone. He grabbed at the stand, but missed the microphone, and it was flung to the floor. The loud electronic whine caused the entire room to cover its ears.

Linc stood straight up at his seat.

"Yes, Mr. Palmer? Do you wish to say something?"

"Ah . . . er . . . No, Your Honor." Linc stammered.

"Then sit down," the judge said firmly.

What's wrong with Linc? Tameka wondered.

Linc sat down briefly, hurriedly whispered something to Simon, and dashed from the room.

Tameka leaned forward, tapping Simon on the shoulder, "Simon," she whispered, "What . . ."

"Shhh!" Simon whispered back, grinning.

Danny had been sworn in. At Baker's questions, he proceeded to tell the longest string of lies Tameka had ever heard in her life. How Tameka had fallen under Ty's spell (the only part of his testimony that was true). How Ty had used Tameka physically and financially. How Tameka had fired Danny, saying Ty was taking over as her manager. How, after Danny had objected, Ty showed up at his home, beat him severely, then shot him, only missing his heart by inches.

"You say Miss Moore fired you on Friday afternoon? Friday, July 24th?"

"That's right," Danny nodded.

"When was the next time you saw her?"

"Today, here in the courtroom." Tameka gasped out loud at this blatant falsehood. The prosecution was apparently aware of Ty's version of the events of that day, and was setting up their rebuttal in advance.

"When was the next time you spoke with Miss Moore?" Baker went on.

"I haven't spoken to her since," Danny said, shaking his head in dismay.

Near the end of Danny's long testimony, Linc came back into the room. When Baker was finally finished, the judge turned to the defense "You may cross-examine."

"Your Honor," Linc said standing, "since it is now twelve-thirty, I would like to delay my cross-examination of this witness until after the lunch break."

"Good idea, Mr. Palmer. I'm hungry, too. Court will reconvene at one-thirty." Judge Applebaum banged her gravel, and left the bench. Danny got up just as quickly, and left the room, his limp mysteriously gone.

Tameka kissed Ty quickly before he was taken back into custody for the break. She then turned, "Linc, what on earth is going on? Why did you run out like that?"

Linc hugged Tameka, picking her up and spinning her around, "Because, Mrs. Songbird Barnett, I've got it!"

"Got it? Got what? Where did you go?" Mama and Randy were just as puzzled.

"I had to go call Milo. She's on her way down. Now, listen . . ."

* * *

"Mr. Palmer, I believe before the break you were about to cross-examine the last witness?"

Linc stood. "That's correct, Your Honor, however, with the court's indulgence, I would instead like to reserve my right to cross-examine Mr. Dorsey, and instead call my first witness."

"This is rather unusual, Mr. Palmer. The prosecution has not yet rested it's case. Mr. Baker?"

Danny had returned to the courtroom alone. He looked back and forth at the speakers, like he was at Wimbeldon, clearly wondering what was going on.

"Mr. Dorsey is the state's last witness, Your Honor," Baker said. If it will help speed the proceedings, I have no objection to my learned colleague's request, with the provision I may reserve possible redirect of Mr. Dorsey until a later time."

"Very well, gentlemen. Mr. Palmer, you may call your witness."

"I call Tameka Barnett to the stand."

Tameka rose quickly from her seat, flashing Ty a brilliant smile as she approached the witness stand. After Tameka was sworn in, Linc began, "Please state your full legal name."

"Tameka Morgan Barnett."

"Are you married to the defendant?"

"Yes." Tameka said this with as much joy as one short word could hold.

"When were you married?"

"Last Friday, July 24th. We were married very late that evening, in Las Vegas."

"And are you known by any other names?"

"I am a professional entertainer. My stage name is Meeko Moore."

"Do you know Daniel Dorsey?"

"Yes. Mr. Dorsey was my manager."

"Was? Mr. Dorsey is no longer your manager?"

"No," Tameka said firmly, staring straight at Danny, who began to grind his teeth. "I fired Mr. Dorsey last week."

"When was this?"

"Last Friday, the 24th."

"The day you were married?"

"Yes. I fired him early that afternoon."

"Where did this take place?"

"At Mr. Dorsey's office in downtown L.A."

"And did you have occasion to see Mr. Dorsey again that day?"

"Yes, he came to my home in Beverly Hills."

"Did you invite him?"

"No, I did not." Tameka said emphatically.

"Did you let him in?"

"I most certainly did not."

"No? Why not?"

"I wanted nothing further to do with Mr. Dorsey, and I had told him so that afternoon. Also, I was afraid of him."

"Afraid of a man you had worked with for years? Why so?"

"Because he had become very angry when I fired him, and threatened me. Also because Mr. Dorsey had been making improper and unwanted sexual overtures to me for years, throughout the course of our working relationship."

"I see. So you would not let him in. Did he get in anyway?"

"Yes, he did. He had gotten a key, and the combination to my home alarm system."

"Did you give them to him?"

"No. I never would have given Mr. Dorsey access to my home under any circumstances, not even when he was still my manager."

Linc seemed puzzled. "Then how did he get them?"

"I don't know. But he *said* he got them from the owner of the company that installed my alarm and security door."

"Objection!" Baker popped up. "Heresay."

"It is not heresay, Your Honor," Linc said calmly, "since the statement was made to Mrs. Barnett directly by Mr. Dorsey."

"Objection overruled. Please continue, Mr. Palmer. I'm finding this extremely interesting." Judge Applebaum stared at Danny, who gulped.

"Thank you, Your Honor. Mrs. Barnett, you said you are an entertainer. You're a vocalist, a Grammy award-winning vocalist, are you not?"

"Yes," Tameka replied simply.

"Naturally, you have to rehearse. Do you rehearse at home?"

"Objection!" Baker was on his feet again. "Irrelevant."

"Mr. Palmer, we all know of Mrs. Barnett's professional career. Although I am enjoying this glimpse into the entertainment world, I admit I fail to see the relevance."

"It will become clear shortly, Your Honor."

"All right, Mr. Palmer. I'll allow you some leeway. But move it along. Objection overruled. The witness may answer the question."

"Yes, I frequently rehearse at home."

"And do you do anything special to help maximize your rehearsal time?"

"Yes. I usually record my rehearsal sessions, so I can listen to myself, and make any corrections or changes indicated. This is a common practice among entertainers. Football players watch tapes of their games for the same purpose."

"Interesting. What were you doing the night Mr. Dorsey illegally entered your home?"

Baker started to rise at the word *illegally*, but apparently changed his mind.

"I was rehearsing."

"Exactly!" Linc quickly strode over to the defense table,

and pulled a reel of tape out of a large envelope, holding it high above his head. "Your Honor, we would like to enter this tape as evidence, and as a part of Mrs. Barnett's testimony."

Danny actually turned ashy pale as his lower jaw dropped down to his chest. His eyes darted around like an animal's caught in a trap.

"Mr. Baker, any objection?"

"No, Your Honor." Baker turned sideways in his seat, and crossed his legs as he threw a hard glance Danny's way. "I'd kinda like to hear that tape myself."

Linc nodded at Milo, who had crept into the courtroom after the session had begun. When Danny turned and saw Milo, he looked as though he might faint.

Milo went to the door, and Sandy entered, lugging Tameka's heavy professional reel-to-reel tape recorder. Sandy sat the machine on the defense table, and Milo plugged it into an outlet under the table, before following Sandy back out.

"We're ready, Your Honor," Linc said quietly. "This is a six hour tape, but it's been cued to the pertinent section."

Judge Applebaum nodded, leaning forward eagerly.

Linc hit the Play button. The sound of Tameka's clarion soprano filled the room, with a piano accompaniment. After about 15 seconds, the beautiful sound stopped abruptly as a man's voice said, "Hey, now, I like that. Is that dedicated to me, baby?"

"How did you get in here?" a woman's voice replied.

"Like I told you before, sweet thang, I got connections in lots of places. Have you forgotten who recommended your alarm company? The owner and I go way back. All it took was a call."

As the tape played on, all eyes turned to Danny. He seemed to collapse within himself.

When Tameka's desperate screams began, the judge's mouth hardened into a thin line as her eyes narrowed.

The tape ended with the loud electronic whine caused by Tameka's microphone breaking as it was flung to the floor.

Linc shut off the machine. Not a sound could be heard in the courtroom. Then Linc said, "Your Honor, in light of the evidence just presented, I move the case against Tyler Barnett be dismissed."

Baker rose slowly, "Your Honor, I admit the evidence we've just heard establishes my primary witness . . ." he turned and looked dead at Danny, "as a brazen liar and a degenerate . . ." he paused, as if daring Danny to dare to deny it. Danny couldn't even look him in the eye.

Milo came rushing back into the room, and almost ran up to the defense table, whispering something to Simon.

"But the protocol of justice must be followed," Baker was continuing. "The evidence does not indisputably prove Dr. Barnett innocent of the crime of which he is accused. The jury may find insufficient evidence to indite.." he swept his arm toward the jury box, "But the state cannot withdraw charges based on this evidence alone."

The judge nodded, seeming to reluctantly agree. Simon had pulled Linc down to his seat, and rapidly conferred with him while Baker was speaking. Before the judge could rule, Linc stood once again. "Before your ruling, Your Honor, another witness has just been located that may lend further credence to my motion."

"You're just full of surprises, aren't you, young man?" the judge observed. She sighed, flopped back in her chair, and threw up her hands, "Well, if your witness' testimony can shed any light on this situation, bring it on!"

"Thank you, Your Honor. I call Deirdre Slayton to the stand."

Tameka whirled in disbelief. The door opened, and in came Dee-Dee, followed by her mother and Pastor Hawkins. Pastor Hawkins and Mrs. Slayton took a seat next to Tameka as Dee-Dee unsmilingly approached the witness stand.

"Pastor!" Tameka whispered fervently. "What . . . how . . ."

"The Lord works in mysterious ways, child," Pastor Hawkins whispered back, patting Tameka's hand. "After your visit, her mother forced the truth out of Dee-Dee, and then called me."

Dee-Dee had been sworn in, and stated her name and connection to Ty and Tameka.

"And after you followed Reverend Barnett to the airport, what did you do?" Linc questioned Dee-Dee.

"I didn't know what to do. I had no idea where he was going . . . until I heard Tameka had left town." Her face hardened, "I knew he was going to her, but I didn't know where to find them. Then Saturday morning, I went to the church to pick my mother up from her usher board meeting. Tameka's mother had left her purse alone on a pew, and I . . . I took it."

"Why?"

"To get Tameka's address in L.A. It was there, in Mrs. Morgan's address book. Then I flew out to L.A. myself."

"Again, why?"

"I don't know. To confront them, to catch them together, to prove they were shacking up." Dee-Dee bowed her head. "I didn't know then that they had . . . had gotten married."

"And did you catch them together?"

"Yes, I did. And neither of them left the house Sunday night. I could see them having dinner on the terrace."

"You're sure of that?"

"Yes, I'm sure. I watched the house all night long."

Linc paused. "Miss Slayton, I know this must be difficult for you, but I must ask this question to clarify your testimony for the court. Why did you wait so long before coming forward?"

Dee-Dee seemed near tears. "I . . . I was embarrassed. And I was angry because Tameka took Ty away from me." Dee-Dee gave a mighty sigh. "Well, I guess he never really belonged to me in the first place. But I was hurt and I wanted to hurt them back.''

"And what made you change your mind?"

"My mother overheard me arguing with Tameka after Ty was arrested. She kept after me as to what we were quarrelling about until I broke down and told her the truth. And anyway . . .'' she looked forlornly at Ty, "whatever Ty may think of me, I really do love him. I couldn't let this happen to him when I knew he was innocent . . .'' a tear slid down her cheek, "even if it means watching him walk away with another woman.''

Linc looked at Dee-Dee sympathetically. "Thank you, Miss Slayton," he said softly. Linc turned to the judge, "Your Honor, I renew my motion that the case against Tyler Barnett be dismissed.''

The judge looked at the prosecution's table, "Mr. Baker?"

Baker stood, "Your Honor, the state has no desire to prosecute innocent citizens, nor to waste the court's time. We have no objection.''

The judge banged her gavel, "So ordered.''

"Your Honor!" Baker wasn't finished. "I know this is irregular, but I hereby place Daniel Dorsey under citizen's arrest for perjury, fraud, and attempted rape under my own recognizance. I take this drastic step because I believe Mr. Dorsey may flee justice if not immediately detained. I ask that Your Honor order the bailiff to take Mr. Dorsey into custody, and that all evidence in this case be retained for further court action.''

The judge banged the gavel with a vengeance, "So ordered with the greatest of pleasure! Bailiff . . . .'' she stood and pointed to Danny, "Arrest that guy!''

Danny tried to run, but the bailiff, assisted by Baker and his assistant were too fast for him. As Danny continued to struggle, the guards right outside, who had accompanied Ty to the courtroom, also lent a hand.

Seeing he was outnumbered, Danny stopped struggling,

and submitted. As he was being taken away, he stopped in front of the witness stand where Tameka was still seated. "I just did this because I loved you, baby," he said quietly. "I really loved you, but you never gave me a chance."

Tameka just stared into his eyes with sad revulsion. His captors led him from the room.

"Dr. Barnett," the judge said, "you are free to go. Please accept my apologies on behalf of the state, and rest assured, we do not take lightly the manipulations of those who would attempt to use taxpayer's money for their own loathsome purposes." She banged her gavel one last time. "Case dismissed."

Cheers and applause rose in the courtroom, even from the jury and judge, as Tameka flew to Ty's waiting arms.

" . . . so when he dropped the microphone, it hit me like a lightning bolt," Linc was saying around mouthfuls of his peach cobbler. "Both Tammi and Ty said when Dorsey picked up that stand to throw at Ty, the microphone made a loud whine. It's only going to whine like that if it's on. Which meant Tammi had never hit the Stop button when Dorsey came into the room."

"I used to get mad at myself for always forgetting to turn off that machine. I've never been so happy to have a bad habit in my life!" Tameka declared from her perch atop Ty's lap. As she spooned more cobbler into his mouth, he kissed her hand.

"I really feel like a chump it took me so long to realize that though, man," Linc went on apologetically.

"And of course, Tammi would have realized it herself the next time she went to use the machine, and found it was still on, although of course the tape had run out." Mama put in, finishing her own cobbler.

"That might have taken a very long time, Mama," Tameka said. She put her head on Ty's shoulder. "I didn't feel much like singing while my man was jail."

"But I should have picked up on it as soon as I heard your statement, Ty," Linc insisted, shaking his head.

"Oh, Linc, stop fishing for compliments," Randy said from her seat at the table next to him. She put her arm around his shoulders, and kissed his cheek. "You were magnificent, and you know it!"

"No, sis. He's right. He's a lousy attorney, and a worse friend, and I'm going to deduct it from his fee," Ty teased, throwing a piece of crust across the table at Linc.

"Right," Linc came back sardonically. "Tammi, have you got any Billy Preston albums?" He rolled his eyes at Ty. "I feel like hearing 'Nothing From Nothing Leaves Nothing.' "

The entire table burst out laughing at that, poor Milo almost choking on her cobbler.

"But I tell you what, man," Linc said softly. "If you really want to help me out, you can talk your sister into going out with me. She doesn't seem to want to pick up on the hints I've been dropping for years."

"Hints? What hints? Linc, I know you're just fooling around with that stuff. I'm too old for you," Randy laughed.

Linc wasn't laughing. "How old are you?" he asked bluntly.

Randy was caught unaware, "Why, I'm . . . I'm thirty-three."

Linc looked her in the eye, "I'll be thirty-one next month."

Randy looked at him like she had never seen him before. A smile slowly crossed her face, "Well, fancy that," she said softly, gazing into his eyes.

After a moment, Mama said, "Ah . . . would anybody like more cobbler?"

"Not me," Milo said. "I'm stuffed! I haven't had a meal like that since I left home."

Tameka looked thoughtful, "I wonder what's going to happen to Danny?"

"Who cares?" Randy piped up. "Personally, I hope they put him *under* the jail."

"I'll co-sign that," Linc said with feeling.

"They seemed really interested when I told them Danny kept a gun in his office," Milo volunteered.

"Yes, and I bet they find it, and when they do . . ." Ty's eyes were grim, "I bet the only fingerprints on it . . . are his own." Ty was silent a moment, then said, "I wish the Hawk could have stayed, but he wanted to escort the Slaytons home. He knew they needed his support right now." Ty paused again. "I wish the Slaytons had stayed, too. We don't bear them any ill will."

"Honey, you're too kind to bear anybody ill will," Tameka told him. "But, after today, even I can forgive Dee-Dee. It took a lot of courage for her to do what she did." She looked into Ty's eyes, "And I understand the pain she must feel. I don't know what I'd do if I ever lost you."

Ty kissed her forehead, "You'll never have to worry about that, Mrs. Barnett." He suddenly brightened, "Hey babe, your lord and master's home! We got any buttermilk?"

"Yep. Had it delivered just for you." Tameka jumped off his lap, and went to the refrigerator, but wobbled for a moment, holding on to the door.

Ty was instantly at her side. "Honey, what's the matter?"

"I don't know, Ty. I just felt light-headed for a second." She touched his chest and smiled, "I'm fine, baby, really. Just too much excitement, I guess."

"Yeah. I guess." He picked Tameka up in his arms. "Well, good night, folks," he said, making for the stairs, "I'm taking my overwrought bride up to bed, so she can get some rest."

"I bet," Randy said under her breath.

Tameka waved at them happily from over Ty's shoulder as he bore her away, "Good night!"

"I hope she's all right," Milo said worriedly.

"Don't worry, honey," Margaret Taylor Morgan said with a mother's wisdom, looking wistfully after her only child. "There's nothing wrong with Tammi the next several months won't fix!"

Epilogue

Milo was taking dictation.

" . . . and I would be most pleased to be your graduation commencement speaker. My wife will be getting in touch with you soon concerning her selections. She would very much like for your wonderful women's gospel choir to sing with her.

"As to our fee, about which you expressed concern, that is no roadblock. My wife and I do not charge fees for our speaking engagements. We appreciatively accept your kind offer to cover our travel expenses, but that is all that is necessary.

"My office will be in touch concerning arrangements as the time approaches. Until then, I remain, Yours in Christ . . . You got that, Milo?"

"Yes, Pastor Barnett."

Ty pushed back from his desk, looking at his watch. "It's getting late, Milo. We better stop now so we can get some rest. We've got an early flight tomorrow.

"Pastor," Milo said shyly, "I can't thank you and Sister

Barnett enough for all you've done for me. And now to be going to the Grammy awards! I just can't believe it!''

"Well, we've got a major meeting with the network about the expansion of *Sweet Hour* to the west coast. And all those speeches. Tammi and I wouldn't be able to keep anything straight without you. It's getting dark out. Want us to drop you home?"

"No, Pastor." Milo blushed. "Calvin's coming by for me."

"Again?" Ty smiled, "I'm going to have to start charging that boy rent if he doesn't stay out of my lobby."

"Who, honey?" Tameka asked, breezing into Ty's office.

"Calvin," Ty told her.

"Oh," Tameka said, with a knowing look at Milo. "Well, don't be late for the flight tomorrow, honey. Would you like the pastor and I to pick you up?"

"No, thanks, but I already have a ride out to the airport with . . ."

"Anybody home?" Calvin stuck his head in the door. "Hello Pastor, Mrs. B. You ready, honey?"

"Yes, Calvin." She turned to the Barnetts, "Good night. See you in the morning."

"Good night, honey," Tameka called softly. "Well, Pastor," Tameka continued, after the young people had left, "I'm just too pooped to participate, as a wise man once said . . ." She plopped into Ty's lap, putting her arms around his neck, "So let's go home!"

"I hope you're not 'too pooped' when we get home," Ty said, putting his arms around her waist.

"You know, for some reason.." Tameka kissed him lightly, "you have the strangest revitalizing effect on me."

"Oh, really?" Ty whispered, rubbing her nose with his. "How would you like an energy burst right now?"

They were just really getting into the kiss when a small voice said, "They're doing it again. Uck!"

"Moe, haven't I told you to knock before you enter a room?" Ty said.

"I'm sorry, Daddy, but the door was open," said Tyler Morgan Barnett.

"Yeah, but that's just because he pushed it open, Daddy," Taylor McDougall Barnett volunteered.

"Tattletale." Moe stuck his tongue out at his brother.

"Moe, you stop that this instant," Tameka got up from Ty's lap. "Mac just told the truth. That doesn't make him a tattletale. Now you tell your brother you're sorry."

Mama stuck her head in the door, "I just wanted to make sure you knew they were back, Tammi."

"Where's Jesse, Mom?" Ty asked.

"Out in the car. Seems like a day at the zoo with his grandsons was too much for him," Mama laughed. "I kept telling him 'Man, you're sixty, they're six. You can't keep up with them.' But would he listen?"

"Thanks for taking them today, Mama," Tameka said, coming over to give her a kiss. "I was able to get by the doctor's for my check-up, and still have time to get us all packed and ready."

"No thanks needed, honey. I love taking care of my boys. But I'd better get out of here and take care of my big boy. He's probably going to need a good liniment rubdown if we're going to make it to that plane in the morning." Mama bent over from the waist. "Come kiss Grandma good night, boys!" The twins ran to their grandmother, smothering her with kisses.

"She's going to spoil those hellions," Tameka said after Mama had gone.

"Of course," Ty replied. "Grandma's her name, and spoiling is her game."

"Mama," Mac piped up. "Are Aunt Randy and Uncle Linc going to meet us in Sangles?"

"That's 'Los Angeles', honey. And yes, they will."

"Is Aunt Randy bringing that baby with her?" Moe was obviously not looking forward to the possibility.

" 'That baby' is your cousin, young man. Of course they're bringing her. Anyway, little Barni's grown a lot since you last saw her. She not a baby anymore. She's almost three now.''

"Three *is* a baby," Moe insisted. "And why do I have to have a cousin named after that purple dinosaur?"

"She's not, Moe, as you know very well," his father told him. "She has our family name. Don't you think Barnett Palmer is a pretty name?"

"No, I don't," Moe stuck to his guns. "And the last time she was here she spit up on me."

"What about Aunt Eddie and Uncle Purse?" Mac wanted to know.

"Aunt Eddie can't go on an airplane right now, Mac. Not until her baby comes."

"Why do we have to go out there, anyway?" Moe pouted.

"Well, dude," Ty said, picking the child up, and putting him on his knee, "remember when you and Mac and Mama went to the glass room with all the microphones, and you put on headphones, and sang 'Jesus Loves Me' with Mama?"

"Yeah," Moe's eyes lit up. "That was way cool. I wanna do that again."

"You probably will, son. You two inherited your mother's voice, as well as her dimples."

"And they've got their father's good looks," Tameka winked at Ty.

"Be that as it may," Ty continued to the child, "you and your brother and Mama have been picked for a special honor for singing that song. You may even get what's called a Grammy."

Moe looked up at his father with large worried eyes. "But if we get another Grammy, do we have to give the old one back? I'd rather keep *her*."

Ty and Tammi burst out laughing. "No, that's not what I meant, son," Ty finally said, putting Moe down. "I'll explain it more when we get home. Let's get outta here."

The boys ran off down the hall while Ty was putting on his jacket.

"Honey," Tameka said thoughtfully, "my grandmother's maiden name was Tucker." She smiled tenderly up at Ty, one hand on her tummy. "Tucker Barnett. Has a nice ring to it, don't you think?" she whispered.

Ty's jacket wound up on the floor as he took Tameka in his arms.

ABOUT THE AUTHOR

Raynetta Mañees has been an administrator with the federal government for almost 25 years. She is a graduate of Wayne State University, with a degree in Mass Communication. She has been a solo vocalist since childhood, performing in numerous venues in the Northwest and in the Caribbean. She is also an accomplished actress and former on-air radio personality.

Raynetta welcomes your comments at her E mail address, *Rmanees@aol.com*, or via "snail mail" at P.O. Box 648, Inkster, MI 48141.